NEVER
TRUST
THE
HUSBAND

BOOKS BY JESSICA PAYNE

Make Me Disappear
The Lucky One
The Good Doctor

JESSICA PAYNE

NEVER TRUST THE HUSBAND

bookouture

Published by Bookouture in 2024

An imprint of Storyfire Ltd.
Carmelite House
50 Victoria Embankment
London EC4Y 0DZ

www.bookouture.com

ISBN: 978-1-83790-568-3
eBook ISBN: 978-1-83790-567-6

To Sara, without whom this writing journey would be far less fun

PROLOGUE
MADELINE

Four Years Ago

The sky is the darkest I've ever seen it. Darker than it is in the city, darker than any destination I've visited on vacation. Our little group is utterly isolated so far from civilization.

Any other time in my life, I'd find that frightening. But crawling from the tent—taking one last look back at Benji—*my husband, my gosh, I have a* husband—I don't mind. It's romantic. And besides, I trust everyone here. Well, mostly.

Grass and rocks crunch beneath my shoes as I step out into the cold night, and my gaze catches on two other tents pitched not far from ours. I'm here with the people who matter most. The people who love me—my husband, Benji. My best friend, Gwyn. All of our close friends.

So why was I so sure one of them had it out for me? That secrets tore their way through these precious relationships.

Bracing mountain air rushes up the side of the nearby cliff, and I hug my jacket tighter, trying to push away the thoughts.

It's paranoia, that's all. And out here, what's there to fear?

Though the sky is dark, a sliver of a moon and a smattering of stars mean I can see where the tree line is.

Bears are out there. Mountain lions, too.

I hesitate—maybe I shouldn't leave the tent. Maybe I should stay safe beside Benji, safe within our little camp. But my camera strap weighs heavy over one shoulder. I have something I want to do.

I turn away from the tent and back to the cliff, climbing the rocky surface toward the edge. I'm going to capture the perfect image to surprise Benji. I'll blow it up, frame it, and it can go on the wall above the hearth in our front room. It'll take some time to get the photo—a time-lapse image does—but the result will be incredible.

Behind me, a noise like scurrying, and I glance back, but it must be the wind, the trees. Maybe the marmot we saw earlier. I try to let go of my nerves and enjoy the Milky Way overhead.

I go about setting up my tripod, my camera, selecting the settings for the time lapse. When it's ready, I hit the button and step away to gaze out at Seattle, far beyond the mountains—a mirage of golden lights glowing in the distance.

I'll get this photo then return to my tent. I'll snuggle back into my sleeping bag beside Benji, and in the morning, my best friends will emerge from their tents, and we'll eat breakfast and drink coffee together and reminisce. I twirl the two rings on my left hand, and a smile grows on my face, staring out at the universe. I'm a lucky girl.

Another breeze sweeps my hair over my shoulders and rustles the branches of the trees. In the midst of it, a footstep—the crunch of rock under boot, and I swing around, adrenaline soaring, heart thumping, not sure whether Benji followed me out here or it's a mountain lion—

But before I can see anything, a hand lands between my shoulder blades. Suddenly, I'm not on solid ground. I'm flying—

flying forward, over the cliff, and before I can do anything to save myself, grim realization cuts through the panicked gasp wrenched from my throat.

One of them did have it out for me. I'm not so lucky.

And now, I'm going to die.

ONE

REBECCA

Now

I prefer not to be called a voyeur, and definitely not a peeping tom. Call me an observer, a regular woman who happens to enjoy running after the sun has set, leaving my Seattle neighborhood in the cover of dark.

It's not as though I get off on what I see. I can't help that the human eye is drawn to light, that my neighbors leave their curtains wide open, their lights on, practically turning their home into a stage for passersby to watch the show.

A bracing wind flutters my ponytail, and I hold back a shiver as I lock my front door. Clouds roll in overhead, making the night darker if possible, insulating the Puget Sound against cooler temperatures. It will rain, which is hardly surprising given it's Seattle, but that's fine—the rain means fewer people out to see me.

Besides, I like the rain. I've missed it.

I scan the road one way, then the other. No neighbors out. No headlight beams flashing my way. Complete darkness. I stroll across, clenching my hands inside my shirtsleeves. Somewhere, a metallic *drip-drip-drip* as water drops onto steel. A pine tree brushes over my shoulder as I step onto the sidewalk, the needles dampening my shirt, the scent of the tree filling my nose with one thing—*home.*

It's the perfect night for a run, and I break into a slow pace.

As I move from one neighborhood to another, televisions flicker over monotonous expressions of the home's inhabitants. Cell phones are personal spotlights, illuminating smiles and expressions of boredom alike. They watch a screen—and I watch them, creating stories inside my head of who they are, what we might talk about if they were my friends, my family.

But only one house and one person gets me to halt my run.

His voice, husky and warm, carries through the night, and my shivers go away when I hear it. I ease along a fence line and press my face to a hole in the wood—he's lit up by outdoor hanging bulbs, plus a bonfire licking over the top of logs inside a steel basin. The fire illuminates a stubbled jaw, then flickers over his eyes, which I know are a deep brown, bright with laughter as he holds one end of a thick rope—and his German shepherd mix holds the other end. They're locked in a game of tug-of-war, the dog settling into her haunches, yanking back, Chris's laughter booming as he lets the dog win. Despite the cold, that laughter warms me.

I suck cool air into my lungs, and the scent of the wood fire comes with it.

I close my eyes and step into an alternate version of reality. If Chris were truly a part of my life, I'd be there with him. I'd sit on the porch, wrapped in a blanket, drinking a beer around the fire while he threw a ball for the dog—*Izzy, I'd heard him call her*—and he'd turn and lean in, and we'd kiss, and the dog would be back, jealous for attention. We'd laugh.

I stand here for at least ten minutes, imagining it, watching him.

The problem with Chris is I know that's his real name,

unlike other neighbors I make up stories for. Because I see him regularly in real life, though I make sure he doesn't see me. Which makes this a far more dangerous game. A game I can't afford to play.

I step away from the fence and sweep down the alley, not letting myself fantasize about Chris anymore. I have somewhere to be.

My goal is another house, one I've yet to observe, but am all too familiar with.

Your house, Madeline.

The familiar streets open before me—the one with new houses and almost no trees, sprinklers hissing on as I pace by, because someone forgot to shut them off in the winter months.

A left turn, then a right, along a trail system that dips into a wooded park. The gentle sweep of my shoes over damp pavement. A murmur of branches overhead with the breeze. The trail detours to another neighborhood, and this one is older, nicer, a mix of Victorians and fancy glass-walled modern homes. A new scent washes over me—the scent of sea, of saltwater and the tang of seaweed and fish. These homes back up to the Puget Sound, facing west, the ideal view for the silky clouds and brilliant colors of sunset. Longing fills my veins, and I pause to soak it all in. To remember how things used to be, back when life was *good*...

But the past is gone.

This was once your neighborhood, where your husband still resides, where his new fiancée has moved in, where I'm drawn to, like a creature caught on a fishing line, reeled in against her will. But I'm done fighting. Now, I'm swimming with the current.

I may have mixed feelings about the person you were, Maddy. But you didn't deserve what they did to you. I won't stop until I find out what happened.

I halt beneath a tree and run a hand over my body, my face,

re-memorizing my new features. Your death was no accident. If I'm going to find out who tossed you over the side of a mountain cliff to your death, they need to believe I'm someone they've never met. A complete stranger. Someone they can trust.

It wasn't easy, and it wasn't cheap. But I did what I had to in order to become someone new.

"Rebecca." I whisper my new name out loud. I touch my new face. My new body, with weight added, some of it muscle. My new hair is straight and sleek instead of wavy down my back. Everything has changed. And yet, returning to Seattle, it feels like nothing has. Will I turn this corner and see your home, and will you appear in the doorway as if nothing ever happened?

No. You won't.

I'm not delusional. Just... yearning.

Another hundred feet to the corner, and I take it at a slow jog. Not long ago, I wouldn't have been caught dead running. The idea of strapping on a bra to hold my breasts down—putting anti-chafe cream in places I don't like to think about—but I've taken a liking to the exercise. The act of motion. The miles go by fast when something is on your mind.

Plotting revenge is all-consuming like that.

Breathe, Rebecca, breathe.

And then I'm on your street. My stomach rolls, and I slow to walk the last block in the shadow of a fence line. No cars parked on roadsides here—it would be against homeowners' association rules—and so they are tucked into garages, or second driveways around the back, or even an alleyway. No, the road is wide and clear, and even in the dimness of 9:22 p.m., this neighborhood is perfection. At least, it pretends to be.

Your house appears in front of me. A broad sweep of lawn and a white mansion beyond. A row of tall, rounded windows. Columns supporting an eave. And no Madeline. Because you're gone. My chest feels heavy as I take breaths and come to a stop.

I can't think of you right now. If I do, I'll spiral. I'll think of how you should have known better, how you should have read the signs and left him before the wedding.

And now, your grieving husband has asked your grieving best friend to marry him.

Only three words sufficed: *What the fuck?*

And I knew then, it was time. The scars had healed. I'd become Rebecca. One—or both of them—are guilty. I suspect your husband. It's always the husband, after all. But first, I'll make sure. Gwyn wasn't such a good friend to you, either.

I can't change what happened to you, Madeline—but I can do something about it.

TWO

MADELINE

Four Years Ago

When tall-dark-and-handsome strode through the doors of the club, the only thing I thought was, *Happy birthday to me.* Just as I'd order champagne that night to celebrate, this man would satisfy a want.

Or maybe, considering those broad shoulders and confident grin, a need.

I knew better than to assume this would be more than a one-night stand. The perfect match was an illusion of perfection, a ticking time bomb until reality hit. Daddy had been through three wives and plenty of mistresses. His version of love was *smile and look pretty, do what I want, and you can have anything money can buy.*

Love, I learned, was an exchange of *you help me, I'll help you.* Simple.

Tall-dark-and-handsome approached the bar. I tilted my head, admired the square jaw, the slender waist under a crisp white oxford tucked into tailored pants. Dress shoes that looked like they cost as much as my heels—which was saying something.

Maybe I was being too cynical. I knew Daddy loved me. But he always said learn from others' mistakes instead of making your own. So that's what I did. And if I learned anything from him, it was that relationships weren't the way to happiness.

"Elena," I whispered, nudging my sister with my foot beneath our high-top table. She shrugged me off, looking at her phone in one hand, holding her gin and tonic with the other. Elena had her heart broken by her college boyfriend and had sworn off dating altogether. She did her best to be a sister and fill in as my mother, but she wasn't much use as a wingwoman.

He stood at the bar, leaning casually, elbow propped on the polished wood, laughing with the bartender, a hint of flirtation in the way he smiled at her.

Oh yes. He'll do nicely.

He handed over cash and accepted two rocks glasses—bourbon? Scotch? It didn't matter. I didn't need to know his drink of choice, because with any luck I'd have my fun and never see him again. He turned, and I caught those electric blue eyes as he searched the bar for someone. I followed the line of his gaze. I didn't mind a little competition, but if he had a fiancé, well, I wasn't going to bother with that. I did like a good time, but I wasn't a homewrecker.

"Elena," I said again. She looked up, and I nodded at him. She took a single glance, then returned her full attention to her phone.

"One sec, I have to finish this..." Her voice trailed off as she typed.

We were out to celebrate my twenty-eighth birthday. My best friend, Gwyn, was in the bathroom, again—probably texting Alex. She needed to just break up with him and have fun with me, but she wouldn't. She still hadn't figured out that he was an asshole. I searched the room for my other friends, but they had yet to arrive. And Elena had left her office early to meet me, meaning she was effectively still at work, texting a patient considering a facelift. Unlike her patients, she came by her own good looks naturally, all high cheekbones and angles, set off by dark hair swept up in a bun that somehow looked chic instead of messy. I wondered if her patients resented her for possessing for free the beauty they had to pay for.

The man walked in the direction of my table, apparently finding the person he was looking for on the far side of the restaurant—a man in his sixties, balding, probably someone my dad played golf with. Country clubs are their own small world like that.

I sighed, signaling my discontent to Elena, and finally, she looked up.

"Too attractive. He's trouble." She absentmindedly swirled her gin and took a sip. "Now will you quit bugging me? Some of us *work* for a living."

I shot her a glare. I worked plenty, as an influencer, which was hard work, despite what my sister thought—and as her temporary receptionist, since hers deserted her a week ago. Besides, it was her job to *make* people attractive, so holding that against a man hardly seemed fair.

I caught sight of him again—weaving through tables, nearly to ours. He really did look like the perfect birthday present. *Twenty feet away. Ten.* I tried to catch his eye, but he was busy dodging a child who'd escaped his parents and sprinted in from the family dining room.

Maybe I was just annoyed at my sister and friend for making my birthday about everyone but me. Or maybe it was the wine. But in that flash of time, I thought, *What do I have to lose? It's* my *birthday*.

I stuck my foot out.

My heel caught on his pant leg as he stepped into it.

Surely, he could have dodged it if he wanted to. Fire-engine-red heels are hard not to notice. Then again, maybe we were playing this game together.

Oh, I like that idea.

My foot jerked, forcing me off the barstool and into him. My hands came up for balance and landed on his button-up shirt. Hard muscle tensed beneath the fabric. He stumbled, recovered, somehow spilling only a few drops of the amber liquid. When he managed to get upright, we were close. So close. I could feel his warmth, smell the masculine scent of sweat and expensive cologne.

My birthday present set the glasses down and touched a hand to my elbow, bare skin on bare skin. He steadied me, in more ways than one.

Across the table, Elena finally noticed me. "Seriously?" she hissed.

I ignored her. Instead, I focused on him—those blue eyes blazing into mine.

"Sorry," he murmured. His voice soft and husky. "Did I spill on you?"

I leaned back against the table, a glow of satisfaction warming my whole body, his attention on me like sunshine on a chilly day.

I didn't bother with witty, flirtatious lines—direct always worked best for me.

"It's fine." I held out my hand. "I'm Madeline."

He took my hand in his, but not to shake it—instead, he pressed a kiss to it. Elena didn't waste a second scoffing, but I thought it was sweet.

"I'm Benjamin." His brow quirked playfully, a hint of a smile on his lips—oh, I was almost *sure* he'd let me stop him on purpose. He'd walked into my foot knowing full well it would lead to this moment. Our meet-cute, so to say.

"Benji?" I asked.

He laughed and took me in with his gaze, and I was sure he felt it too—that slow simmer that meant we'd have one hell of a night together.

"Sure," he said. "Benji it is. For you, anything."

Anything. I liked the sound of that.

THREE

REBECCA

Now

The best view of the interior of the house is from the thick woods that edge the property or, if I'm stealthy enough, the backyard. Behind the house sits the Puget Sound, and the entire rear wall is glass. I find my place among the shadows—a row of tall, slender pines, that separate one property from another—creeping around the house to the back. A motion sensor light turns on. I reach up, unscrew it until it dims.

Darkness. Stillness. No moon to light the backyard, and the waters are deep, murky, fading infinitely into the night. My hands tremble, adrenaline coursing through me, heart thumping frantically in my chest. I'm afraid of what I'm about to see, a sight I've put off until I can no longer ignore it. But see it I must —it's why I came back to Washington, after all. To see him, to see her, to see them *together*. I exhale and keep moving forward.

The mansion glows, golden light pouring from every single window. It's as though global warming isn't a thing, as though he hasn't a care for money in the world. And he hasn't. North

Wineries has taken off. Your money will soon be in his bank account since you've been recently declared dead—three years after it happened. A flush of heat at that thought. The possibility it was Benjamin himself who killed you, going after your money, or maybe going after your best friend—the best friend he's now engaged to. If he wanted her, he could have just said so. Calling off the wedding would have been far simpler than murdering you.

Or maybe, he wanted both. The money and the friend. I fight back the rising rush of anger, thinking of it. There's no space for that here and now.

I saw the photos on social media, and that's when I knew it was time to come back. To finally make my move. The kneeling man, his hair longer than I remembered it. The new fiancée, hand pressed over her O of a mouth as though she hadn't seen the moment coming. Women *always* see the moment coming.

I bite my lip to keep the memory of your own engagement from surfacing.

My eyes have to adjust, the house is so bright, lit up like a theater production, or maybe a dollhouse—in the spotlight, just like they like it.

Benjamin. Gwyn. *The couple. The actors.*

And I'm the audience. I settle onto the cold wet ground and wait for the performance to begin. Soon, if I play my cards right, I won't be on the outside. I'll be in there, laughing *with* them. Welcomed into their home, their lives. Maybe Gwyn's newest BFF. But tonight is about watching, learning. Sizing up my prey before I begin the chase.

Benjamin appears first, stealing the breath from my lungs.

I'm here, years later, to witness it. To witness *them*, but it's been so long that seeing him is like seeing a ghost. The long strides he takes across the kitchen to the wine rack. The furrow to his brow as he runs fingertips from one bottle of wine to another. The nod when he selects one, and the wide, easy smile he tosses over one shoulder when someone else enters the room.

When she enters the room. Not you—the woman who should be there—but Gwyn.

It's how he used to look at you.

He raises the bottle for her approval, but she only smiles, coy. Disgust roils in my gut as she snakes around the room, by the chunky farmhouse table you picked out, passing the matching bar, to find her place at his side, where she presses her cheek to his shoulder and murmurs something.

I wish I knew what she was saying. I wish I knew what he said in return.

Their lips brush one another's, smiles tracing their mouths as they pull away and Benjamin motions at the back door. The perfect couple, ready to enjoy an evening on the patio.

That sends fire through me. Hot, scorching fire, the sort that I suspect fuels crimes of passion. It should be you there, Maddy —living your happily ever after. Not *them*.

I force steady breaths in and out. The glass door slides open. Their voices go from a silent film to actual sounds—his warm, confident; hers too high, too flirty. Like Gwyn always was.

I have to get out of here.

The words strike me, and panic makes my breath come up short, suffocatingly short. But there's nowhere to go—left or right, they'll see me. The other option is to run for the Puget Sound, but it's no higher than fifty-or-so degrees, which means I won't get far before I freeze.

Crazy talk. Crazy thoughts.

Me, spiraling. A crush of anger and grief and other emotions I can't afford to let take control. *I* have to be in control —otherwise, how will they believe the lies I tell them?

I squeeze my eyes shut and push you away. *Go away, Madeline.* Focus on the moment, the salty breeze, the quiet lapping of water behind me.

It's okay. It's okay.
Because I can fix this.
I exhale, my pulse slowing to normal.
Well, not fix.
But avenge.

FOUR

MADELINE

Four Years Ago

Benji walked away, and all Elena could say was, "I don't like him." But she didn't like anyone I dated, so I just rolled my eyes. Besides, I didn't plan to *date* him exactly.

He joined his friend, stopping once to glance over his shoulder at me. To wink.

"He's the sort of guy who would come to me for Botox at thirty. *Thirty*." She pressed a manicured hand to the table and leaned forward to give me that serious look she got from Daddy. I wasn't sure what her point was—I thought it was perfectly acceptable to get Botox at thirty, and she didn't mind giving it to women that age, so really, what was her problem?

I shrugged. "If I don't like him, I'll never see him again." Which was the plan all along.

"Maddy—" Elena extended a hand, placed it over mine, gave me that mothering look that made me feel like a rebellious teenager.

But then Gwyn returned, face flushed, and I had to wonder if instead of arguing with Alex, they'd just finished a round of phone sex. Elena pulled away fast—she didn't like Gwyn, so she promptly turned back to her phone, ignoring us. The only reason she agreed to come out with Gwyn in tow was because it was my birthday.

"What happened?" Gwyn took in my self-satisfied smile.

"I just met my future husband."

Elena's eyes went wide, but I was only saying it to annoy her—and my mouth curved into a smirk Gwyn returned. She knew as well as anyone marriage was not in my future. A flutter of motion at the table's edge—other friends, arriving late after an afternoon of shopping.

"What are you two grinning about?" Leah asked. She plunked her purse on the table, stole a nearby stool, and pulled it up next to Gwyn. She still wore scrubs from her job as a pharmacist, but I knew she had a quick change of clothes tucked away somewhere. Natalie, who worked as a dietician at the same hospital, chose to stand, her go-to, because she swore it burned more calories. Her eyes shifted my way, then to Gwyn, probably trying to figure out if she could find a way to swap seats and be next to me. While Gwyn was my ride-or-die, Natalie coveted the position, which Gwyn seemed to not so secretly enjoy. I personally found their constant attempts to one-up each other tiresome—we were all nearly thirty, couldn't we drop the high school popularity contest already?

"Oh nothing, Madeline just met her future husband." Gwyn shared a wink with me. Elena sighed and muttered something to Leah, my only friend she didn't actively dislike. Leah leaned in, raising a brow, conspiratorial.

"He had the nicest eyes." I let my face go dreamy, but the words snapped Elena out of her conversation with Leah.

"She kicked him!" Elena said.

"I did not kick him."

"He's creepy," she added.

"Creepy's kind of in," Natalie said, coming to my rescue, flashing me a smile.

"Only true-crime-obsessed weirdos think that," Elena muttered.

They continued among themselves, but I looked across the bar, catching sight of him. Benjamin was such a classy name. And he hadn't balked at *Benji*. Which told me plenty about his confidence. A lesser man would have cringed, would have complained. In all likelihood, Benji wouldn't do the Hallmark things that annoyed me—asking permission to kiss me, when I clearly *wanted* him to. Asking if I was okay every five seconds during sex, the ultimate turn off.

Heck, it would almost be worth it—to go on a second and third date—to be around someone as confident as myself, just to annoy Elena. I hesitated at that thought—it was childish of me. But her overprotective-sister thing chafed. It was her attempt at a relationship with me, and I recognized that. I, too, sometimes wished we were closer. That we really connected in a meaningful way. But for whatever reason, no matter how much effort we both put in, we ended up antagonizing the other.

I bit back a laugh at the realization—maybe that was what real sisterhood was and we were succeeding without realizing it.

But regardless, he wasn't creepy. If anything, Elena was jealous.

She caught me watching him and leaned toward me, whispering like my friends wouldn't hear. "He's exactly the sort of guy you should watch out for. I'll bet he doesn't even have money. He's probably here trying to snare someone like you, someone with a trust fund and an inherit—"

"Oh stop." More "sisterly" love. I hated it when she brought up the trust fund, something my mother left me when she died, when I was only a toddler. Elena might have been jealous, but she still had a living mother, and besides, as a plastic surgeon, she made more money than she knew what to do with. Not to mention the two of us were Daddy's only heirs.

We bickered awhile longer, Elena playing stand-in mother, me wishing I hadn't invited her. Finally, she got up and left in a huff—probably started the whole fight to have an excuse to go back to the office, anyway. God forbid she spend time not making money. No wonder she'd been single for so long. I still wasn't entirely convinced her former boyfriend actually existed —she'd never once brought him home in the two years they'd dated.

"Maybe you should be careful." Natalie circled around the table to take Elena's seat, a few inches closer than where she'd been. She lowered her voice and reached out, touching my arm. "You don't know anything about him."

"So, he's cute?" Gwyn pretended Natalie hadn't spoken. I didn't miss the daggers they shot at each other in a quick sideways glance.

"Hot? Rich?" Gwyn raised her voice a notch just as Natalie opened her mouth to say more. I might have been Queen Bee, but Gwyn wanted to be next in line to the throne. With a flick of her hair, she effectively relegated Natalie to an onlooker instead of part of the conversation.

A beat passed, and Natalie gave in, as she always did, leaning in alongside Leah to wait for my response. Their gazes rested on me, shining with admiration, smiles of anticipation waiting for what I would say next. For a moment I basked in being the center of attention. I couldn't help it, being a Leo, after all.

"Hot, yes. Rich, does it matter?"

Benji was cute and confident, but I had my own money—I didn't need a man's.

I sipped my drink and smiled because I never went after a guy. The first rule of finding a worthy man: let him come to you. If he wasn't willing to put in the effort, to risk being turned down, he wasn't worth your time. Daddy told me so, and it's true. Besides, it wasn't as though I'd asked him out. I simply gave him the opportunity to notice me—and he hadn't disappointed.

Thirty minutes later, we finished our drinks. I snatched up my phone and posed for selfies, then photos of all us girls together, editing and posting on Instagram for my followers—*Happy birthday to me!*—with a handful of hashtags.

Gwyn went to pay the tab, and Natalie sidled closer.

"What's the birthday girl want to do?" she asked. At her hand was an empty glass, her lite margarita drained. She was hoping I'd say go dancing, but she wouldn't suggest it until I did —an excellent workout, she'd be sure to mention at some point. And I actually *did* want to go dancing. With Benji.

It was some of the best foreplay there was.

As if on cue, Benji caught my eye from across the room, his mouth widening in a smile. I beckoned him to join us.

We left the country club bar—which we'd planned pre-drinks at for the sole reason it was one of the few places Elena deigned worthy of her presence—and made our way to a real club, where Benji and I wandered to the floor together. And okay, so, he didn't dance so much as sway. But he did buy drinks, and he did stand out in the crowd, tall, broad-shouldered, confident. Gwyn and Leah and Natalie danced together, then with the best-looking men who approached them. And I was tempted to go with them—to find someone who really wanted to dance, to *move*, but something about him kept me by his side.

I hated to admit it might have been the conversation. The way my whole body tingled when he turned his confident gaze on me.

We found a quiet table, and he waited for me to sit before sliding in beside me and asking, "What do you want to do with your life?" and "Have you been to Napa?" and lastly, "Did you play soccer growing up?" At my inquisitive look, his eyes dropped to my heels, and he raised a brow—

Oh god, he's going to ask me about my childhood. Such a lame first-date question.

But his lips curved into a grin. "Well—" His tone dropped to a whisper. "I couldn't help but notice you're quite good at kicking men."

I almost couldn't stand it—the heat that rose to my cheeks, flushing them a deeper pink than the blush I'd applied earlier that evening. This man had accomplished something no one had in, well, forever. I nearly spit my rum and Diet Coke, hand flying to my mouth as I held back a laugh until I could swallow the drink down.

"You caught that?" I didn't deny it—in fact, a warm glow filled me as he held my gaze. Our knees brushed. We leaned closer in, and my heart beat faster and faster. I wanted to look away, but I didn't.

At least, not until Gwyn bumped over and shouted louder than was necessary, as this was a club in *Seattle,* not *L.A.,* "Come *dance* with me, Maddy!"

She was drunk. *Very* drunk.

"I found the cutest guy," she crooned.

"You have a boyfriend," I said, not because I cared, but because she would in the morning. But this wasn't abnormal for her—hell, she'd stolen Alex from one of our college friends years ago.

She stuck her tongue out, then glanced at Benji. Her casual drunk-girl act faltered for a moment. She narrowed her eyes, blinked. "Who's that?"

"This is Benji," I announced, realizing she hadn't met him at the country club.

Benjamin gave her a wave hello. She just blinked at him again, then shrugged and flounced off.

When our eyes met again, it was as though the moment

between us had broken. We talked some more—skirting the edge of anything too serious, but not small talk, either. Benji and I sat in that corner, where the music wasn't so loud, and I realized I kind of liked this—sitting back while my friends played on the dance floor, relaxing with him. I liked that he was someone I actually *could* relax with. I couldn't remember the last time that happened.

Which was about the time alarm bells sounded in my head. This was exactly how Daddy felt, before my mother died, before his most recent wife divorced him, how he felt when Elena's mother, one of his many mistresses, had enough of his shit. How Elena must have been before her boyfriend walked out. *Comfortable.* This sort of feeling was only an illusion. Chemicals in my head, fooling me into thinking we had something, when in reality, biology only wanted us to have sex then find someone else.

An hour later, when Benji said, "I'm so sorry, I have an early meeting tomorrow. But I'd love your number. I'd love to—" His hand beckoned, as though to indicate *do this again*, but what came out of his mouth was, "Maybe do something just the two of us? Early this coming week?"

And I said, "Sure, that would be great," while inside disappointment left me craving more. I *should* have found someone to dance with. As it was, I was nearly sober, and about to be alone at a table instead of tipsy with my friends on the club floor. Not the way I thought my birthday night would end.

He passed a card over, and just as I was about to blanch—was he really going to give me his *business* card?—he extended a smooth, heavy pen, and said, "Write your number down. I'll call you."

I wrote down a number and slid both back his way. Benji leaned in, pecked me on the cheek, and murmured, "For the record, I'm glad you kicked me."

And then he stood, gave me a last smile, and walked toward the exit. Gwyn wandered over, a man in tow.

"You didn't really give him your number, did you?"

He disappeared around a corner. I realized I was watching, waiting to see if he'd change his mind about leaving.

"Of course not."

I had given him a number—the wrong number. I didn't want or need a boyfriend. Or a real date, for that matter.

"Come dance!" Gwyn said, and I took her hand, let her pull me into my circle of friends. Leah passed me a drink—god knows what—and in minutes, I caught up to them, drinking, dancing, enjoying my last night as a twenty-seven-year-old.

So imagine my surprise, when the very next day, against all odds, Benji called me.

FIVE

REBECCA

Now

I stop a block short of the tiny home I've rented on a corner in the Queen Anne neighborhood, just close enough to Benjamin and Gwyn's house I can run there in ten minutes. A gas station glows with fluorescent lights, and like with their home, I can see everyone inside through the glass. I size them up, but there's no one I know from before. An attendant, a young college man sporting a Seahawks cap. A middle-aged woman frowning as she stares at the assortment of beverages inside a cooler. It's safe.

My clothes are soaked by rain, but the attendant doesn't give me a second glance as I push inside, the heat making me shiver, making me realize just how cold I let myself get as I witnessed their adoration for one another firsthand. My shoes squish down one aisle, then another. "Do you have today's newspaper?" I call out.

The attendant says nothing, only points, and I follow the line of his finger to a newspaper stand. There's one left. I open it, flip through, make sure the article in question is there, but don't bother reading it. I've read it three times already on my computer, but I want a physical copy for the album. Your album.

I hand over cash, asking for a bag to keep it safe from the rain, then head outside and stride down the dark sidewalk. Gwyn and Benjamin fill my mind—the image of them together scalded into my brain, something thick and grimy caught in my throat, keeping me from taking a full inhalation. I feel like one of my patients at the hospital who can't get a full breath, whose lips have a tinge of blue due to lack of oxygen, whose eyes take on that wild look like they're on the verge of something big—for them, usually death.

Except the big thing happened three years ago. Since then, I've been watching from afar. Planning. Becoming Rebecca. Considering the people who could have killed you and planning how I will in return kill them. There is no other suitable revenge for taking your life. You finally had exactly what you wanted before it was yanked out from beneath you. And whoever did it deserves to pay.

There were plenty of people with motive, Maddy—you were such a social butterfly. Your friends, who watched you with adoring, envious eyes. Kip, who in hindsight obviously wanted you but couldn't have you. Alex, who blamed you for Gwyn ending things right before he asked her to marry him. Even Benjamin's brother, Aaron, who missed the good old days, being a bachelor with his winery-owning brother.

A bungalow on a quiet corner waits for me, a rental like every other house I've lived in—a small house that could use a paint job. A yard that could do with some sprucing up but is mowed regularly. The sort of place people don't notice. It's enough for me these days. My needs are far simpler than they used to be, my goals pared down.

Inside, I strip naked and dry off, not bothering with a shower. I wrap myself in a robe and pour straight gin into a glass and sit on the futon that came with the place. The book sits on the scuffed coffee table, a brown faux-leather photo album, the sort popular around the time I was born. Creamy pages with sticky backs and a film of plastic to protect the photo pressed upon them. Except this book isn't about childhood memories or wedding photos.

I like to stay organized, everything in its place. This book has every piece of information I've been able to collect on what happened to you, from newspaper articles to your wedding announcement photo. Even transcripts of podcasts, the true crime sort that made a big buzz when you, a woman worth millions of dollars, went missing two days after her wedding.

In the end, it was presumed you drowned, caught in a river below the cliff you careened from, your body likely eaten by wildlife or caught between rocks underwater.

I gulp the gin, then pause long enough to grab ice and tonic and lime, throwing them together in amounts that are probably more gin than tonic but suffice as a mixed drink in a pinch. The drink palatable, sweet, I drain it, then make another. The newspaper sits at my knee, a pair of scissors beside it, yet I can't help flipping through the pages, reviewing every detail, making sure I haven't missed a thing.

I've spent three years obsessing over you. Wishing you had listened. Wishing you had chosen a different path, one that didn't lead to you being declared *dead in absentia* on a day not far off from what should have been your third wedding anniversary.

On your first anniversary, I was still recovering from the changes that would allow me to become Rebecca. On the second, I'd become Rebecca, become a nurse, and slowly learned my trade. On the third, well—you were announced dead, officially. I have the newspaper article clipped and pasted in to prove it. I couldn't help but notice the timing coincided with Benjamin and Gwyn's engagement, and between the two events, I knew it was time.

I turn another page, which contains the first article published on your disappearance, the one that came in the days after the feature that ran on your wedding. *Madeline Hughes Marries Benjamin North in Ceremony Fit for Royalty* is followed by *Madeline Hughes-North Missing, Presumed Dead.*

I don't read it. I don't need to. Instead, I stare at the familiar faces—you, Madeline. Benjamin. Gwyn. Your bridesmaids.

When I've gotten my fill of memories, I unfold the paper and cut it carefully, keeping the newspaper's name and the date at the top. I like to know where my sources come from. I press it into the sticky backing and finally let myself read it one more time.

Madeline Hughes Declared Dead in Absentia After Three Years Missing

Madeline Hughes would now be 31 and worth roughly $12 million thanks to her family's fortune. At the time of her disappearance three years ago, she had recently married Benjamin North, owner of North Wineries, Seattle's first zero-carbon-footprint vineyard. Ms. Hughes went missing on August 18 while backpacking the Wonderland Trail with her husband and friends.

The article reads like every other one, adding the line: Ms. Hughes was declared dead in absentia earlier this week.

Ms. Hughes is believed to have disappeared the night of August 17 on the fourth night of a 10-day backpacking trip. Her fellow adventurers reportedly woke in the morning to find her missing. All of her belongings except her camera and phone remained in the tent. She had reportedly stayed up late to photograph the night sky but likely never returned to camp. It is believed she fell over a cliff into the Carbon River.

Hers would be the third death at this specific cliff in the past decade, which has led to several suggestions that signage be placed to warn of loose rock and the risk of falling. It is not uncommon for hikers and climbers to go missing in Mount Rainier National Park. Dozens go missing every summer and a handful are never found.

Below the article are blurbs from old interviews, but none of the lines are new—all pulled from previous interviews. No new information. Nothing for me to analyze or memorize or consider.

I flip back to the wedding photo, remembering that day.

Benjamin. Gwyn. They stand on either side of you. His brother, Aaron, stands behind him. Your friends and family fill in, creating what should have been a moment you'd look back on for decades.

You chose to ignore the warning signs—and there were plenty of them. Benjamin, perfect man you thought he was, hid more than one secret from you.

Your face says you're certain this is the first day of the rest of what will surely be a perfect life.

You couldn't have been more wrong.

SIX

MADELINE

Four Years Ago

He called twice—because I ignored him the first time. An unknown number calling in the evening? No, thank you. But if the number called again, it might be something important—like a hair appointment needing to be rescheduled or Daddy losing his mobile yet again.

"Hello?" I sat in the window seat of my bedroom, staring out at the rain. It held off long enough to let me turn twenty-eight, but no longer, and the autumn downpour officially canceled my first stand-up paddleboard yoga class. Gwyn had texted, *Just called, it's canceled,* and a moment later, Natalie lit up the group text: *Dang it, now I have to drive to the gym. Anyone wanna go with?* Leah replied with an eye-roll emoji, but to the *other* group text, the one that excluded Natalie, because Gwyn and Leah liked to talk about her behind her back sometimes.

"Ms. Madeline Hughes. It's lovely to hear your voice."

The back-and-forth inner chatter of my brain debating how

to respond to my friends went dead silent as it tried to identify the male caller's voice.

"Speechless, I see," he continued, and that's when it hit me —*Benji*.

Another beat, as I verified my own memory—yes, I *had* given him the wrong number. So how was he calling?

"Benji?" I said.

"Oh, is that nickname going to stick? How fortunate for me. I'll have to find an equally annoying one for you."

"Annoying?" I snapped back, "Are you kidding? It's adorable."

My words rushed from my mouth as blood pounded through my body, equal parts dopamine and adrenaline. A grin worked its way over my face—he'd *found my number*. No one had ever done that before. Quite frankly, I was impressed. Flattered. And also, a little creeped out. But it showed he was *capable*, and that was more than most men in Seattle could say, especially the spoiled trust-fund ones who ran in my circle.

"So, how was the rest of your evening? What did you ladies do?" His voice, utterly relaxed, settled my own nerves—not the voice of a creepy guy stalking me. Rather, the self-assured tone of a man who didn't *need* to stalk a woman, who maybe merely knew the right people to get my number.

"More dancing. More drinks. Daddy sent a car to take us home." The moment *Daddy* rolled off my tongue, I cringed— Jesus, why did I still call him that? I wasn't a child.

"Good birthday, all in all, I hope?"

"It was great."

"What was the best part?" His voice held a smile—a teasing smile—as if daring me to mention him. I considered, but if we were going to play this game, I intended to win.

I pretended to think it over. "Definitely the champagne."

A chuckle.

"Well, if the champagne beat me out, perhaps I should take

you out. Show you a *proper* birthday celebration. And then I'll call again and ask the same question."

My head buzzed. My heart sped faster. I was hot, too hot, even though I wore only a tank top and joggers. When had a man affected me like this before? Never. But before I could dart ahead to my next thought—which would have likely been something along the lines of *Jesus, is this feeling why Daddy kept marrying women?*—he said, "Great. Pick you up in thirty minutes."

And he hung up.

I blinked at my phone. Replayed his words—realized he was coming *here*—how did he know where I lived, anyway? But then, it wasn't hard for him to find my number, which meant—

Text me your address if you don't mind, he messaged.

Relief left me loose and woozy—okay, so he wasn't creepy, merely resourceful—but then I remembered that meant he'd be here soon, and realized I now had *twenty-nine* minutes to get ready.

Benji arrived in a sleek black Land Rover, and I was out the front door, clicking in my red heels down the walkway before he could even make it around the SUV.

"You're early," I called.

"Better than late." His gaze flicked behind me, taking in the house, freshly painted with picture windows and artful landscaping and a view of the Puget Sound. Did he want to come in? Maybe. But it was too soon. Hell, in a month would be too soon. He was getting a real date—that was more than I gave other men.

Daddy was inside, toiling in his office—I wanted out of here before he could make an appearance, before the two of them could shake hands and go through the man-to-man process that society seemed to necessitate between a woman's father and the man she was dating—or at least, going on *a date* with. Not to mention I didn't want to emphasize the fact I still lived at home, even if it was to keep an eye on Daddy, whose health was questionable.

"I wasn't expecting you to call so soon," I said.

He opened the passenger door, and I slid in, soft leather beneath me. I crossed my legs, pulled the hem of my dress down, and fought to not play with the platinum bracelet at my wrist.

I watched him take in my words—hopeful he might divulge where he got my number. But he just smiled, and that was all the answer I was going to get.

"I'm glad you were available." He pulled a U-turn to take us out of the neighborhood toward downtown Seattle. I expected him to launch into how excited he was to see me, or some follow-up to his first statement, but that's not what I received. "I'm leaving town in two weeks for Europe. Wine tour." A glance my way. "I don't think I mentioned that I own a vineyard and a small winery, focused on zero-carbon footprint and renewable packaging. And good wine, of course."

"How very Seattle of you," I said, infusing my voice with enough warmth he'd know I wasn't making fun.

A wide, pleased smile spread across his face, but not the annoying sort—the sort that told me he really was proud, and he wouldn't be embarrassed by that fact. I liked that. Owning what was important to him. "I'll be gone for a month."

His statement settled between us. My first reaction, hardly knowing him, was disappointment. It didn't *matter* though, I reminded myself, because tonight was a onetime thing.

But then he surprised me again. "So, I want to see you a few times before then."

I blinked. *A few times?*

Daddy flashed through my mind—the box of wedding photos I'd once found in the hall closet, from not one, not two, but *three* weddings—his first wife's, then my mother's, then the awful step-mother—and photos of the other women he'd been with but never married.

Elena's mother one of them.

Unease pooled in my stomach. I looked away, out the passenger window, at lights twinkling over Lake Union. But this wasn't a wedding. This was a few dates.

"Presumptuous of you," I murmured.

He laughed. "Fair enough. So, I hope you don't mind, but I thought we'd do something a little different tonight."

"Define *different*."

"Well—" His gaze dropped to my bare legs. "I probably should have mentioned it'll be chilly. But I have blankets. And it will be worth it, I promise."

I raised an eyebrow, and his fingers drummed over the steering wheel. "I know, I know—you're all dressed up for a proper date, but I think to make an impression I'll need to do something different than your other suitors."

I wanted to say, *I don't have suitors*, as a badge of pride, because most men who ran in my circle knew better than to try to bullshit their way into my life. I held those words back, though, because it sounded like a complaint, which it wasn't.

"I'm taking you to my boat."

"Your boat," I repeated.

"Have you ever been out on the water at night? It's incredible. The Seattle lights—how quiet it is. Don't get me wrong, it's cold, but it's worth it. Think you're up for it?"

I didn't relish the idea of freezing my ass off, but his words were like a challenge—and though I'd been on plenty of cruises, I'd spent very little time on the Puget Sound. And never at night. The Space Needle rose up over a hill, lit up blue and green for the football team. What would it look like from the inky black waters of the Puget Sound?

"Let's do it," I said.

Fifteen minutes later, we parked in front of a sign that read

Elliott Bay Marina—a little stretch of land skirting the Sound, a tiny parking lot, and rows upon rows of boats. The dock stretched out in perpendicular lines, a narrow plank down which to walk. The moment I stepped from the car, the wind hit me, cool over the Puget Sound, despite the late summer air. My dress flared, a Marilyn Monroe moment, minus the length, and I slapped the fabric back down, laughing.

Wild, free.

The words streamed through my consciousness, and I realized the last time I felt that way was dancing in New York the winter before, at New Year's. I was drunk, far too much champagne, and so were Gwyn, Natalie, and Leah. Elena and Daddy were *somewhere*, but the city was far too crowded for us to have a chance in hell of finding them. We'd danced and drank and partied until the club shut down, which felt like practically dawn.

But this was different. A quiet, focused *wild* and *free*. Not a drop of alcohol in my system. Another cold breeze, my fingertips going numb, my legs knocking together with the chill, but Benji came up beside me and wrapped an arm around me.

"Come on, boat's over here—let's get you out of the wind. The cabin's heated."

And I didn't dare let myself dwell on the thought, but I'd be lying if I didn't admit the thought flitted by that *I could get used to feeling this way.*

That night, we motored out of the marina, into the gently lapping waters of the Sound. "I'll turn the lights off so you can see how dark it is, but just for a second—not safe to leave them off for long with other boats out here," Benji murmured.

Then the world went dark.

In the absence of all that light, as my eyes adjusted, I could see quite a lot—West Seattle. Downtown. The Ferris wheel, the lights from the stadium. A salty breeze carried the scent of the ocean. The sound caught me, so much silence, save the water, the peaceful sort of murmur I could almost fall asleep to. We stepped out onto the deck and sat, a thick wool blanket wrapped around us both, our bodies pressed together, warm, cozy.

And I felt the pull of him, the desire for the first time ever to stay with someone. To simply *be* with them. It had to be an illusion—that combination of hormones raging through my bloodstream—and yet, the not-so-rational side of my brain kicked this knowledge aside. But I knew better than to think that truly meant anything. So I liked a man. I liked being on his boat staring at the lights. I was impressed at his resourcefulness, at his ability to flatter me without annoying me. That made him different than most, but that didn't mean I *needed* him. Not how Daddy needed someone, how Elena thought she needed her ex, and she was just doing fine without him now, wasn't she?

I decided to enjoy the moment—the experience. Because I knew after tonight, I'd never step foot on this boat again. I'd let him take me back to his place, or we'd grab a hotel after we docked, and I'd get him out of my system. And then, I'd move on, because I didn't believe in love.

SEVEN

REBECCA

Now

Taking someone else's identity should be difficult. And maybe it would be, without the right connections. As it was, becoming Rebecca Johnson, RN, was exceedingly simple. The real Rebecca died overseas in a surfing accident. She lived a spartan life as a night-shift travel nurse, and had no family and few friends, all easily dispatched with rude texts.

The nursing part was both good and bad—on one hand, it made traveling and coming to Seattle easy. On the other hand, nursing is a unique career field, and because I never actually trained to be one, nothing else could have fully prepared me for it. But she already had spent six months working in Spokane and had a nursing license in Washington State. It required some research, some "on-the-job training," but it wasn't hard to figure out the rest. And because travel nurses are never fully trusted, no one really knows you or how good of a nurse you are—I'm never given difficult patient assignments.

I look up from my computer as the charge nurse walks by, as

though she heard me thinking about her. Her gaze, icy blue, rests on me a moment too long as she crosses the unit to her patient's room. It didn't take me long to realize the pecking order on this unit—Riley, the nighttime charge nurse, followed by everyone else. She could be your best friend, or enemy. She'd taken a disliking to me on day one, and since then, watched for an opening—a weakness, a single screwup—probably in the hopes of getting me fired. I watch her disappear into the room, curly dirty-blonde hair bouncing around her shoulders.

Mostly, I lie low. I don't talk to people, don't make friends. Her rabid attention on me could become a problem, a problem I need to avoid. Fake identification and pretending to be someone else worked just fine so long as you weren't under heavy scrutiny. I'd worked hard to become Rebecca, to create this pretense that would place me here in Seattle and allow me an income while sorting out who killed you. To have it crumble around me would be the worst-case scenario. It would mean starting over.

I came to Seattle a month ago, and have five months left on this travel assignment, which means plenty of time to figure things out. Though if Riley had it her way, that would happen sooner.

The computer screen glares at me, and I type in vital signs, entering blood pressure, heart rate, double-checking for errors.

I mindlessly type in more numbers and think about my options.

I have a hard time believing it would be Alex or Aaron, though Aaron was jealous of your relationship with Benjamin. And your friends, well—they envied you, but would they have killed you over it? They had nothing to gain, at least not that I can think of. They mourned you in the aftermath of your death, though knowing them, that might have been all show—all *woe is me, I'm so sad.*

But Gwyn, Gwyn wanted to *be* you, not just be like you.

And everyone says, "It's always the husband."

So it must be Benjamin or Gwyn. There is no other option.

You died days after your wedding. It was convenient. Too convenient. And then Benjamin and Gwyn decided to fall in love. To get married. And I couldn't help but wonder if it was a long game they had played with you. Marry Madeline, kill her once what's hers was his, then live happily ever after, together, with all her money.

Part of me had held out hope Benjamin was still in mourning—Gwyn, grief-stricken. That you still resided in their heads, and I'd realize I was wrong, that maybe it was an accident, or it was someone else who'd shoved you over that cliff. Maybe they bonded over the loss of you and ended up together.

Wishful thinking.

Naïveté, maybe.

I have to do this for you, Madeline—I won't be able to move on until it's done. No one else seems to have noticed or cared that there's no way you *accidentally* tumbled to your death. It's like I'm the only one who knows, whose eyes are wide open. And I'm unable to stop thinking about what happened. It's driving me slowly mad. There is no option to fail.

An alarm sounds down the hall, distracting me again. The hospital is never silent. Nor is it ever dark, except maybe in the morgue. The computer I'm charting at reads 2:03 a.m. Other nurses sit all around me, and we click at the keys of a dozen computers. I wonder what they are thinking.

I bet I'm the only one thinking of murder.

A call light chimes, green light blinking above the patient's room. My patient's room. Before I can so much as stand, Riley sticks her head out of her patient's door, looks to see which room it is, and turns to give me a dirty look—like I'm neglecting them. I pretend not to see her and lock the computer, step across the tiled floor, my shoes louder than anything else. I step into the room and shut the door behind me. A small lamp illuminates the far corner, but otherwise the room is dim. My patient lies in bed.

"Who are you?" She blinks up at me, sheets clutched beneath her chin. Fearful.

"Hi, Louise, I'm Rebecca, and I'm your nurse." I pull up a chair and sit near her. "Everything all right?"

Her eyes are wide, and they flick around the dim room—touching on the television, the monitor above her head, where her vitals tick across the black screen—evidence she is alive.

"I don't know where I am."

I take her hand in mine. "You're in the hospital. You fell. You had a hip replacement, and the medications can make it hard to remember."

Louise does another scan of the room. When her eyes rest on me, they are still wide, but not so fearful. She takes a deep breath, then presses her hand over the nasal cannula pressed into her nostrils, as though she didn't know it was there.

"That's right. I fell." She nods and focuses on me once more. "You seem like a nice young lady. Can you stay here a little while? It's lonely."

I hold her hand and ask her questions about her life, and after a while, she falls back to sleep.

A moment later, a gentle knock comes at the door. I step forward, pressing a finger to my lips as a tall form enters.

"She just fell asleep," I whisper, but before I can say more my breath catches in my throat. I want to run. I want to stay.

"Evening," a doctor in blue scrubs replies in a quiet voice. He stands there a moment, looking at the patient, at the monitor *beep-beep-beeping* above her head.

I have to focus to hold still. To not make an excuse to leave, though it's really not a bad idea. Eventually, the doctor's eyes come to rest on me. His gaze feels heavy, like a hand-quilted blanket. The sort of thing I could wrap myself up in. But that won't work.

"Hi." I look down, playing the shy nurse. Playing Rebecca. Pushing back the surge of hope and knowing it can never happen in equal measures.

He rubs his hands together, sanitizer making them slick and shiny. He frowns. "I don't think I recognize you. Are you new?"

We haven't met. I've made sure of it, finding a reason to leave the floor whenever he consults on the patients in my unit.

"No," I say in a soft voice. "I'm Rebecca. I'm a travel nurse."

He takes a step forward, extending his hand. I take it tentatively, relishing that I can finally interact with him. His hand is warm, smooth. "I'm Dr. Neilson, but call me Chris. Nice to meet you." Then he adds, "I wish I'd done that. They have travel gigs for doctors, too."

"Why don't you?"

The smile falters, then comes back with twice the wattage. Something deep inside me flutters. "I suppose I could. I just feel so established here. Got the job. Bought a house. Adopted a dog."

"Sounds nice." I want to say more—want to engage him in a conversation. But I can't. Now is not the time. "Your patient is doing okay. A little confused, but her vitals are stable." My voice comes out shaky, like a teenager on her first date.

Chris presses his lips together, gives me another lingering look, as though he expected something more than an update on his patient. For a moment, I almost give it to him—I want to ask about his dog, or his plans for his house, or what he does in his spare time. He pulls his stethoscope from his shoulder to press it to Louise's chest. I go back to charting, only relaxing when he gives me a nod and exits the room. But that relaxation turns to a feeling of loss—as though I had an opportunity at hand and let it get away. But that's my life now. I live for you, Madeline, not for me.

I stay a few minutes more, to make sure Louise is out, then straighten the covers and move around the room, picking up trash and tidying—making the room a little more pleasant for her to wake up to. It keeps my mind busy, instead of focusing on the adrenaline trilling through me at Chris's sudden appearance.

I should just be glad he didn't recognize me.

EIGHT

REBECCA

Now

When my shift ends at seven, I change from scrubs to running shorts and top, swap my clogs for Nikes, and head out into the morning. Sometimes, mornings are better for observing than nighttime. Evenings are lazy, predictable. Families eat dinner; mothers care for children, fathers find a means of escape, single people talk on the phone or play video games or watch Netflix. But mornings are more purposeful.

I glance in windows as I run the sidewalk from downtown north back toward the Queen Anne neighborhood—gulped coffee, hurried breakfast, children shooed toward the front door. Backpacks and briefcases, running to catch a bus, phones pressed to ears with shoulders as jackets are deposited on sons and daughters, and rarely, someone with a hint of a smile, staring at a newspaper or book, undisturbed by the rush of the morning.

These are the people I enjoy watching most. It's calming. Seeing someone else in their element, taking their time with life. Something I was never very good at but am striving for.

Everyone else just makes me sad—rushing through life. Not enjoying the people who care for them.

I don't stop to watch, though; my goal is Gwyn and Benjamin's, and in twenty minutes, I'm there. To the east, the sun has just broken over the horizon, sending streams of pink and red across the ends of the earth. But it's just dark enough I can tuck myself in that line of pine trees and watch, wait.

The house is still lit up, but more lights come on at a side door—seconds later, the mechanical whirring of the garage door opener, and I settle deeper into my hiding spot behind a tree, perched on a rock, watching as a black Tesla pulls silently out.

Benjamin.

One thing hasn't changed—his taste in expensive vehicles. He stops at the end of the driveway, mouth moving, and I realize he's talking to someone through the car's Bluetooth. His voice is inaudible, but over the speaker, I can just make out the other voice.

"We should close Woodinville."

I lean forward, straining to hear. Something about *overhead* and *cost* and Benjamin's mouth sets in a straight line. But he mutters something back, and pulls from the driveway, and he and the Tesla disappear around the next turn.

North Winery appears to be flourishing. The Seattle tasting room has expanded, taking up an extra shopfront. Its wines can be found anywhere that sells wine in the Seattle area, and parts of Oregon, too. But it sounds as if they're discussing closure of the Woodinville location—Seattle's closest wine destination.

Interesting. There were money issues early on, but you made sure those were taken care of with your family's money. Despite the big house, the Tesla, the giant rock on Gwyn's finger, perhaps not all is well in Benjamin's world. The thought makes me smile.

But the smile fades. Money issues might also be the reason Benjamin had you declared dead after only three years. I'd assumed it was so he could marry Gwyn. I turn that over in my head, trying to sort it out. You hadn't signed a prenup, so everything became the collective *yours* when you married Benjamin. Or at least, that's what I assumed. Perhaps there was money he couldn't touch unless you were declared dead.

When I look back at the house, the garage door is still open.

My heart speeds, and I consider it—consider stealing inside and waiting for Gwyn to leave so I can begin my search. There are two things you always carried with you, recording your life —your diary and your camera—neither of which were recovered when the search for you began. It was believed you had them on you when you disappeared. The other option? The guilty party took them, meaning those items might be in the house with your murderer.

I eye the house. I need to get inside.

The problem is I don't know Gwyn's schedule—she might be right inside the hall that leads to the garage. She might be making breakfast in the kitchen that connects.

Or, she might still be asleep in bed.

She always did like to sleep in. At your bachelorette weekend, she'd slept till nearly noon. But it's a Tuesday. Surely, she has work.

My phone vibrates, and I glance down—it's work. A mere half hour after I've escaped the walls of the hospital, that's not good. It might be the day nurse with a question. It might be management asking if I can come early. It could even be Riley, calling to inform me I forgot to do something or made some error. The thought makes my stomach cramp with nerves. But whatever it is, I can't answer here. I let the call go to voicemail and refocus on the house.

The garage door still gapes open—inviting me. I creep another ten feet through the line of trees to get a better look— Gwyn's Porsche Cayenne is still there, though from the looks of it, she's upgraded to a newer model. I bite my lip and consider worst-case scenario: She finds me. She calls the cops. I'm arrested.

That would be a problem. That would screw up everything.

My heart pounds louder in my ears at the thought.

Best-case scenario, she never knows I'm in the house. It's big, and I know my way around. I know where you and Benjamin stored things—either the hallway walk-in closet or in the basement, neither of which I can imagine Gwyn spending much time in. She's more of the *ask the maid to do that* sort of woman.

I'm about to do it—about to dash forward across the driveway to swoop into the garage, to listen at the door, then let myself in the hall—but a sound makes me stop a millisecond before I go, a rhythmic beating of footsteps coming closer at a fast pace. I pull back. I halt my own breath and go as still as humanly possible.

Gwyn.

Gwyn, in a white running skirt swishing around her thighs, a turquoise sports bra peeking out beneath a V-neck long-sleeved running shirt, her white-blonde hair in a high ponytail, a pink visor with the word *Runner* in fancy cursive across the top.

I wonder which magazine suggested the sporty style.

She slows to a walk, shakes out her limbs, grins. A glance down at her watch, and the grin grows wider. Her phone comes out of nowhere—a hidden pocket? Her bra? And she says, "Text Benjamin," and then, "New PR! Ran the last mile in eight minutes."

Gwyn's fingers jab over the screen. The breeze comes up off the Sound, carrying with it her smell, that same combination of deodorant and hair product and, now, sweat. I wrinkle my nose, and she turns on her heel. It's the moment I've been waiting for.

I've got her.

NINE

MADELINE

Benji did the best and worst thing a man could do to me that night.

We docked the boat, got in his car, and drove north—I presumed to his place. I imagined where someone like Benji might live—a little bungalow in West Seattle? Maybe an apartment closer to the city. Possibly, given his affinity for the water, a houseboat, off one of the beaches. Or maybe we were headed to a hotel. I imagined walking in with him, hand in hand, heat radiating between us, and what we'd do when we got to the room. My body tingled, imagining the possibilities.

As we drove, he told me about his hobbies. "I love getting out in the mountains. I go with my brother, Aaron, all the time. Mount Rainier is beautiful from here, but it *towers* over you out there. Stars are brighter, food tastes better. You eat dinner around a campfire," and "The boat was my dad's. We used to take it out for days at a time. When he died, he left it to me. Besides the mountains, out on the Sound is where I'm happiest."

I listened, taking in the details, but focused on my end goal: Him. Me. Naked. When he held out his hand, I took it. The connection was like electricity shared between us, like we were one, and we were a live, crackling wire. I couldn't wait to find out what it would feel like with more than just our hands touching.

But then the familiar streets of my neighborhood appeared. My stomach flipped as I realized this wouldn't lead to an hour flirting over drinks in a hotel bar, or in his kitchen where he'd insist I try one of the wines his vineyard made—there would be no going up to the room, or kissing in the kitchen until it turned into something *else* in the kitchen.

No.

Overwhelming disappointment left me dismayed—left the pit of my stomach hollow, left me searching every nook and cranny of my memory: *What had I done wrong? Had I given him the wrong signal?* He *called* me. He *was holding* my *hand.*

Maybe this was what rejection felt like. I bit my lip as I stepped from the warm interior of his car, sure we'd never see one another again. But then he wrapped me in the sort of hug I'd never gotten before—long, drawn out, tight. His lips tickled at my ear as he whispered, "I had a great evening. I'll call you. Maybe we can do one of those fancy restaurants next time."

And I murmured, "Sure," because I was too dazed to find other words, and his lips brushed my cheek, and then he was gone. The evening was over. I was alone.

When had a date ever ended with me alone?

I called Gwyn to talk it over, but when she answered, it was obvious she'd been crying.

"Hello?" Not a gaspy voice, but a flat one, Gwyn after she's used up all her emotions.

"What's wrong?" I asked.

"Alex and I got in a fight. He stormed out. It's been an hour and he hasn't come back." Her voice cracked. "Maddy, why is it always like this? Why can't we just be happy?"

My mouth opened, closed. Yesterday I'd have said we were too young to be in serious relationships. That they were a waste of time anyway, look at our parents, divorced, dead, unhappy. And I still believed that. But the words wouldn't come out.

Instead, I found myself saying, "Gwyn, you two have been doing this for years. Maybe it's time to take a break. He shouldn't make you feel this way. You should find someone who makes you happy."

Gwyn got quiet, then a shaky breath came over the line. "You're right. You're totally right. But I can't imagine life without him."

We talked for a while longer, but I couldn't mention Benji to her. Not today. Not when her own relationship was on the verge of ending. I called Natalie next, and she sounded breathy, too, but I knew it was for a far different reason. "Hello? Maddy? One sec, let me turn down my show."

"What are you doing? Bike or elliptical?"

"Elliptical," she said, and the background noise faded to nothing. "Wanna go hiking this week? I'm tired of working out in a room. It'll probably rain, but there's a trail with a spectacular view."

That was different. Natalie was usually too focused on how many calories an activity would burn, not so much the experience. Maybe this was a good sign, maybe she was seeing her therapist again, maybe she was ready to admit that her obsession with calories was on the verge of unhealthy. Or maybe she was just trying to edge in around Gwyn. I could never tell.

The thought of trudging through rain to a questionable view that would almost certainly be obscured by said rain didn't sound like a good time to me. But Natalie and I didn't spend much time together, just the two of us, and if this was a step in a healthy direction for her, I could support that. "Sure, let's do it. Um, do you have a second to talk?"

"Of course! Anything for you, babe, but let me call you back. I have thirty-second sprints coming up. Call you in an hour after I shower and make a smoothie? Or, better, want to come over? I know it's late, but I can put edible lavender in our smoothies, and I swear it'll help you sleep. Oh gosh, that would be fun. Like a sleepover!"

I pressed a hand to my eyes, tried not to let frustration come through in my voice. "Um, maybe just call me back."

We disconnected, and I sat on the edge of my bed, drumming my fingers as though that would somehow solve the problem that neither of my closest friends had time to talk to me. I tried to think of what I wanted to say to them exactly, and come to think of it, I wasn't actually sure: That I'd gone on a second date? That I kind of liked Benji? That *he* had left *me* wanting more, and I wasn't sure how to handle that?

I tried Leah—the newest addition to our friend group, who sometimes felt like more of a hanger-on, mostly because I suspected she more wanted to be in our circle of friends than actually be a friend—but she didn't answer.

That left me with two options: Daddy, who was down in his study, working, even at eleven on a Saturday night, or Elena. Elena, who wanted so badly to be a good sister to me, who wanted to feel like part of our family, which she *was*, and I didn't know why she felt she had to try so damn hard. It would please her if I called and asked for big-sister advice, even if it irked me to imagine her soothing tones.

My finger hovered over the call button, then I pressed it.

Elena answered on the second ring. "Hey, Maddy, what's up?"

I shut my eyes and breathed, picturing him—feeling again the rush of wanting *more*, but instead he left me at my doorstep with the promise of a proper date.

"I went on a date tonight." I filled her in on the details. For once, Elena didn't interrupt or prod for more information. She just listened, silently, making appropriate noises. I ended with, "I don't get it. I thought we were going to—" I pause, think of how to put this to my sister, who I don't share these things with usually. "I thought the date would go further tonight, but he just *left*."

"Did he say anything?"

"He said he'd call me. He kissed my cheek."

Elena chuckled, but I failed to see what was so funny.

"What?"

"Madeline—he's *into* you."

I replayed the scene in my head. "He kissed my cheek, Elena."

"And said he'd call you again after taking you on a romantic date." She made a noise that might have been a snort. "He didn't want a one-night stand, Maddy. Don't you get that?" Her tone dripped with something. Not quite sarcasm, not quite approval, either. She'd suggested he was the type to get Botox at thirty. That he was after my money, but he already had his own damn boat, so I couldn't imagine money was a problem for him. Which meant that he didn't want sex. He didn't want my money. All that left—if Elena was right—was me.

He wanted *me*.

I was used to a lot of people wanting me. But not for more than a night or two. Not for more than my social circle, or to be featured on my Instagram. And usually, I didn't want them at all.

"It sounds like he's got your game," Elena murmured after a beat.

I frowned. "My game?"

A trickle of laughter. "That's it. Maddy—he's playing hard to get. Leaving you wanting more."

Her words echoed in my head. *Hard to get.* That's not how I would have described Benji, exactly, and yet there was a bit of truth to that—how many times had I been on a date, knowing exactly what the guy's end goal was, holding it back to tease him along, to get what *I* wanted?

Benji, handsome and confident, had turned my own game on me.

Heat ran through my veins thinking of it. A slow smile came to my lips. Just like he'd played along in the bar, when I'd stuck my foot out, inviting him to accept my invitation of a meet-cute.

He was good. And I was determined to prove I was even better.

"Thanks, Elena."

We disconnected, my mind already scheming.

This game would be far more fun with both of us playing.

TEN

REBECCA

Now

The line of trees is to Gwyn's back. I press against the rough bark, listening as she talks into her phone, enunciating each word so the voice-to-text picks up what she's saying, and I take advantage of the noise to creep along the wall of pines. When I reach the street, I stand straight and begin to run again, but take only a few steps—because what matters here is *falling*.

I hop from the road to the sidewalk but let my foot catch on the curb—I hit hard, forearms and elbows scraping over cement, the skin on my knees tearing as they touch the asphalt of the road. Sharp, exquisite pain sears through me, blood red, but nothing compared to what I went through to make me who I am now.

Silence.

The cold, unforgiving road beneath me. My heartbeat roaring in my ears, body tense with anticipation—did she see? What will she do?

I collapse into that moment after the fall when your body realizes what has happened. Your brain says *pain* and *this will hurt* and the roil of embarrassment that follows, knowing I've hit the ground hard, like a toddler who's still learning to walk.

"Oh my gosh." Gwyn's words echo up the driveway. The slap of her footsteps louder, closer. "Are you okay?"

I stay on the cold wet concrete as she comes up behind me. Fingertips touch my shoulder.

"I'm—I'm not sure." I keep my face down, out of the glare of headlights passing us by. The sun is up now, but it's that golden hour light that leaves the world ever so slightly fantastical. Here in Washington, it means pink and blue intertwine across the sky, and the light is dim, but present. My hands tingle from the pain, the adrenaline. My heart beats a frantic rhythm, because in seconds, Gwyn will see my face.

I should have waited. I should have watched and learned more about them first. Or tried this new appearance on someone else before seeing them—someone unimportant in the bigger scheme of things. If this fails, there are no other options. I suppose I could report my suspicions anonymously—but there's no guarantee anything would come of that.

This has to work. For you, Maddy.

"Gosh, let me help you." Gwyn's hand cups my elbow and pulls me to standing. I wince as my knee straightens and look down to see torn skin with a trickle of blood running down my shin. "Yikes."

I finally look up and meet her gaze, her lower lip thrust out in a pout of sympathy. Our eyes meet. I know mine are no longer green, but instead a dark brown. I know my freckles are long gone, thanks to a bleaching cream. My face is heart-shaped now, instead of oval, and I'm thirty pounds heavier, a combination of simple weight gain, but also lifting weights, filling out my body instead of the slender build I had before. But there will always be similarities.

"Have we met?" She tilts her head.

Change your voice, I remind myself. I'd spent weeks

learning to make it higher, breathier—less intimidating. Someone a person will instinctively trust and find harmless.

"I don't think so. I just moved here," I answer calmly, hoping my internal panic does not seep through.

That same grin breaks through, curiosity replaced by enthusiasm. "Where from?"

"Kansas City, originally." It's not the truth, but it is somewhere I've spent enough time that I could answer basic questions about it. "But I just moved from St. Louis."

"Well, welcome to our little corner of Seattle. I'm so sorry you fell." She puts her hands on her hips and glances down at my knee. "You all right?"

I breathe out, clench my teeth, nod. "It stings, but yeah."

"How far from home are you?"

"A couple miles. I'm—" I think fast. "Training for a race, so—"

Gwyn's eyes go wide, and this close, I can tell she too has had work done—the fine lines she already had by thirty have disappeared, and she's closer to thirty-five now. "A race? Which one?" But before I can answer she continues. "I just signed up for the Seattle Marathon. It's at the end of November."

"That one." Another tight smile. "Moved here and thought it would be a good way to meet other runners."

"Has it been?"

I laugh. "Well, not really. I work night shift, so I run in the mornings around now, but it seems like everyone else is already at work."

"Oh, girl, I know. My friends run at 5 a.m. or 5 p.m., when it's dark or there's all that pollution from traffic." She scrunches her nose in a gesture so Gwyn my heart palpitates for a moment; all I can think of is her complaining about her damn boyfriend. She was always the most annoying of your friends.

"I'm Gwyn by the way. Want to come in? I'll get you

cleaned up. Least I can do after you fell on our little patch of sidewalk. I've got coffee, too."

I let hesitation flash through my eyes and wait a full two seconds before responding—as any woman invited into a stranger's home would do—but then I nod. "That would be great, thank you."

"You should run with my friends and me sometime. We mostly run on the weekend. Have you done a race before?"

I carry on the conversation the best I can, sharing that, no, I've never run a race, but I'm excited; that I've been in Seattle about a month, and I love it, but gosh, where is the sun? By the time we're through the garage and inside her house—the house that used to be yours—the sun is just turning the view of Mount Rainier opposite the Puget Sound orange and red and baby blue —a gorgeous sunrise for the start of what will surely be, if not a beautiful friendship, a useful one.

She was within my sights.

Now, she's within my reach.

It's the beginning of the end for your killer, Maddy.

ELEVEN

MADELINE

Four Years Ago

We played the game for the two weeks before Benji had to leave for Europe.

Dates infused with thick, delicious tension, where even holding his hand left me wanting more. Texts alternating between sweet and suggestive. Stolen moments when we hadn't planned a date at all, stopping by his winery because I was "just passing through," or him inviting himself along to drinks with the girls, where he'd charm all of us with his banter, where he'd insist on picking up the check.

We were like one of those early-2000s classics of romance and passion, living in the moment, enjoying the person before us, not thinking about what happened next. Or at least, that's what I told myself.

I ignored my friends, and he ignored his business and his brother. We packed two months of dating into two weeks.

And then abruptly, the game ended. We'd known it was coming—that Benji would leave for Europe, and we wouldn't see each other for a month. In the quiet moments after I went home from his condo or he left my house, I couldn't help but wonder if it was his own personal way of playing the game—maybe this was how he dated. He set a deadline, which allowed him to gracefully bow out, the woman knowing from day one things would, if not end, at least take a long pause, during which time they would cool off.

I had to remind myself, that's what *I* was doing, playing that game. And I hated that.

It led to our interactions taking on an almost frantic pace. And all the while, I told myself it was fine, it didn't matter, because he was leaving, so I could let myself be this open, this vulnerable. It would end, and I would go back to my normal life.

Then the night before he was to go to the airport and leave Seattle—leave *me*—arrived. Our final date. Our goodbye.

Benji was late to pick me up. I stood in the foyer, peeking through the marbled glass, wondering where the hell he was, my stomach churning, my eyes dropping to check my phone for messages from him over and over.

"What the hell has gotten you so riled up?" Daddy asked. He leaned in the doorway that connected the foyer to the galley kitchen, a glass of Scotch held in one hand. His eyes took me in. "Let me guess, finally, a man has gotten to you." I didn't answer, and he went on. "I've seen you these last two weeks. Distracted. Dreamy look in your eyes."

I forced myself to stand still, to stop fidgeting with my phone, my purse, the hem of my silk shirt.

"It's not like that," I said, but I heard the lie in my voice. Daddy did, too.

"I know you don't approve of how I've lived my life." Daddy stepped farther into the room and found a place to settle his glass on a built-in bookshelf. "But let me tell you something, Maddy. Your mother was it for me." He stared at me, a direct look he usually only leveled at someone trying to give him a bad deal at work. "Every woman I've been with since then was me trying to find that feeling again. The feeling your mother gave me. So if you've found the right person, don't let them go just because you're a little bit scared. Love *is* scary at first. It's a big deal."

"I don't love him," I said, my voice fast, defensive.

Daddy's lips twisted into a smile, and I could almost hear the word *liar* cross from him to me.

Was I lying?

A gentle *rap-rap-rap* on the door. My breath caught in my throat. I spun. Daddy made a noise that might have been a chuckle, but my attention had already shifted from him to Benji, even with a thick door between us. I opened the door and slipped out, avoiding them meeting yet again.

Our last date was to mirror our first real one. The night on the Puget Sound in the boat. It had grown colder, the wind slicing through our layers more acutely, but it only meant we snuggled closer.

"You know what my goal was when I first brought you out here?" Benji said after we'd finished cider spiked with rum and the smoked salmon and brie he'd brought along for dinner.

"What?" I asked, wishing I could live in the moment this night, too, instead of considering a future without him. It was only a month, but a month could change things. What if this spell broke during that month, and I returned to considering men beneath me? I wasn't afraid to admit it. That's how I'd felt all these years. And then I met him, someone on my level. I'd experienced what Daddy and Elena had fallen so deeply for, and Daddy's words echoed in my head, telling me not to let go, but this didn't feel in my control. This felt entirely *out* of my control.

How lucky I had been to come across Benji. What were the odds, really? What were the odds of any two individuals meeting and connecting and falling in love? Not that this was love, but it was *something*.

Benji took a long time to respond, like he wasn't sure he should say what was on his mind. Then he took my hand, pulled me closer, and in a soft voice as he stared out at the dark waters, whispered, "It was to make you fall in love with me before I left. I know, I know—it sounds like a movie or something. Two weeks to fall in love, right? But that was my goal. You have a reputation for not being patient with men, and with me leaving for a month—" His voice faded off. He didn't have to say the rest. His fears mirrored my own.

But what was more was his goal: to make me *fall in love* with him.

God, why were people so obsessed with *love*? With *falling in love*? It felt like a ridiculous pressure to put on two people, especially when love apparently meant you were supposed to commit for a lifetime or something like that. And yet...

"Anyway," he said, "You don't have to answer if I've succeeded or not. I suspect two weeks isn't long enough for most people, especially people like us."

My whole body tensed. Was this where the *this has been fun, but...* conversation came in? God, he was good. What a way to let a woman down easy.

"So, I bought you a ticket to go to Europe with me. I know it's short notice, and if you need a few days to collect your things, I can change it. But you do social media, so you could work from anywhere. In fact, it might be *good* for your social media, some of the places I'd love to show you in Europe would photograph beautifully."

Static filled my head. I pulled away, turned to stare at him, my pulse in my throat as I replayed his words. I have no idea what my expression was, but his changed in an instant—from earnest hope, eyes wide and vulnerable, to something akin to fear.

"Too soon, I guess. Damn." He stood in jerky movement. "I get it. It's okay."

But I was still processing what he'd said.

After a moment I finally said something. "Did you just invite me to go to Europe with you?"

Benji turned, looked at me from where he'd braced his hands on the side of the boat. "I did."

I grinned, throwing my arms around him. "Yes. Yes, yes, yes." His returning laugh was full of joy and relief.

When I got home that night, elated, packing a bag furiously, texting Elena she'd have to find someone to fill in for my temp job as her receptionist, I thought through every moment of our short time together. How incredibly lucky and perfect we were. How two weeks wasn't enough, and maybe I *could* fall in love. Europe would be perfect.

TWELVE

REBECCA

Now

My initial impression is that Gwyn is happy. She has everything she ever wanted, so she should be. She got Benjamin. She got the house, her own fledgling interior design business, the car, the time to spend training for a marathon. Not only that, but it's clear with you gone, your friend has become Queen Bee instead of the Queen Bee's bestie. She whips around the kitchen, pouring coffee, fielding texts from friends, chatting away.

She practically *glows*, filling your shoes. It makes me want to shake her—to demand answers. To see her eyes widen as she realizes *I know*.

"I plan our run routes." She slides a mug my way. "We always start from here, because it's the most central location, and we head north to either Discovery Park or Green Lake. Green Lake is my favorite, because the best coffee shop is right by the local running store, and sometimes—"

As she drones on, I observe her from inside the house now, accepting the coffee but not sipping it, letting my hands close over the mug until they burn from the heat. It keeps me focused, keeps me from slipping into the past when it was you in this kitchen.

You loved this kitchen, even if you never went so far as to learn how to boil a pot of water.

"Cream? Sugar?"

Gwyn waits across the counter, that big welcoming smile on her face.

"Cream, please," I say. "Thank you."

"So polite." She waggles her eyebrows as she goes to the giant stainless-steel fridge. "Must be a nurse thing."

I've never been called polite in my life, but she's right. *Please. Thank you.* I'm putting on a performance for her—the breathy voice, the vulnerable young woman. It is *I* who is apparently the actor in her house, now. But there are no do-overs, so I paste on my best estimation of a happy-go-lucky smile. "Definitely. They teach it from day one."

Gwyn sets a carton of half-and-half in front of me and finds the stool opposite. My knee is forgotten, but that's fine—my goal is to use this time to get close to her.

"So, what brought you to Seattle?"

"I've heard good things," I say.

"About Seattle in October?" A half laugh. "You're here a few months too late, I'm sorry to say. The summers are incredible. But fall is when the rain starts. And doesn't stop until the next summer." Gwyn peers over the lip of the mug, looking up at me, tracing my face with her gaze. Seeing something she finds familiar, maybe. I force myself to relax. To ignore that my body is rigid with nervous anticipation of being found out.

Don't worry, Maddy. I won't fail you.

"How is marathon training going for you?" I ask. "I'm really struggling with the long runs."

Gwyn waves me off with one hand. "Not anymore, girl. You

working this Friday night? Could you come run Saturday morning?"

"I have Friday night off." I don't. But I'll call in.

"Well, we start here at 7 a.m. It's our rest week, so we're only doing eight miles. That work for you?"

I nod. It's more than what I've been doing, but I'll struggle through. It's an opportunity to get to know her, to get to know her friends.

"The key to running long is having friends to chat with. And we will chat your ear off."

"Thank you for the invite." More politeness, more playing along. "Do you have a restroom I could use?"

"Of course." Gwyn hops off the stool and leads me to a half bath down the hall.

I step inside and go still, my mind drawing a blank. I expected the white tile and teal-blue trim and photographs of the Puget Sound on the walls—the way you decorated and proudly displayed it—but it doesn't even resemble the room it used to be. The tile has been replaced with flat gray walls. A beach and lighthouse theme, complete with a miniature lighthouse at the top of a towel rack.

It's been three years. *Three* years. They never found a body, and you were declared dead days ago. It's all happened so fast, so easily, almost like someone wanted it to be that way. How convenient you were never found—no body, no crime, as they say. And your husband, your best friend, they gave up hope after a mere three years. Almost like you never existed to begin with.

Gwyn, as far as I can tell, just recently moved in, around the time they got engaged mere months ago. Did Benjamin do this? Start erasing you one room at a time? I think back to the kitchen. I'd been so focused on anticipating what Gwyn might ask, how to turn the conversation the way I needed it to go, I hadn't looked carefully around—what else has changed? The refrigerator was still there. The countertops remained granite. The floors were large tile, the same tile that came with the house when you bought it.

I force myself to move—to wash my hands and dab the blood off my leg. Meanwhile, my eyes never stop roving the room—new towels, seashell-shaped soap, a soap dish that *is* a seashell. My throat closes up, and I turn the cold water back on to splash my face, to keep myself in the moment.

It's just a bathroom. But I remember how proud you were after you remodeled it. How you showed off the colors, the theme, the tile. And now it's all gone. Every trace of you.

Through the door, Gwyn's voice rings out in words and laughter. The name *"Maximillian's!"* breaks through the otherwise too distant words—the name of a downtown restaurant. She must be on the phone. I crack open the door, and the hall is empty—but two doors down is a closet where your things might be stored. *Hidden.*

That said, Gwyn, another perfectly good source of information, waits for me in the kitchen. I take another look down the hall and ease into it. The floor creaks beneath my footsteps—Gwyn's voice silences in the kitchen.

My eyes dart toward the kitchen, then back to the closet. I swallow. This isn't the time. I need to wait until she is better distracted. Though that assumes I'll be invited into her house again. Your house. I *have* been invited back, though—Saturday morning.

I leave the hall and stroll back into the kitchen, doing my best to turn on a bright smile. Gwyn smiles back and murmurs into the phone. "Gotta go. Can't wait for tonight. Love you, too." She sets the phone down. "Sorry, fiancé called. He always checks to make sure I get home okay from my runs. Isn't that sweet?"

"That *is* sweet." I sidle up to the counter and sip my coffee and turn on whatever old-fashioned nurse charm I can muster. In reality, every nurse I've met swears like a sailor and doesn't take shit from anyone—but Gwyn likes the theatrical.

"When did you get engaged? Can I see the ring?"

Gwyn positively glows as she launches into the story, and I listen, freely given the information I've been so curious about these past weeks. Months. *Years.*

If I'm lucky, she'll let something incriminating slip. I gaze at her and see the friend she was to you—the fun gossip who never failed to text back or like a social media post. Who was your bestie above your other friends, though I can't understand why. She was certainly not the most likable. I see the girl who's become a woman, who's grown confident with her new place in life, replacing you. Would you have ever guessed she'd do that? Do you think she did it on purpose? Arranged for it? I'll think of a way to ask the right questions, if not now, then in a few weeks, when we've grown close. When she trusts me.

She flashes the ring my way, and I take her hand in mine as though it's precious. I exclaim and tell her it's the prettiest one I've ever seen, and damn, she is *lucky*. The rock is bigger than yours was, Maddy, but not in a good way—in a gaudy, overly flashy way. Just like Gwyn.

"Is it your first marriage?" I ask, and when her eyes widen at the question, quickly add, "I was married for a while. That's why I ask." My lip juts out just a bit with these words—letting her know as kind as I am, I'm also deep. I have pain in my past. She eats it up.

"Oh, you poor dear. Yes, it's my first marriage. His second." She tilts her head and reaches for the coffee pot, filling my cup. "How long did it last?"

I launch into a story about a man who never existed. "But he died, and—" I shrug and look anywhere but her, and she takes the hint.

"I'm so sorry." A hand touches my shoulder, and I give her a little nod, let our eyes meet. Let us have *a moment*, because that's what friendships are made of.

"So, what does Benjamin do?" I ask after a suitably long silence.

"He owns a winery." Her eyes flash with pride. "North Winery. Have you heard of it?"

"Oh, I drank a bottle from there last week." A lie. I wouldn't touch the stuff.

"He opened it all by himself after he got his MBA. I'm so proud of him, and it's been *so* successful."

"That's impressive," I say. All by himself, my ass. With the help of your money. "I've heard new businesses fail more often than not."

"He's so business smart."

That's not what his conversation this morning might have meant. But I could have taken it out of context. Or Gwyn might not know about it—if Benjamin would kill you for your money, he'd certainly lie to his fiancée about money troubles.

Coffee lasts half an hour before the exhaustion of working night shift hits. I yawn, and Gwyn offers me a ride home. I accept, because it's only fair—if I know where she lives, she should know where I live. That makes me easier to trust. To be seen as the person I claim to be. Rebecca, the travel nurse training for a marathon, staying in a tiny house on the edge of the Queen Anne neighborhood.

"Do you think you'll come on Saturday?" she asks as we pull up in front of my place.

"Definitely. Here, I'll text you." We exchange numbers. She pulls away with a flutter of fingertips. I watch her go, the cool air warming around me as the sun rises in the sky, a rare sunny October day. Maybe it's a good omen—a sign that this will go according to plan.

My lips quirk up as she takes a corner and disappears from

view. I've done it. I've met Gwyn and fooled her with my new identity. I've been invited in.

THIRTEEN

REBECCA

Now

In preparation for my entry into Gwyn's new life, I call in sick Friday night. I can't work an overnight shift then go run eight miles and be on my game.

Of course, Riley answers.

"You didn't waste your excess morphine the other day," she says by way of greeting. "I tried to get ahold of you to come back and fix it, but you didn't answer your phone."

I go still. It's a controlled substance. Failing to account for the part I poured down the drain can get me in *real* trouble—and a real nurse wouldn't have forgotten that.

"Anyway, I took care of it, but be more careful. Or your job will be in jeopardy. Maybe your license, too, *Rebecca*."

I bite my tongue, then grovel. "Thank you. I'm so sorry. I won't let it happen again. But I'm not feeling well. I need to call in sick. I can make the shift up next week."

Riley heaves a sigh. "Hold on, let me get the patient assignments. I'll see if we can shift things around." In my head, I see her standing over the binder with staffing assignments, running her finger down the list of nurses to find my name.

"Did I mention I knew a Rebecca Johnson once?" Riley clucks. "Back when I worked in eastern Washington a couple years ago."

My breath catches in my throat.

"Rebecca? I lose you?"

"It's a common name."

"A strange coincidence, I guess."

I'm standing in my bare-bones living room, phone pressed to my ear, putting together what this means, when it hits me— Riley worked with Rebecca. The *real* Rebecca. It may be a common name, but eastern Washington is where Yakima is. Yakima is where Rebecca worked back-to-back travel assignments.

We hang up, and I tell myself it's nothing—it will be fine. There's no reason for Riley to put two and two together. And yet, Riley's already watching me. Already giving me the side-eye over the smallest thing, like she somehow *knows* I'm not a real nurse. And now this.

It leaves me uneasy, and I spend the hours I can't sleep pacing the streets rather than running them. I watch as a mother reads a child a bedtime story beneath soft light. I listen as a couple argues back and forth about money. I find my way inside a home for sale, the back door left open, and wander the rooms, one at a time, imaging what it would be like to own a home like this. I pretend to be anyone except who I am. Especially since who I am is just a lie.

When I start to grow tired, I find Chris's alleyway. I hear his dog before I see him, a scuffle of feet, an excited *yip, yip, yip*, Chris's rumbling laughter. A knot in the fence line is my opportunity, and I smooth my fingers over the rough wood to peek through.

A rope is in Izzy's mouth—the other end in Chris's hand. A

game of tug-of-war, the dog, her haunches lowered, her legs taking her slowly backward, clearly the winner, though I suspect that is because Chris lets her win.

In another life, where I got to know Chris for real, I'd knock on the outside fence gate. Or maybe, I'd text him ahead of time. *I'm coming over*, or, he'd text me: *You busy? Want to have a beer* I'd say yes, and there would be no make believe. It would just be me and him, and the truth.

Heat radiates through my chest, swirling through my insides, imagining the text. The invitation. The warmth of a familiar face when I arrived.

But before I can bask in the vision, there's a nose through the fence line at my knees—a snuffling sound, and then a bass growl—and Chris yells, "What is it, girl?" and I've nearly been caught.

I slip through the alley to the house behind Chris's and slip through the gate, as though I live there, as though I belong.

But I don't belong here. Or anywhere, really. Maybe when this is all done, when I can rest easy, I can find a place I belong again.

I ease along the side of the house—an empty one, no lights on inside—and to the next street. I'm headed home when a familiar shape lopes across the street not fifty feet from me. My whole body goes still—a deer frozen before its doom—but he doesn't so much as notice me. And as his form becomes one with the inky blackness of night, I forget my plans to not make this a run. I break into a jog, then a sprint, running lightly on the balls of my feet to catch up with him.

Because the Benjamin I knew never ran, too obsessed with his work to do little more than catch a quick session with his personal trainer. Is this a new side to him? Or maybe he's running for the same reason so many people run, to escape their inner demons that might otherwise claw themselves out from the inside.

When I find him, I drop back half a block and follow at a distance, ready to turn and run a different route if he notices me. I time my footfalls to his, eliminating the risk he will hear me. And I watch his body move, striding forward, a powerful motion I wouldn't have guessed could come from your husband. I wonder what other secrets he keeps—sides to himself he never showed you.

We pace a mile to a beach, then run along a trail that parallels it. When we turn off, it's to enter a wooded park, and here, I hesitate. It's the sort of place women don't run by themselves, especially with men who might be murderers. But he doesn't know I'm here. And I'm dressed in black, sticking to the shadows—even someone who would harm me likely won't so much as see me. So I follow him in, assuming it will be a quick breeze through back to the road, where he'll return home.

The moisture in the air builds as we enter the forest. The heavy scent of moss and pine creates the illusion we are somewhere far away from Seattle, with its traffic and overloaded highways and Pike Place and tourists. We could be anywhere. Even back in those woods where Madeline disappeared.

When Benjamin comes to a stop, I do, too, assuming he's going to stretch or take a breather—what I don't expect is for a second form to join him—a tall, slender form, with a ponytail.

I can barely contain the gasp that works its way up my throat. Benjamin and the woman move closer, voices murmuring, joining with the wind, obscured entirely. I can't see her face, can't tell who she is—but I can tell she is *not* Gwyn.

I step from the shelter of my tree and move closer. I'm nearly to the next tree when a twig snaps beneath my shoe.

Crap.

The voices stop. Even the trees seem to go still, as though I've interrupted their conversation. My skin tingles, and I squeeze my eyes shut, breathe slowly, reach out and touch the ruddy bark of the tree. I press myself close to it.

"Come on," Benjamin says after a beat. "Probably a junkie."

Footsteps pace away.

I hold back the curse at my lips—an opportunity lost. I could follow them. My body aches with the anticipation of lunging forward in pursuit, this time being more careful. But the worst thing that could happen is I'm noticed. Then this would all be for nothing. I wouldn't do that to you, Maddy.

Their shadows recede into a bend in the trail. I'm left with the trees and questions, like who Benjamin is meeting with in secret. Maybe he's not a runner. Maybe it's merely an excuse for something else. But what? It could be an affair, and the real issue he's unable to settle down with one woman, always looking for someone else. Maybe he cheated on you with Gwyn, and now cheats on Gwyn with—well, whoever that was.

I sag against the tree. My watch tells me it's just past midnight. I've got to be up in six hours, so I turn toward home. My heart won't slow, though, reimagining the woman's appearance. I try to replay the way she moved in my head, try to identify who it could be—but it was too dark, and they were too far away.

More than anything, I want to know who this mystery woman is and why Benjamin is meeting with her in secret, days after his wife was declared dead, while his fiancée sits alone at home.

FOURTEEN

MADELINE

Four Years Ago

We went to Europe, and Benji took me to London and Florence and Paris, and it was magic. One moment I was fighting against myself, the next I knew my life wouldn't be right without him.

I even used the L-word. I told Benji I *loved* him.

When we returned, I stopped hiding him away. No one knew what to think. Madeline Hughes, coupled.

Daddy, of course, adored him. Elena was happy for me, though I noticed the way her eyes lingered on him—wondering, maybe, how she could have been so wrong about him that first night. Gwyn doubled down her efforts to make things work with Alex, panicked, I suspected, at the thought her best friend might have yet another thing she didn't have—a boyfriend. Leah seemed newly interested in me, seeking me out for yoga classes, walks along the waterfront, even inviting me to her family's cabin in the San Juan Islands. Natalie, meanwhile, assured me she never thought he was *really* creepy, and took to texting me every day, checking in on how our relationship was doing.

We attended parties, galas, and hosted a few at Benji's flagship tasting room in Woodinville. There were times our life felt not like our own—between him traveling to Woodinville, Walla Walla, Napa, and occasionally other locations, the unending invitations to attend events, and my own life, which swirled around creating content for my social media and resuming my part-time job at Elena's practice. Our time together was minimal. But we'd decided every Sunday night would be ours. The entertaining was done for the weekend, the new week yet to start.

And on such a night, he took me out on his boat, gave me a new Nikon DSLR, and said, "Do you know how to work this thing? Will it work for your social media?"

I nodded, staring down at it with wide eyes. "Yes, of course."

He knew that my love for photography and Instagram didn't come from a desire to merely show the world my life, but my love for the art form itself. As I turned on the new camera, played with the settings, and set it up on the boat deck with the sun setting behind where he sat watching me, I wondered why I hadn't bought myself a real camera before this moment. I loved to capture moments of life that have that extra sparkle. It was kismet that Instagram became a thing when I was a teenager, and that it became my go-to way of sharing my life. But I also took photography classes in high school and college. My phone was easy, always with me, but a fancy Nikon I was still working out how to use? That was all him.

I snapped a photo of him, his eyes on me, twinkling with joy.

"What's the special occasion?" I asked. Benji stood, shoved his hands in his pockets. Shrugged. "Just a little gift to say I love you."

"Well, I love you, too." I advanced to press a kiss to his lips, then took a couple more experimental shots.

"Is there a timer on that thing?" he asked.

"Of course. I can do..." I squinted at the screen. "Three seconds, ten seconds, or thirty seconds."

"Let's do ten. Maybe get a photo of us in front of the sunset?"

I scrunched my nose. "The light of the setting sun will probably overpower us. Maybe to one side?"

"Show me where to stand."

I approached him, unsteady on my feet as a wave slapped against the boat. His hand clasped around my arm, and he pulled me close, steadied me.

I pointed out the best spot, which caught the edge of the sunset and a pile of blue and purple puffy clouds in the distance. We weren't far from shore, only about ten minutes of slow going, so we could still see the piers of Seattle, the jutting peninsula of the edge of West Seattle.

"Let me check it." I held the camera up, then knelt to find a steady place to put it. I'd have to buy a tripod. Once I had it safely on a seat where it couldn't fall overboard if another wave hit us, I looked up. "Ready?" I called.

His eyes never left mine, steady, heated.

"Let's do this." His words carried a weight that left my gaze lingering, curious about what exactly he meant.

But he waited, and the camera sat ready, so I pressed the button and hurried to his side. I tried to snuggle in against him, but he murmured, "Here, sit right here," pressing me a foot or so away. The camera was about to flash, so I didn't argue, just turned toward it, put on a bright smile, and—

"Maddy." Benji's voice, urgent, made me whip my head to look at him, worried a boat was headed our way, maybe the giant ferry that shuttled tourists from—

"Oh my god." My jaw dropped.

The flash went off. The shutter snapped open and shut.

But I couldn't move. Benji knelt before me, holding up the

ring in a Tiffany-blue jewelry box. He'd tricked me into taking our engagement photo.

"Maddy, will you marry me?" he asked.

Of course, I said yes.

FIFTEEN

REBECCA

Now

Sleep doesn't come easily. When I wake at six to prepare to meet Gwyn, my eyes are puffy, and my mind drags.

My album about you sits on my dining room table, and I can't help but stare at it as I pull on a sports bra and fill a water bottle.

Madeline Hughes Missing.

Madeline Hughes Presumed Dead.

Madeline Hughes Declared Dead.

I mentally add my own headlines.

Benjamin North Engaged to the Best Friend.

Benjamin North Meeting Secretly at Night with Another Woman...

And in the middle of all this, *Madeline Hughes's Diary and Camera Never Recovered.*

I rub a hand over my face, over my neck. Today I have one simple goal—to infiltrate Gwyn's social circle. It's the ticket to Gwyn, to Benjamin, to their home. And it's the way to my ultimate goal—avenging you.

I know you wouldn't approve of what I'm doing. You wouldn't like that I had it out for your husband—that I plan to lie, to worm myself into his life, and that once there, I plan on taking revenge. Do to the guilty what they did to you. But you were a scared little girl, always looking to please everyone while maintaining the status quo at the top of the social hierarchy, a hard balance to strike. If I've learned anything, it's that it's not possible to do both. And you couldn't. Somewhere in the ranks of who you thought were committed friends and family, someone had it out for you.

I reconsider the possibility it was someone besides Benjamin—that it was Gwyn or another friend I forgot about, jealousy getting the best of them, or even a family member, someone who might benefit from the money you stood to inherit. But if that were the case, they'd have shoved you over a cliff *before* you said, "I do," *before* you married Benjamin North, legally giving him the majority of anything that was yours.

You should have signed a prenup like your father begged you to. But to you, it meant a way out—like every relationship your father ever had. You were young, dumb, and dangerously, stupidly, in love. Not that I blame you. Benjamin reeled you in. He seduced you into trusting him. Anyone would have fallen for him.

It's always the husband.

It's 6:58 a.m. when I arrive at Gwyn's, where three women gather in her driveway—slender, tanned legs, running skirts on two of the three, formfitting purple leggings on the other. High ponytails and bright splashes of color, and I realize I chose wrong with my braid and normal dark shades. I want to fit in—not show how different I am. But it's too late now.

I pry my fingers off the steering wheel, cut the engine, force a cheerful smile on my face. But the key to acting is *feeling*, not pretending, so I think about something that makes me happy— Chris; his dog, Izzy; the idea of spending an evening wiling away the hours with them in a world where I can knock on his fence gate and let myself right in.

Sometimes, the only thing that gets us by is illusion. So I fool myself that someday that could happen, and it works—a warmth comes to my cheeks and heart at the thought. Enjoying someone. Trusting them.

Gwyn catches sight of me, her eyebrows climbing an inch, a grin breaking out, and it's all but impossible to keep the mirage from crashing down like the set of a puppet show, the strings cut through with a knife.

"Rebecca," she calls. "You made it! Hurry, come meet the girls!"

I skip over, like a teenager excited to meet her new best friends.

"Laura," Gwyn motions to one woman—her hair a dark shade of auburn, in an efficient ponytail, her shoulders muscular in a way that tells me she spends as much time in a gym as she does running.

"Nice to meet you," Laura says, but her face doesn't reflect much other than *can we get running, already?* Her gaze shifts to the road, then back to me, the tiniest of forced smiles coming to her mouth.

"And I'm Abigail," the other chimes in, before Gwyn can introduce her. Abigail's face is the opposite of Laura's—friendly, open, inviting. I realize I recognize her, someone I used to see at the country club gym, though we never spoke, only exchanged nods in passing. Abigail takes my hand in a soft shake, and relief I hadn't expected drifts through me, as I've met two more people who haven't recognized me.

"Nice to meet you, thanks for having me along." My words come out easily, but I wring my hands, because Rebecca is a little shy—a little unsure.

"No problem." Laura's gaze still drifts around, and she

stands with her hands on her hips—done with introductions and ready to go.

"Well, let's get started." Gwyn motions down the road. "We'll run through Discovery Park first."

Laura takes the lead, and Abigail and Gwyn fall in beside me.

"So, Gwyn said you're a travel nurse?"

I sugarcoat my voice and answer Abigail's questions one by one—where I'm from, what working as a travel nurse is like— exciting, but also lonely at times. I ask her questions in return because people like answering questions about themselves.

"How long have you lived in Seattle?" I ask Abigail. I pull my hands inside the sleeves of my shirt as a breeze hits, and we quicken our step as a group, as if we all feel it.

"I'm from Olympia, but I came here for college. Met my hubby. Never left." A quick grin sprints across her face. She's pretty—and too nice to be friends with Gwyn. She reminds me of you, actually. "I think you'll like it here. Have you thought about settling down? He's got a brother I could introduce you to."

Gwyn chuckles. "Don't mind Abigail. She just wants to see everyone as happy and in love as she is." Her words are kind, but she catches my eye between strides, and her teeth clench as she nods at Laura, who's a few paces ahead of us. The message is clear—*Laura is not happy and in love.*

The run goes by quickly—first through the trails of the park, then along a waterfront path. I manage to keep pace, though I can tell my legs will be sore after eight miles. The wind picks up, but the rain holds off as we log our miles. Conversation strays to Laura's new job—she's an attorney who's opened her own practice—and then to Abigail, who's trying to get pregnant. This brings up the topic of pregnancy, and Gwyn laughs when Abigail lobs the topic her way.

"So, you and Benji."

If I weren't an object in motion, staying in motion, I'd go still—*Benji.*

Your name for him. A name I haven't heard in three years.

Gwyn makes a face, and it might be my imagination, but I swear a flicker in her gaze carries grief or darkness or—or *something.* "*Benjamin,*" she corrects, "doesn't want kids. And I'm fine without them, too."

"Really?" This time, from Laura.

"Yeah. I mean, we're having fun. He owns a winery and like three vineyards, and—" She shrugs, waits a beat, catching her breath as we top a hill. "I'm just getting my business going. We're happy. I don't think we need kids to keep us that way."

There's strain in her voice, and I wonder what secrets she keeps from them. Secrets I will find a way to get out of her.

"Yeah, but—" Laura begins.

"I totally understand." My voice seems to startle them, hopping in on a conversation on a topic that is maybe better suited to Gwyn's closer friends. "I don't want kids, either. Nothing against them. I just don't feel the need to have them. It's like because it's an expectation, everyone thinks eventually you'll want them."

"Yeah." Gwyn's eyes catch mine, grateful to have someone on her side. "Exactly like that."

Satisfaction creeps through me—one step closer to her trusting me.

Laura and Abigail stay silent, and I wonder if in endearing myself to Gwyn, I've put myself on their bad side. Or maybe, Gwyn told them about my pretend husband dying.

"Well then, you'll just have to be an auntie when I have one!" Abigail says as she glances my way. "Both of you, if you decide to stick around, Rebecca."

Something inside me loosens for a millisecond—feeling a flash of acceptance, of *friendship*—but just as fast, I recall why I'm really here.

"Gwyn, when's the wedding?" I ask.

"Oh, we got engaged not that long ago, so I'm just starting to plan. But we're thinking next September, somewhere here in Seattle. The weather is usually pretty good still, and—" She prattles on about locations and color schemes. Abigail chimes in ideas for bridesmaid dresses.

"How many bridesmaids do you think you'll have?" I ask.

"These two." Gwyn nods at our fellow runners. "I have a cousin I'll ask. A sister." She scrunches her nose, and a bead of sweat rolls off the end. A beat where she pauses to think, only our panting breaths filling the cool morning. Overhead, the pale light of morning has faded, a gray cloud cover taking over.

"What about a best friend?" I let the words on the tip of my tongue tumble out, a streak of satisfaction coursing through me. I can't help but think of other women who used to be in her life —where have they gone?

Laura surges up a hill, and Abigail chases her. There's a moment when Gwyn and I stride pace for pace, and I think Gwyn will read into me, but she just laughs. "Honestly, Benjamin is my best friend. And these two. We talk about everything while we run." I'm caught on her claim that Benjamin is her best friend, but she looks up at the sky.

"Oh, you just seem so—" I pretend to fight for the right word, shoot her a sheepish smile. "Social. In a good way."

Gwyn glances in my direction, indecision in her eyes. "Honestly, my other friends—they don't approve of me and Benjamin, so... we've sort of lost touch." She swallows, then eyes the sky again. "Storm's coming. Let's sprint to the end. Then I'll make coffee. Laura brought scones."

That streak of satisfaction becomes a pool so deep I could practically swim in it. So, everyone jumped ship, Maddy. *Good.* Just as I hoped. Gwyn doesn't deserve your friends.

SIXTEEN

REBECCA

Now

We arrive back at Gwyn's, and she busies herself pulling out plates and forks and pouring mugs of coffee. Laura excuses herself to the bathroom, and Abigail and I are suddenly next to one another, watching the Puget Sound through the big windows at the rear of the house.

"Look at the water," she murmurs, all wide eyes as she clutches her coffee mug in her hands.

I follow her gaze, and sure enough, with the wind blowing in over it, actual *waves* have formed, crashing against the beachfront at the end of the property. The gray waters swirl, full of sand and mud. Fog has rolled in, giving the illusion we're staring at the ocean instead of the Sound, and the water fades into infinity in the distance.

"So, have you met Benjamin yet? He's *so* nice. His wines are incredible, and sometimes he does tastings and tells us so many interesting details—"

Abigail is still talking, rambling about a Riesling or maybe it's a chardonnay. I turn, pretending to listen, watching her intently, this woman who's become Gwyn's new friend. Someone I don't think Gwyn knew *before*.

"I told Gwyn I'm impressed," I say. "I've heard most businesses fail in the first year or two."

Abigail nods eagerly. "Right? It's so incredible."

"So he hasn't had any trouble?"

She turns, looks at me questioningly.

"My husband—before he died—owned a business. He really struggled." I shrug, look down into my coffee. I hope that smooths over my line of inquiry into something that's none of my business.

"Oh, that must have been really hard." Abigail touches fingertips to my arm. "I mean, I think every business struggles sometimes, especially at first. Gwyn did say he had an infusion of money early on, but things seem to be going okay now."

I start to ask another question, but Gwyn asks Abigail for help with something, and Laura returns, effectively ending our conversation. I murmur I'm going to go to the bathroom—and as the other three get comfy in the kitchen, I go down the hall, shut the door to the bathroom, and instead close myself in the nearby closet. I'd hoped to get more from Abigail on the business, but in all likelihood, she doesn't know anything. The last thing I want to do is make her suspicious I'm snooping. I exhale and search the darkness of the closet, ready to search for your diary and camera, the two things that might hold the answer to who wanted you dead. Having Laura and Abigail here is the exact distraction I need.

The closet light flicks on with a *snap* that makes me jump. We used to hang our coats in this closet, and nothing has changed—storage for all the crap from Benjamin's former life, before he married you. Down the hall, the rapid-fire chatter continues, an occasional laugh breaking through. My eyes adjust to the dim light, catching the patterns of coats and jackets, an umbrella leaning against a backpack stowed in a corner.

Clear totes line a shelf along the back wall, and I take two steps, closing the distance. I whip my phone out for the extra light, turn it on, inspect the items, squint at the black marker where labels are scribbled. Titles like *Winter Clothes* and *Backpacking Gear* and *Freeze-Dried Camping Food*.

None of these are right, so I squat down to inspect the lower rack.

Gardening Supplies.

Extra Dishes.

Another boom of laughter down the hall makes me jump. My hands tingle with a flush of adrenaline, and I search faster, running my hands through a chest of drawers, checking in cardboard moving boxes. But nothing. I settle back on my haunches, biting my lip, trying to think. *Think.*

Benjamin's closet. Or his office. That's where I need to search next. My eyes dart toward the door. The main bedroom is at the end of this hall, whereas his office is back the other way, past the kitchen where everyone is gathered. With Gwyn distracted by her friends, maybe I could make it there and back.

I have to try.

I ease the closet door open and wait, listen. More laughter. The refrigerator opening and closing.

"Do you want hazelnut or cinnamon creamer?" Gwyn asks one of them.

I inhale, exhale, and turn toward the bedroom.

And run into—*shit, shit, shit*—a man. His hands land on my forearms, and I pull away fast, stepping back to put space between us, hitting the wall behind me. It's then I look up to see his face in the dim light of the hall, to see—

"Benjamin." I say the name without thinking.

"Sorry about that. You get turned around?" His brows furrow. "You must be Gwyn's new friend. Rebecca?"

"I—I am, yes." I wipe my palms on my running shorts and extend a shaky hand, trying to recover from my obvious shock. I raise my voice a note, remembering to sound young, harmless. "Nice to meet you. Yes, sorry, I forgot my glasses. Which way—"

"Rebecca? Benjamin?" Gwyn's head pokes into the hall. "Oh, there you are. Guess you met each other, then. Who wants coffee?"

We turn toward the kitchen, the skin on the back of my neck prickling as he walks behind me. As someone who might have killed *you* strolls mere feet from me. A murderer.

"You're the travel nurse, right?"

"I am." I move to stand closer to my new friends and spin, pressing my back into the kitchen counter, summoning a smile that I hope makes me look less stunned. If he'd come five seconds later, I'd have been halfway down the hall. To the door. God, I might have walked in on him in the bedroom...

"Welcome to Seattle. Gwyn said you're training for the Seattle Marathon, too?"

"Yes." I add a splash of cream to a fresh cup of coffee and stir. "Ever done one?" I ask.

Adrenaline still sizzles in my fingertips. I need to be interesting, captivating Rebecca. Engaging to converse with, someone they want to spend more time with.

"Me?" he asks with a laugh.

Laura snorts but doesn't say anything. Abigail gives her a light smack on the arm and pulls her away to go watch the storm rolling in again.

"Gwyn's such a runner," I gesture at her, offer them both a smile. "I thought maybe you run, too."

He chuckles, and in my head, I'm reliving the night before —following him in the darkness, the moment I realized he was meeting someone, another woman. Is he putting on an act right this moment, too? My eyes flick to Gwyn. She's busy making another pot of coffee, measuring ground beans with a scoop, seemingly comfortable as can be.

"Rarely. I don't mind it in the summer months, but once the rain starts—" He bares his teeth in a grimace.

"Get used to it," Gwyn calls to me. "We're lucky we didn't get rained on today. It starts in October and doesn't end until April or May."

"I don't mind a little rain," I say.

"Brave," Benjamin says and smiles at me.

For all my nerves, relief floods through me. Benjamin thinks I'm Rebecca. I've fooled him, too.

SEVENTEEN

MADELINE

Four Years Ago

Our engagement party was a month later. Daddy wanted it to be held one of his business partner's yachts, but we decided to go the other way. Instead of a fancy uptight party with champagne served by uniformed staff, we held it in the space Benji recently acquired for his newest winery and tasting room near downtown. A large, high-ceiling concrete building, that long ago had served as a fire station, but now would undergo renovations to be a winery. Hired catering staff in khakis and button-up shirts stood out against the industrial background, and tablecloths covered every surface. White flowers stood in simple vases, and silver platters of food were set out here and there.

"Is this too much?" I asked when Benji finally disentangled himself from his mother and sister, both of whom caught my eye with bright smiles. I gave them a little wave as Benji led me away, fingers brushing the small of my back. I turned toward him, toward his touch, and he pulled me in for a kiss.

"For our engagement party? For the party that celebrates we intend to spend the rest of our lives together?"

He beckoned with his arm, a sweeping motion inviting me to look around. The space was still rough gray walls, no drywall hung to create rooms or an inviting reception area. But it was a lovely space, and we'd hired Gwyn, who worked as an interior designer, to decorate for the party. It was just past New Year's, so she'd gone with a holiday theme, adding touches of purple and silver to make it distinctive. Sommeliers stood behind tables on either side of the broad room, offering wine tastings. Between them, a table laid with self-serve appetizers in preparation for an actual meal that would happen later.

Only thirty or so people were in attendance—our nearest and dearest, but Benji hadn't been able to resist sprinkling in a few potential investors for the business, and they stood out from the rest of the crowd, more dressed up in suits than our friends, who were Seattle casual, jeans and flannel.

"Unless you're having second thoughts?" Benji's lips brushed against my ear as he whispered it, but I only smiled.

"You know me better than that."

"I do."

Our gazes locked, and we shared a look, a knowledge that, despite our pasts, we were meant for one another.

"Benjamin, you promised me a tour." Aaron appeared at his side. "Where are these oak casks hidden away? Are you certain I can't convince you to try your hand at whiskey, too?" He sniffed and took another look around. "You sure this is what you want to be doing with your weekends? We could be on the mountain trying out those new snowboards right now."

I sighed. Aaron took every opportunity to remind Benjamin of the life he'd supposedly left behind by coupling up with me. Besides, the casks weren't hidden—they were in plain sight, lined up on giant shelves in the back of the space that in six months' time would become his flagship winery, hopefully attracting the Seattle crowd, more than doubling the business's income.

Benjamin ignored Aaron's jab. "I'll show you. Let me grab a couple people first. I'll do a whole tour." Benji leaned in, pressed his lips to mine, then walked away to gather the potential investors he'd invited. Mostly men, but one woman, tall and slender and not much older than him, with sleek dark hair down her back. I'd seen her at social events before, though I didn't recall her name. A twinge of something—*jealousy?*—hit me as she laughed at whatever he said to her, but I quieted it. We'd talked about many things in Europe, including our past relationships, which for me were a series of first dates that convinced me I didn't need a man in my life, at least not until *our* first date. For Benji, it was singular—a woman he'd almost started his winery business with, as they had graduated college together. Benji had gone so far as to consider asking her to marry him, but in the end, decided not to.

"Jealousy," he'd told me. "She was jealous of everything. Of everyone. To the point it was suffocating. She went through my phone. I couldn't hire a single female employee without her asking a million questions. The final straw was when she had one of her friends I'd never met come on to me in a bar, to see what I'd do. She was paranoid about it, and it destroyed our relationship. And the thing was, I never once even considered cheating on her. I'm not like that."

So as I watched Benji walk away with Aaron and the investors, including the stunning woman with long hair, I squashed my unnecessary emotions and instead looked around for Gwyn. But she was nowhere to be found.

I sent a quick text: *Your decorations are perfect! When are you and Alex arriving?* I tucked my phone away and went to give Daddy a quick kiss on his cheek, to find Elena and ask another partygoer to take a quick photo of the three of us.

"Congratulations," Elena said to me, after Benji's mother snapped a shot and handed the Nikon back to me. "I was wrong about him, and I'm happy for you." She held up her glass of wine and offered me a toast.

"You were just looking out for me." I said the words, letting her off the hook, because she was trying—I could see that. And after a lifetime of being the overprotective big sister trying to fill the shoes of big sister *and* mother, that was something.

Benji was making me realize just how lucky I was. I had a family who cared for me. I had *him*.

"Let me know if you want help picking out a wedding dress. I'd love to go." Elena gave me a tight smile, then on impulse, a half hug. I couldn't help but wonder if this was a sign of a new beginning for Elena and me, a chance to build an easier, more comfortable rapport. She stepped away quickly to greet Leah, who'd come over with Natalie in tow. Natalie slipped me a bright smile, waving as though she'd already had several glasses of wine. I waved back, but I was worried—still no Gwyn.

"I'm glad you and Elena are getting along better." Daddy approached and raised his own glass—Scotch, we made sure we had a bottle of his favorite on hand. "And I'm glad you decided to take a chance on Benjamin."

We sipped our respective drinks, as I looked for someone else to greet, but Daddy kept talking before I could. "So, have you considered going back to school for your MBA? It would be helpful with Benjamin's business. It could become a family business, the two of you."

"Daddy—" But I caught sight of Gwyn across the way, entering through the front door, alone. A young man offered to take her coat, and she handed it off, exposing jeans and a short flowy dress, almost identical to the one I'd worn the last time we met for drinks. A streak of annoyance ran through me—there's no way it was an accident—but the redness around her eyes struck it from my mind. Besides, wasn't imitation supposed to be flattering—or something like that?

"Sorry, I have to go," I said to Daddy, and crossed the room to meet Gwyn.

"This place is amazing," she said before I could get a word in. Her eyes were too wide, too dramatic. She held her hands up for dramatic effect. "Like—*wow*, Benjamin, *wow*."

I frowned—she was deflecting. Trying to pretend everything was okay. And besides, it wasn't like this was her first time coming to the winery. She'd decorated for this party. A second later, Alex walked in behind her, slinking along like he didn't belong there. Which I was starting to think he didn't, especially if he'd left Gwyn in tears—again. He tried to catch my eye, to share a smile with me, but I glanced back in the direction Benji had wandered off instead. "Benjamin's giving a tour, Alex, if you want to join in."

"Oh, thank god," Gwyn breathed the second Alex left.

"What?" I snagged a glass of chardonnay from the nearest table and pressed it into her hand. She took a long sip, smoothed a hand down the lookalike dress—*Jesus, Gwyn, really?*—and shook her head.

"He never came home last night. I think the only reason he showed up today was because he wanted to come to this." Her eyes flicked around. "This is really nice. Think Benji needs an interior designer for renovations, too?" She bit her lip. "I'd love to work on it for him."

My stomach hardened, imagining her in the winery with him—just the two of them. Benji taking her on a personal tour, Gwyn discussing lighting and colors and— "Anyway, he's probably already hired someone. Maybe I'll ask, though. I bet I could do it for less."

I turned to look at him across the room, to hide my face from Gwyn. Benjamin really was perfect, and I would not become like his ex. I wouldn't be a jealous fiancée or wife. Besides, Benji never once gave me reason to doubt him, and I was Madeline Hughes—I was the one other women were jealous of. That said, I couldn't help recalling how Gwyn wormed her way between Alex and his girlfriend back in college. The way it happened so casually, I don't think anyone realized it until she was on his arm, his ex forgotten. And now, she was on the verge of ending things with her current boyfriend. I couldn't help but wonder who she'd try to steal away next.

She took stock of the room. "Anyway, we can talk about it later. This is your engagement party. You should be having fun." A forced smile.

"Gwyn," I whispered. I hesitated, but she was my friend. "You need to end it."

"I know. I know, *again.*" Her eyes turned watery. "I just—I just feel like he's all I have."

"You have me. And Natalie and Leah." I beckoned to where they stood together near the sommelier, waiting for fresh wineglasses, chatting. Elena stood with them, and when she saw us looking, gave a little wave. "Even Elena."

Gwyn snorted. "Elena hates me. So does Natalie."

"No, they don't, they just—" I thought to that same afternoon, when I'd worked a half day to help Elena organize patient charts she still hadn't hired a receptionist to take care of. She'd been grateful for the help, but couldn't help micromanaging me, telling me what I could be doing better.

"She's just not great with people," I finished with. "She means well." I didn't bother arguing about Natalie—it would have been too obvious I was lying. They'd never gotten along well, their competition for best-friend status growing ever more heated.

"Seems to be doing just fine." Gwyn raised a brow, and we watched as Elena said something that made Natalie and Leah laugh.

Ten minutes later, Benji approached and I did the right thing for a friend to do. "Benji, have you hired an interior designer yet? Gwyn had some ideas to discuss with you if you haven't."

He didn't hesitate. "I've been meaning to, actually. I should have asked you in the first place! That would be great. Want to come by Monday afternoon? Say, one o'clock?"

Gwyn smiled, like there was a ray of hope in her otherwise shitty evening dealing with her cheating boyfriend. "Perfect. It's a date."

I ignored the flash of nausea in my stomach. I trusted him, and Gwyn was my friend. I had nothing to worry about. Absolutely nothing.

EIGHTEEN

REBECCA

Now

My Sunday night shift goes by in a blur, admitting new patients, texting with my new friends, who have included me in their group chat, trying to understand who they are and what they want, and how I can better become one of them.

It seems to come down to this: choosing to run thirty miles a week, but complaining about it; drinking coffee and alcohol, both in questionable amounts; acting terrified and excited about our upcoming marathon; always supporting each other, regardless of what's going on.

When Gwyn texts *Ugh, Benjamin has another business dinner tomorrow. Girls' night?* I have to clench my hands into fists to keep from typing back *Yes, I'd love to!* I don't want to appear too eager. Instead, I redirect my gaze at the patient monitor. I'm in Louise's room, but Louise isn't home—she lost consciousness last night and hasn't woken up. When I came in for my shift, she'd been started on meds to keep her blood pressure up. For a travel nurse, she became a complicated assignment, and I was surprised Riley hadn't given me a different patient.

Only after Abigail responds do I allow myself to message, *I'm in! Where and when?*

My gaze comes back to my patient, and a tiny hole opens up in my chest I recognize as worry for Louise. Worry for someone who it's not my job to care about. Or maybe it's just loneliness, and I'm grasping on to the closest thing I have to a friend. Which is sad. She's my patient.

How long has your ghost been my only companion? Three years, holed up in one rented home after another, poring over the album of photos and articles and images—relistening to podcasts describing the backpacking adventure you never returned from. Imagining what Benjamin or Gwyn had done, how they'd planned to get you out there alone.

Three years.

And now, a grave will bear your name, no casket, no body buried beneath it.

I gnaw on the memory of today—the run, so easy and carefree. For a moment, I'd forgotten why I was there, right about the time Abigail slung an arm over my shoulder and told me I was officially part of the group.

Gwyn's face had lit up. Even Laura's face vaguely resembled a smile.

Benjamin had chuckled from his corner, where he leaned and drank coffee and watched his fiancée's friends clucking about their running, as though this was the new bridge club or knitting circle. Maybe it was. Fitness is in, right?

Had he done that with you? I can't remember.

I'm an hour out from my shift ending, getting Louise cleaned up and turned on her other side, when Riley slips into the room. My body tenses, but I offer her a smile.

"How's your night going?" I ask.

She brushes curls from her face, tucks them behind her ear,

and watches as I get Louise tucked back in. Her gaze is critical, and for a moment I feel like she's waiting for me to make some fatal error—is there a correct way to tuck a patient in that I'm failing at? I've been working as a nurse for over a year now. Long enough that I tend to blend in just fine. But her gaze makes me fumble, and I nearly drop the pillow I'm positioning under Louise's arm.

"Fine." Riley's reply is curt.

"Do you need something?" I turn to face her, clearly pausing in my duties to give her my attention. Forcing her to get to the point or leave.

Riley twists her lips, indecisive, then mutters, "Never mind." She turns on her heel and exits the room. I stare after her, my stomach clenched. Riley is a wild card, one I wasn't expecting.

Down the hall, an alarm sounds. A scuffle of feet outside the door, as nurses run to make sure the patient is alive, or to code them if they're not doing so well. I don't respond. Don't even think twice about it—when you respond to a code, you put yourself in the spotlight.

I do a final check of Louise's room, then slide out the door. I head for my computer to do my end-of-shift charting, but my gaze catches on the computer across from mine—unlocked, the monitor shining bright. Left open when the alarm sounded. It's the computer the charge nurse sits at, but it's not the charting software pulled up. It's an internet search.

Rebecca Johnson Washington State registered nurse is typed in the search bar. My heart goes rapid-fire, and I lean in. Images of a dozen different women, from an actress to a doctor. And right in the middle is a picture of the real Rebecca Johnson, RN. The one whose identity I've taken. I exhale, reminding myself these are *all* Rebecca Johnsons in Washington State. There are dozens of us. But then I see a second tab open.

Washington State Department of Health.

My stomach bottoms out. I risk a glance up, but everyone's still down the hall, and from the sound of it, the patient's crashing. I'm alone in the nurse's station, and I take advantage, clicking to that tab. Riley's done a search for registered nurses named Rebecca Johnson. There are exactly three. Two with birthdates decades before the real Rebecca was born.

And then, Rebecca. Singular.

The license I'm working under is Rebecca's. But if she worked with a Rebecca in Yakima, there should be two of us listed with birthdates in the 1990s. Not one. I sink heavily into the closest chair, staring at the search.

Does this mean Riley knows?

Maybe expired licenses drop off. Maybe she will assume the Rebecca Johnson, RN she knew moved elsewhere, let her license expire since she was no longer using it.

Or maybe, she's onto me.

I itch to delete the search history and close the window, but that might make her more suspicious, so I turn and force myself to chart Louise's care. I ignore the fact that my hands are trembling. That my identity may be on its way to expiration. That it might be best for me to slip away now, before she calls for an investigation into who I really am. But who would she call? What would she say?

My shift finishes with no further interaction with Riley, who goes back to ignoring me. I whisper goodbye to Louise after I sign out to the oncoming nurse, because if I've learned anything, it's that sometimes death swoops in the moment you look away. It's what happened to you.

In the brisk morning air, I stretch and listen to the leaves rustling through the trees, thinking about what I found on Riley's computer. If anything, this means I need to hurry up—finish what I came to Seattle to do. And in the meantime, I can't let it distract me. I exhale, pushing thoughts of the real Rebecca from my mind.

Just as I'm about to set out to do a quick tour of the neighborhood on foot—ending at Benjamin and Gwyn's, where I hope to get a glimpse of them—my phone chimes. I go still. It's not just a text message or a reminder. It's a news notification, the sort I set up to tell me whenever your name is mentioned in the news.

The last time my phone made that noise was mere days ago, when you were officially declared *dead in absentia*. My mind searches for reasons you might be mentioned again so soon. Occasionally a local paper picks up your story and reviews it— or maybe an *in memory of* piece, now that your death is official.

I pull my phone from the sports bra I changed into before leaving the hospital, but a scuffle of feet startles me, and I drop it. I swing around, looking for a person—but other than three nurses leaving out a side door some fifty feet away, there's no one. Only the exterior of the hospital, a campus full of shrubs and landscaping and block pillars holding up a covered parking area.

But still, my heart is in my throat, and I can't stop searching my surroundings. It wasn't my imagination. Something or someone was close by, moments ago. I run at night, by myself, all the time. The darkness has become my friend. But I know what I heard, and it seems impossible there's not a single soul behind me.

When my pulse slows, when I'm certain no one's about to jump out and grab me—I squat to retrieve my phone. The screen is cracked, a sharp edge piercing my thumb as I run it over the surface. My attention is still on my surroundings, though. Seattle is a nice enough city, but like any city, it has its crime, and hospital campuses, I've found, bring all sorts.

Standing here won't solve any problem, though, and I can run fast—so I take off at a steady pace, listening for footsteps behind me, overly aware. It's only when I'm close to my home, and the fork that leads me to either my place or Gwyn and

Benjamin's, that I slow to a walk and take another long look around me.

That first glimmer of the sunrise courses over the world. Dawn is not far off. I swallow, and giving the shadows one last look, finally give myself permission to breathe normally again, to focus on my phone.

But just as fast, I stop breathing.

I read the headline a second time to make sure I read it correctly.

Body Found, Suspected to Be Missing Hiker Madeline Hughes.

NINETEEN

MADELINE

Four Years Ago

The day after the engagement party, Elena uttered words I'd never have dreamed of hearing from her.

"You two are literally the perfect couple."

Around us, the silent waiting room of her plastic surgery office practically echoed her words; I was so surprised to hear her say them.

"You think so?" I looked up at her to catch a rare vague smile on her face. She perched on the edge of the desk, tucked her hands in her white lab coat, nodded. Daddy was right—she really was trying to be a good sister. "Thanks. What about you? Have you dated at all lately?"

"No, but..." A ghost of a smile. "I've been thinking about it. Feeling inspired by the two of you." Her eyes dropped, this admission maybe too much for her. She was about to leave—to shove away from the desk and retreat back to her office, so I tried to think of something to say to keep her there, to extend the moment.

But my phone chimed, a text from Gwyn, exclaiming *He hired me! OMG, thank u thank u thank u!*

I forced myself to smile at the message. To attempt to feel happy for her. To feel happy for Benji, too, because Gwyn was great at her job, and I'd featured photos of interiors she'd done on my social media fairly regularly. Like any good friends, we cross-promoted.

"What are you doing?" Elena whispered. "There are patients in the waiting room."

My eyes flew from my phone to a fiftysomething woman waiting for a consultation appointment about a facelift. Her nose was buried in a magazine, and not another soul was in the room.

"Seriously?" I set the phone down. "I looked at my phone for five seconds." And we'd just been chatting about something completely non-work related. Inside, I deflated a bit—Elena, my sister, ever mercurial with her moods.

"You're still an employee. You have to follow the rules, like anyone else." She gave me a pointed, mothering look.

"What rules?" A man's voice broke in, coming from around the side of the desk where the entrance was. We looked up to find a twentysomething with a big grin, displaying straight white teeth, excitement flashing in his eyes.

Elena straightened, mouth opening, closing, clearly unable to recall his name.

"Call me Kip. I'm your new resident."

We both stared at him a beat—me, because he had a lovely English accent; Elena, I would guess because she'd forgotten she agreed to take on a resident.

"My new resident?" she asked.

He faltered, eyes darting between the two of us. Did he see the family resemblance? Could he sense she was the one in charge, that I was the younger sister who didn't care much about this supposed job? I kept my gaze on him, but not because I was checking him out—sure, he was handsome—but he wasn't my type. He was, however, Elena's type, the sort that could star on a teeth-whitening commercial, and something about finding love made me charitable in that moment. Especially given her change of attitude and own stated desire to find someone.

"So nice to meet you, Kip." I stood, extended a hand, gave him a bright smile.

"You as well." But his gaze slipped back to Elena, tentative. "We spoke on the phone a couple weeks ago?"

"Right," Elena managed. "I remember. I wasn't expecting you for a couple more weeks."

"Oh." His face fell. "Maybe we got our dates mixed up. I thought—" His hands went to his pockets searching for a tiny calendar he eventually pulled out. "I thought we said—"

"It's fine," Elena said, though her tone suggested otherwise. "Come with me. I'll show you around. This is Maddy, she's— temporary." Elena waved a hand at me as though I didn't matter, but Kip whispered, "Nice to meet you, Maddy. She always like this?"

I gave him a conspiratorial grin. "Only when she's flustered."

Interest sparked in his eyes, and he gave me a nod. Took it as the challenge it was, I hoped. With them in the back, I picked up my phone once again and texted Benji—*Found Elena a new boyfriend!*—then waited almost breathless for his response.

But it didn't come.

I sighed, checked my Instagram, looked to see how many visitors I'd had to my website since our engagement party and accompanying photos, checked the news—but still, nothing. Maybe Elena's receptionists quit because this office was so damn boring. But with a resident, someone who could help with patients, maybe it would get busier. With two doctors, it was bound to.

I texted Gwyn next—*So excited for you! What kind of designs are you thinking?*

And on the heels of that, I even sent Natalie a text. *Hey, Benji is out of town this weekend. Want to go shopping? I need new boots.*

The door chimed, another patient shuffling into the office, this one for a consultation to have extra skin removed along her jawline. I tried not to think about what the procedure might look like.

"Just fill out these forms," I said to the woman, handing over a clipboard and a pen.

Another glance at my phone.

No response from Benji. No response from Gwyn. But Natalie cheerily wrote back, *Yes, please. I need boots, too! Maybe we can do twinsies!*

I swiped back to Benji's and Gwyn's texts. Both of them were quick responders—so why nothing? Were they still touring the future winery? Maybe they were going over plans or the details of costs. Maybe Gwyn pulled out her standard contract and the two of them were combing through it over glasses of chardonnay.

I pushed the thought away and busied myself for the next half hour, arranging charts for the afternoon appointments, half listening to Elena giving Kip a tour of the office.

It was nearly one when I looked up, about to tell Elena I was leaving for a lunch break. I planned to call Benji and check why he wasn't answering his messages, but he walked right in.

"Hey, darling."

"Benji."

He chuckled. "You look shocked." He leaned over the desk, pressed a chaste kiss to my mouth. "I just wanted to swing by and thank you for recommending Gwyn. She had great ideas, far better than the other designer I spoke to. She understands what I'm trying to do with the place. I'm excited to work with her."

And before I could ruminate on his words, a small bouquet of pink roses, baby's breath, and tiny yellow flowers I didn't know the name of were in front of me. The floral scent hit me, and I blinked up at him, and my whole body relaxed. "Thank you. This is such a nice surprise."

Our eyes met.

"You okay?" Benji asked.

I smiled up at him, shaking off my own anxieties. "Perfect."

TWENTY

REBECCA

Now

The time is 7:22 a.m.

I don't pause to think in the seconds after I read the headline that a body has been found—I race for their house. Visions of your body, battered and broken from the cliffside fall flash through my mind. I want to see their reactions firsthand. It may tell me more than anything else.

As I run, I consider how to handle this—to walk through the wooded side yard and get a glimpse inside their home while they are unawares—or to knock on the front door, or text, announcing my arrival. *Just out on a run. Thought I'd stop by and say hi!*, effectively inviting myself in for coffee.

Would Benjamin cry, or would he remain stoic and unaffected?

Would I catch him panicked at the idea a body has been found?

I force my lungs to work harder, increasing my pace. Their reaction or lack thereof might tell me so much. Or, what if with a body found, their behavior is at odds with how they *should* be acting? I'm not even sure what that would look like, but I want to witness it, regardless.

The last corner to turn is in my vision, dim in the early sunrise, and it feels like it takes minutes instead of seconds to reach it. The turn is too long, the trees blocking their house too thick, and I *swear* I should be there by now.

But then a white van comes into view, lit up by the reflection of Gwyn and Benjamin's own home. A second white van, this one with *Seattle News* scrawled across one side, its headlights bright in the partial darkness. Two more, plus random vehicles and a small gathering of people just on the edge of their property line. Shit. Of course. A case that caught the attention of the city for years, and days after you are declared legally dead, a report your body has been found. Of course, the media is here.

My breath comes out in puffs of steam. I scan the yard, the house. Neither Gwyn nor Benjamin is outside—which hardly surprises me. They will likely make a statement at some point, but otherwise, refuse to talk to the press. Just like in the early days after your disappearance, when both were considered persons of interest, as was everyone else who'd accompanied them on that trip. But no charges were ever made.

It was, I had discovered, hard for a charge to be made without a body proving death.

But this find could change all that.

I'm tempted to cut through the lawn of the home nearest me. To settle myself in the thick woods to the side of their house and see if they've left their blinds up, their curtains open, despite the uninvited company. But if someone sees me—and there are a dozen people outside, just looking for news to report on—that would be bad.

My phone is in my hand, and I run a finger over the jagged edge to press a button to call Gwyn. This is the best I'm going to get at the moment.

Two rings. Then, "Hello?"

"Hey, Gwyn, it's Rebecca." Then I remember it's not even eight in the morning yet. "Oh shoot, I forgot it's still early. I worked last night, and I'm out running—I didn't even think about it."

"No worries, I'm always up early. How was your shift?"

I consider what I found on Riley's computer. *Not good.* "It was a good night. Glad to be done for the day. I wanted to see if you wanted to join me if you hadn't gotten your run in yet?"

She takes a second to respond, and I relish the silence—wondering what expression covers her face, if she's staring out a window right now at the reporters just waiting for her to make an appearance. Some part of me hopes I'm wrong, that she's only sad there are people in the world who will use a dead body as an excuse to harass grieving people. Another part of me hopes she's terrified she's left some traces of DNA behind that might lead to her arrest. And of course, these dichotomous thoughts aren't unique to Gwyn. I can't help but imagine Benjamin pacing in his office, thinking the same.

"I can't right now," she finally says. "Wish I could. Next time, for sure."

"Okay." And I can't help it. "Are you okay?" I ask. "You sound... off."

Gwyn lets out a throaty laugh. "Oh, I'm fine, just have a big to-do list today. But I'm excited for girls' night tonight. Benjamin suggested we meet at the winery. It's closed today, but I have a key. We can have our own private party. It's called North Winery. We're meeting at seven."

"North Winery. Seven. I'll be there," I say.

Nice cover, I think. This way, her friends won't see news vans surrounding her house. It occurs to me Abigail and Laura might not even know about you—after all, they are new fixtures in her life, her old friends abandoning her, and for good reason.

We disconnect, and I give the property another long look

before turning on my heel and heading for home. I stop on the way to grab a local paper, but there's no mention of a body found in it—not yet. Likely, the news just came in, hours after the paper was printed. I'll have to settle for a digital copy to analyze, to add to my album on you.

I'm on my doorstep, key inserted and turning, when a peculiar prickle comes at the back of my neck. I look up at the silver knocker the landlord installed, realizing I can see a distorted reflection. And in that distorted reflection, I see myself, the white railing of the porch, and beyond that, a thick oak tree in the front yard. And though it's dark and blurred, I'm certain of what else I see—a person, peering around said tree, watching me.

TWENTY-ONE
MADELINE

Four Years Ago

When Benji called in the afternoon to cancel dinner plans, I was annoyed—who wouldn't be?—but I didn't think much of it. He was growing a business. A *successful one*. Of course things were going to come up.

So I told him I loved him and called Gwyn and my other friends. I even invited Elena, who of course declined, but asked if she could send Kip in her place. "He doesn't know anyone and I'm tired of him acting like *we're* friends. Introduce him to some people, will you?"

I met up with Gwyn and Natalie and Leah, and Kip came, to the delight of the girls, especially when they heard his accent. We met at the competing wine bar in town—checking out the competition—and were two bottles of wine in, sharing a giant flatbread, when Benji's text lit up my phone.

Left my laptop at the winery. Would you mind grabbing it if you're nearby? I'll make it worth your while ;-)

I stifled a laugh and sent a suggestive text back, then set my phone down to turn back to my friends.

"So what's the deal with Alex?" Natalie asked. Everyone was over our engagement news and moving on to more normal topics—like Gwyn's shitty boyfriend.

"Who's Alex?" Kip asked.

"Gwyn's long-term boyfriend," Natalie said. "But we're pretty sure he's cheating on her. We"—she gestured to Leah and me—"think she should end it. But they've been together forever, so..." She scrunched her nose. Gwyn's own face was flat, the cheer of the evening gone in an instant.

"We don't have to talk about it," I said.

Gwyn shot me a grateful smile but shook her head. "No, I'm tipsy, this is probably the best time to talk about it." Gwyn rehashed the whole relationship to Kip, and shockingly for a guy, he listened with real focus—probably the medical resident side of him, taking in the details as though Gwyn were a patient he could diagnose. He and Elena really would be perfect for one another, other than what I guessed was a ten-year age gap and the fact she was technically his boss at the moment. But that didn't stop *men,* so in my opinion, it shouldn't stop her.

When Gwyn concluded with, "But I don't actually know anything," Kip frowned and answered, "Excuse me for being the realist here, but it sounds like you *do* know. You just don't like what you know."

The table went dead silent. I almost wanted to kick Kip for being so direct about the situation, but maybe that's what Gwyn needed—an impartial outsider who didn't have a friendship to consider when offering advice. In two seconds he'd said what the three of us had been thinking for months.

"So, Kip, tell us more about you," Natalie said, trying to redirect the conversation. She glanced my way, seeking approval, and I gave her a little nod, a smile.

He slid a glance to Gwyn, maybe realizing the silence had

become awkward. "Well, I'm from London originally. Came here for medical school. I'm a second-year resident, so—" He gives a few more details I'm already privy to but leaves out the part he's shared with me in the moments between patients at Elena's practice—he's counting down the days until he's a full-fledged doctor so he can help pay off his mother's debt back home. She'd lost almost everything when her job disappeared, and he'd already been in the States for medical school, unable to help. It was a source of guilt for him.

But the conversation never gained traction, the energy of the evening sapped as Gwyn sat silently, contemplating what to do about Alex. That pretty much ended the fun evening, which was sad—I was spending more and more time with Benji, which I *loved*, but I was happy to have a girls' night, to reconnect with my friends. Ten minutes later we were asking for the check.

We all parked in the same lot, but as we exited the winery, I remembered Benji needed his laptop.

"Want us to walk with you?" Gwyn crossed her arms against the chill, frowning down the sidewalk as though it had it out for me.

"I'll be fine. It's just a block over." And besides, it was a busy night, plenty of Seattleites strolling the street hand in hand.

"I'll walk with you," Kip said. "You ladies go ahead."

Gwyn and Leah and Natalie wandered off, no longer concerned for me.

"Thanks," I said to Kip. "And thanks for being so..." I searched for the word, "honest, with Gwyn. I think she needed an outsider opinion. Maybe a guy's opinion, too."

"No one should feel like that." He shrugged, and we turned to go toward the winery.

I searched for a topic of conversation. "How's working with Elena?"

"I feel like she's got a bit of a hard shell to crack. But I'm chiseling away at it." He flashed me a smile. "Any tips?"

"That about sums up how to deal with Elena." I laughed. "I was hoping she'd take a liking to you."

Kip hummed a tune under his breath, and for a moment, reminded me of my grandfather who'd passed years back. "What's her deal?" he asked after a beat.

"Her deal?"

"Yeah." Kip met my gaze for a step then turned back toward the sidewalk, hands tucked into his jeans pockets. "What's her deal?"

"Well—long story or short?"

Kip shrugged. "How far's our walk?"

"Half a mile one way, half a mile back."

"Long story, then."

I don't know why I told him everything—maybe after seeing how he was with Gwyn, so easily getting to the point—*it sounds like you do know. You just don't like what you know*—I wanted to meet honesty with honesty. It was nice for a change to not sugarcoat a situation, and besides, he'd only be working with Elena for a month or two—soon, he'd be gone to his next residency block.

I told Kip how Elena and I shared a father, but not a mother. How Daddy never married her mother, and that somehow made her feel less like family. How she'd left for college and not spoken to us for half a decade, but after graduating medical school, moved back to Seattle, decided she wanted to get to know her little sister, how she tried to fill in as my mother. How we both tried and regularly failed to be good to one another but kept trying. How she'd written off men after a failed relationship in college.

By then we were at the winery, and I let myself through the front doors, edging around several customers waiting to be seated. The front had opened to customers the week prior, still rough around the edges, but with high-top tables placed strategically around the front room. A wall had been erected, separating the front from the back, and I didn't stop to greet the busy staff as I beckoned Kip to follow me to the back—all I needed was to grab Benji's laptop and get back to my car.

"Nice place," Kip murmured. "You own this?"

"Yes," I said. "Well, it's my fiancé's, technically."

"When's the wedding?"

"Next August." I felt a warm blush creep into my cheeks as happiness radiated through me, thinking of it. We'd picked a date just a few days ago—and the numbers felt magical to me, like those numbers indicated the start of my new life with Benji. Which they did.

"That's all you need?" he asked when I tucked the laptop in my bag and beckoned toward the hall.

"That's it."

Kip stepped back into the hallway, his eyes lingering over the photographs I'd taken and framed to decorate the wall, despite Gwyn's opinion that they didn't go with the vibe of the place— photos of Benji at the vineyard, picking grapes and talking to locals. Benji in this building, before the contractor came and changed it from a giant empty space to a warm cozy winery. A photo of us with friends and family at the engagement party came next, and after that, the most recent photo, of opening night.

"Cool photos," he said. "You've done so much with the place already." He looked down the hall, toward the back where we stored the wine and even made some of it.

I bit my lip. "Do you want a tour?"

His gaze flicked to me, then back to the photo of Benji and me, clutched in one another's arms, grinning like loving maniacs, my shiny new engagement ring sparkling in the lights.

"Good-looking fella you got," he said. "And sure, I'd love a tour."

As soon as I offered, I regretted it—Kip seemed nice, and I'd spent a couple days working with him now, showing him how the office computers worked, reminding him when patients arrived. He'd charmed my friends no problem. And that was also the problem—he was easy to get along with, and we were fast becoming friends. That was it, and I didn't want him or anyone else to suspect anything was going on, especially now that Benji and I were engaged.

But I had offered.

I kept it short, showing him the racks of wine, the coolers, the oak casks, the stuff people pay twenty bucks to see—but hey, it includes a glass of wine.

"What kind of wine do you like?"

Kip paused. "Is it bad that I don't know?"

I laughed and pulled down two bottles. "Here. A merlot and a sauvignon blanc. Give them a shot."

We walked back toward the front, the tour taking no more than five minutes, when voices in the staff lounge area, high pitched and incredulous, distracted me. The room was designed to be an office, but I'd argued the staff needed somewhere they could sit and relax and store their belongings.

Any other day, I'd have ignored the chatter—they had a right to take a break, and to do so without their boss's fiancée listening in.

But then I heard, "Apparently, she was his ex. His *ex*. She called twice trying to get ahold of him. She said he was late meeting her, and wanted to know if he was here—"

I stopped abruptly, just short of the doorway. Kip stopped too, our eyes met, and his brows furrowed.

"What did she want?" the other woman asked.

"Other than to talk to Mr. North? I don't know. We kept telling her he wasn't here—because he wasn't—but she was sure we were lying. She kept demanding to speak to him, said she basically owned half this place, whatever that means, and she'd fire us if we didn't get him on the phone for her."

Kip's eyes widened as we listened. "Benjamin?" he mouthed, and I nodded.

"Then what?" the second woman prodded.

"Well, I couldn't make him magically appear. I told her when he *would* be here and told her to call back then. It's not my fault he stood her up. Shoot, I don't blame him."

"Did she call back?"

"I don't know!" she squeaked. "But Jesus, he's so nice, I can't imagine him with someone like *that*. I hope he wasn't—well, you know—with meeting her and all..." The voice led off, the suggestion clear. *She hoped he wasn't fucking her.* "I'm glad he's marrying Madeline."

I could almost kiss her for her loyalty, but I was stuck on the part where Benjamin's ex called the winery and demanded to speak to him—where he had supposedly *stood her up*—why would he be meeting with his ex in the first place? God, was this because we got engaged? It probably was. She was jealous, even now, after all this time. I didn't blame him for breaking up with her. But why would he—

Kip nudged me, and I jumped—I'd almost forgotten him there. I pointed back down the hall, and we escaped out the back door.

I'd never felt that way before in my life—*ever*. And to put it in words, I felt *scared*. Threatened. Like someone from Benji's past was trying to creep back into the present, sink her claws into him, tear him away from me.

"Hey." Kip pressed a hand to my shoulder and waited until I met his gaze. My chest was tight with worry, or maybe it was heavy—like some giant weight was crushing me. "You okay?" he asked.

We stood in the alley behind the winery, next to a giant trash bin that belonged to the cafe next door.

"No," I said. Nausea rolled through me, and I wasn't sure if it was what I overheard or the stench. "Come on." I beckoned him down the alley, and soon we were back on the street, pacing fast toward the cars. I had to talk to Benji about this. Had to find out what the hell his ex was doing calling him. What the hell he was doing meeting with her *in secret*.

"Madeline, wait—" Kip tried to slow me down, but I shook my head and kept walking.

"Madeline," he tried again. "Listen, he didn't *do* anything. And she didn't call his cell phone or his home phone—she called his winery. You know what that tells me? It tells me she doesn't have his personal number. She probably saw something about it in the paper and is reaching out."

"Then she also saw he's engaged," I said. "And she said he was supposed to *meet her*. Which he would be doing behind my back. What if he's cheating on me? And what about the part where she thinks she owns half of it?" I come up short. "Shit, do you think she owns half his business?" I turn wide eyes on Kip, my heart about to gallop right out of my chest. *Shit, shit, shit.*

"I don't know. But I do know you can't go accusing your fiancé of cheating on you."

I held perfectly still then. Did I think he was having an affair? Benji's words echoed in my mind, telling me about how awful his ex was. Kip was right. I had to be smart about this.

"I don't think he's cheating on me," I said after a solid minute of thinking about it. "But he's being weird. I feel like he's keeping *something* from me."

"Like what?"

"I don't know," I said. And I really didn't.

TWENTY-TWO
REBECCA

Now

Sense of survival takes hold. I'm in the door and locking it behind me before I realize what I'm doing. I press my back against it, the only place the broad front picture window wouldn't give my follower a glimpse of me. When I've managed half a dozen deep breaths, I turn and force myself to check the peephole—to stare beyond the whitewashed porch to where a form clearly looked out from behind the broad oak in my front yard.

The scuffle of feet echoes in my head from earlier.

I can draw only one conclusion.

Someone followed me. They followed me from my place of work to Gwyn and Benjamin's—they saw me hesitate when I saw news vans, saw me call Gwyn—Jesus, had they heard when and where I'd be tonight?—and then they followed me home.

The implication has me hurrying toward the bedroom at the rear of the house, grabbing the first bag I find, stuffing clothes in it, ready to escape to any other city but Seattle, except—

I ease down on my bed, the shirts and underwear falling from my hands.

Except I have nowhere else to go. And I won't stop now. I'm finally back in Seattle, I've wormed my way into the lives of my main suspects for your murder, a *body* has been found. I can't leave. I can't abandon you.

I have to do *something*. I just don't know what.

I look up and catch my reflection in the mirror that sits over the chest of drawers, an old-fashioned garish thing the landlord furnished. I catch my own eyes, the color of the contacts I wear, the reflection I've slowly gotten used to over the weeks, months, and now years. Rebecca doesn't scare so easily. Rebecca would want to know who is following her—in fact, I *need* to know who is following me. It's entirely possible it's someone who recognized me, and that would be a problem. It would be even worse if I haven't fooled them—if Gwyn or Benjamin know who I am. If one of them followed me here.

* * *

The news article about the body is mostly a catchy headline, combined with a photo yanked from social media—your face, lit up, mid-laughter, Benjamin beside you. In reality, the body has been *in the elements* for a minimum of three years. It was found two miles down the river from where you are believed to have plunged headlong over a cliff.

> It's not uncommon for bodies to travel miles through water, especially during late summer months when the snowmelt creates rising river levels. They can be pinned for months or years underwater, wildlife feeding on them.
>
> Details on the body were not yet released, but experts attest that after three years in water, it would be highly decomposed and consist mostly of bone at this point. If an

intact jaw was not found with the body, it could take days for
DNA testing—

Bile rises in my throat, and I stop scrolling. After I've
collected myself, I force myself to continue, but there's little
new information—only a recounting of how you were recently
declared dead, and the person you were before that.

I close the news site and do a search for more information.
Outside, a sudden boom all but shakes the house, and I pause.
Thunderstorms are rare in Seattle due to the relatively dry air,
but that's what it sounded like. The curtains are closed, a
symptom of my own pastime of looking through windows—I'm
all too aware of how anyone can look in, and on this dark Seattle
morning, that's as true as ever. I find the window and peek
through, almost hoping my earlier stalker will be there, that I'll
surprise *him* or her—what if Riley decided to follow me?—and
then I'll have a face to match to that form peering around the
tree. But there's only side yard, another house, trees. And in the
distance, a flash of lightning inland.

Rain patters down over the window, streaking it, and I
consider leaving the curtains open. Inviting my watcher to try
for a second glimpse, giving me an opportunity to see their face.
Maybe tonight, after meeting with my new friends at the
winery, I can reel them in somehow. Then again, if they suspect
what I'm doing—but how could they?—they might mean me
harm. I sit with that thought a second, then close the curtains
and get back to my computer, the grumble of thunder an eerie
companion as I search for more information on your case.

At some point, I fall asleep, exhausted after a twelve-hour
night shift.

When I wake, hours later, it's to the pinging of my phone,
signaling another news article about you. I roll over, grab it, peer
through groggy eyes at the fractured screen.

Homicide detectives are investigating the scene where a
body was found in the Mount Rainier National Forest—

I skim the details, stopping only when I reach: Benjamin
North, whom Ms. Hughes married mere days before her disappearance, did not respond to our requests for comment.

It's hardly news. Benjamin did a series of interviews, pleas
to the public to share any information, the whole *somebody
knows something* thing they always say. But that tapered off
eventually.

Outside the world has shifted back toward dark again. I've
slept the whole day away. A glance at the time tells me it's 4:30
—late enough that I should prep for tonight and head out soon.
In fact, if I leave now, I can drive by Gwyn's, get a read on the
situation.

I dress in jeans and a shirt I imagine is like something Gwyn
might wear, take a last look at the photo album, filled with bits
and pieces of you, which I still need to add the newest article to,
and tuck it away beneath my bed next to a stack of medical
textbooks.

I'm about to leave when my phone lights up with an
incoming call—from the hospital. I press my lips together,
staring at it. Debating answering. What if it's Riley? Or, what if
it's worse, and she took what vague information she'd found to
the unit's manager, or even HR? The call rolls over to voicemail
before I can decide, and seconds later, the *New Voicemail* alert
pops up. I steel myself and swipe to listen.

"This is Veronica from the ICU—we are short-staffed at
seven and wanted to see if you'd like to come in for four or eight
hours—"

I exhale. End the message. And lean against the wall,
counting to ten in my head, realizing just how hard my heart
was beating, that sweat has broken out along the back of my

neck. I turn to leave, to go to girls' night, then remember the figure standing behind the tree, watching me.

It's too much.

Riley finding that there was only one Rebecca Johnson when there should have been two. Someone following me, spying on me. It's time to leave Seattle, but I can't, not yet. I need to figure out who killed you, Maddy. I thought I had more time, but I need to figure it out, do what needs to be done, and get the heck out. Fast.

TWENTY-THREE

REBECCA

Now

The drive to Gwyn and Benjamin's is slow going, with rush hour traffic even in the neighborhoods. But soon enough, I'm on their street, crawling along behind a car with a *Student Driver* sticker on it, going well under the speed limit. It's a reason to go slow, though, to take a long look at the stately house. Only two news vans remain, and the rain has driven the reporters inside the van to hold vigil. I wonder how Gwyn will escape without them following her, or if they will take up post outside the winery, peer in through the windows. Thinking of that reminds me of my earlier watcher, and I check my rearview mirror, but not a single car is behind me in the narrow lane.

I chew my lip, passing the house, then pull around the block and come to a stop. A risky thought runs through my head. But it might just be worth the risk—because there's no way Gwyn will be able to avoid discussing the issue with me if I do this. And I can frame it as me helping her. Maybe that will soften the blow.

This time, when I dial her and she answers, "Hello?" I don't dance around the topic at hand.

"Gwyn, it's Rebecca."

"Oh hi, Rebecca." Her voice is strained, tired. Perhaps she's spent the day staring outside her windows, wishing she could escape for a run, unable to.

I again check my surroundings—my windows, my mirror—again, no one nearby. I even scan the trees, and when a bird flutters from one branch to the next, jump, realize I'm holding my breath, almost waiting for someone to pop out.

"Hi," I repeat, working up my courage. "Listen, I'm sorry if this is forward. I'm not trying to stick my nose where it doesn't belong." I make my voice delicate, all politeness and concern. "But I saw something in the news today."

I let those words rest between us a moment.

"And I can imagine that what I read has made today difficult for Benjamin—and maybe for you, too."

Another pause. My eyes are glued on the rearview mirror, one hand clenched around the steering wheel, the other on the phone. Nerves shoot through me, but I can't let them control me.

"It has been a hard day, yes," Gwyn acknowledges.

"I know you have news vans outside your house," I say. "I drove by to check on you, and—I saw them." Relief flutters through me. I drove by to *check on her*. What a friend would do.

"Anyway, I was thinking it might be hard for you to leave and not be followed, and I was thinking I could help you with that."

"How?" she asks.

"Is the tide low enough for you to walk along the beach?"

A pause, then, "Yes, I think so."

"I'm a block down. If you can walk all the way down the beach and go through a neighbor's yard, I can meet you down the road and drive you to the winery."

Ten minutes later, a figure appears between two houses. Gwyn strides across, looking back down the road at her house where the two news crews hold camp. She slides into my car. I watch her, but don't expect it when she leans over and wraps her arms around me. The cloying scent of her perfume hits me hard, and I push back annoyance and instead focus on the fact she's not upset with me.

She blinks at me, and I can tell despite her heavy eyeliner and mascara, there's a puffiness to her eyes, suggesting she's been crying.

Tearful at her friend's body found? Or at imagining the rest of her life behind bars?

"Thank you for this," she says.

I paste on a smile, satisfaction curling through me. "That's what friends are for."

TWENTY-FOUR
MADELINE

Four Years Ago

Benji knew exactly what to say. She was simply a jealous ex. One with whom he'd discussed in his college days starting a winery with—so, one day, his ex decided she was entitled to half of what was his and that they were going to discuss it in person.

"I never agreed to meet with her. But I should have told you she called," he said as we sat down on the leather loveseat in his condo. "But I didn't want you to worry. In hindsight, I've only made you worry more. I'm so sorry." Benji leaned in, kissed me, played with the shining rock on my finger. "I don't anticipate I'll hear from her again. I made it very clear she had no legal claim in the business, and that I am getting married."

Relief rushed over me like cool water. I leaned in, wrapped my arms around him. "Good. I hope I didn't sound jealous. I was just—so—" My voice trembled. "Scared. I've never met anyone else I wanted to be with like this. Like you." His strong arms pulled me in.

"I've never met anyone else I wanted to be with like this, either," he murmured into my ear.

I pulled back, suddenly remembering the other part. "Wait, does she own half the winery?"

Benji laughed. "No, not at all. The original business plan was part of a project we did together, but I wrote a new one long before North Wineries ever became a real thing. She played no part in it."

For the first time in the forty-eight hours I'd had to wait to see him in person, to demand answers, I felt as though I could breathe. When Benji got up to answer the door for the pizza we ordered, I sent two texts, one to Kip: *You were right. Nothing to worry about.* And the other to Gwyn, because of course I'd shared my fears with my best friend. She'd listened, face grave, asking me gentle questions like *does he always text you back? Does he leave his phone face down or change the password?* And half a dozen others, before declaring, "I don't think he's cheating on you, Maddy. I think he's got a crazy ex."

See? You've got a good one, Gwyn replied, and Kip messaged a thumbs-up.

When Benji came back, I settled in beside him, a night of pizza and wine and dreaming about our wedding ahead of me. But try as I might, I couldn't slow the beating of my heart, the flutter of nerves in my stomach. He'd explained it away so easily, had the answer to every question, known exactly what to say to calm my fears.

I believed him, I did. But I couldn't help wondering... what if he was lying?

TWENTY-FIVE

REBECCA

Now

I expect we might have a similar issue with the media at the winery as we did at Rebecca's house, but when we drive down the faux-gas-lamplit street with trees planted every ten feet there are no news vans. It's a Monday night, and most of the neighboring shops are shut down for the evening. Only a coffee shop on the corner stays open, golden light spilling onto the damp sidewalk.

"Best place to park?" I ask, though I know the answer.

Gwyn points. "Just park on the street. I'll pay. Easier than the garage a block down."

We enter through a side door in the empty alley to one side of the winery. Inside, exposed ceiling beams match long narrow tables. I know from memory they are made with a dark wood Benjamin bragged about procuring from a dismantled boat from the Puget Sound—more of his green initiative, to reuse instead of buying everything new.

"We'll use the private room in the back." Gwyn beckons me

to follow her. "You should come another time, though, and I'll give you a tour of the whole place. But this way no one sees us from the street and assumes we're open."

I follow Gwyn in. Nothing has changed—brushed-concrete floors, abstract paintings of mountains on the walls. The drive here took less than ten minutes, and Gwyn clutched her purse so tightly I decided to wait to question her until after she's had a glass or two of wine. As such, I follow her patiently, pretending to be impressed by a winery whose floors I walked during the many special occasions you and Benjamin held here—last of which was your wedding reception. We go down the back hallway, and I notice the walls are bare—pictures taken with your camera gone.

Gwyn leads me to a private room with two long tables. A single window gives a partial view of the sidewalk, but mostly it's alley, the *drip-drip-drip* of rain peaceful in the dim room. She flips a switch, and sconces light up along the walls. Edison bulbs hang from one of the posts, illuminating the tables in that same golden light.

In short, it's lovely.

You never got to see this version of the finished project—you would have liked it.

"You designed this?" I need to get her talking.

"Yes." She looks over at me as she sets her purse on the table, and seeing my look of wonderment, smiles. "You like?"

"I do." I take another step around, staring up at bulbs. "This feels very... *Pacific Northwest*. It's perfect."

Gwyn flushes, as I knew she would.

"What about the art?" I beckon at more abstracts covering the brick walls. "Where is it from? It's so different, but it matches perfectly."

Gwyn launches into a clearly rehearsed speech about a local artist she happened upon, and I listen, nodding along and making affirming sounds as appropriate. Gwyn's words quicken as I ask questions, her passion for the design of the winery showing through, and soon she's taking me on that tour she promised.

The last thing I expect to see comes ten minutes later, as we round an old-fashioned bar original to the building, easily a hundred years old, and your face stares back at me from the wall. A framed photo, a short *in memory of* engraved in a heavy gilded frame.

"Oh." I stop short, unable to help myself. I'm at a loss for words, for thoughts, even. "I'm sorry," I stammer, and simply stare.

So they aren't *pretending you never existed.*

"Madeline," Gwyn says after a beat. "She was Benjamin's first wife. I guess you know that, from the article, but—" She had picked up two wineglasses and started pouring a white wine. She finishes now, emptying the bottle, overfilling both, handing one to me. "Maddy and I were good friends."

"Oh," I say again, and let the silence stretch between us, hoping she continues to fill it. My stomach warbles, staring at your photo.

"So—yeah." Gwyn sighs out and leans back against the bar, arms crossed, wineglass dangling from one hand. "I loved her like a sister."

"And now you're marrying her husband." Again, it slips out before I can stop the words.

But Gwyn doesn't so much as flinch.

"I am." A single, decisive nod. "I know it seems strange." She takes a long sip of her wine. I raise my glass to my lips, too, but can barely swallow the dry Riesling she poured. She's about to say more, but a knock at the front door interrupts us, and I look over to see Laura there, her hands cupped around her eyes to see inside the dim interior.

Before she can go to unlock the door, I grab Gwyn's arm,

stopping her. She looks at me, startled. I watch her for a beat, trying to see what emotion resides there, but I've missed the moment, her attention already on letting her friend in. "I'm sorry you lost your best friend. I'm sorry she died. Today must have been hard for both of you."

Gwyn's face softens. "Thanks, Rebecca. I appreciate that." And she gives my hand a squeeze before going to let Laura in.

* * *

We're two bottles in, and Laura's recounting a particularly difficult client at her office that day. "They didn't *believe* me when I told them they have to hire a different type of attorney to help with their taxes." She shakes her head. "You wouldn't assume that a dermatologist could double as a heart surgeon."

"Ugh, that's annoying." Gwyn sets a dish with sliced cheese and a variety of crackers down between the four of us. Abigail reaches for the knife and cuts the brie carefully.

"What did you say Benjamin was doing tonight?" Abigail asks. "It was so fun when he was here that time and told us all about the wines." She pointed at my glass, currently filled with a cabernet. "For example, if that's the same cabernet we had last time, those grapevines are like—" She twisted her lips in thought. "Like forty years old or something?"

"That's why he always tries to buy existing vineyards," Gwyn says. "He says they produce better grapes. And he had a meeting with potential investors, to answer your question."

Something flickers in her gaze, and I wonder if he's meeting with investors because he needs the money—or if it's not a business meeting at all, and he's getting together with the woman from the woods again. Or maybe she tried to get him to cancel it, to be home or here with her instead, given the news. I sneak my phone out, checking for more news, but there's none.

"Where's the restroom?" It was one spot on the tour she

hadn't mentioned, and I'm sober enough to remember I shouldn't already know where it's located.

"Just out the door, go down the hall, take a right." Gwyn points. "They're all gender neutral."

No one watches as I take my glass with me and exit the room. More conversation, this time about whether they should book a hotel by the race start for the night before. "Wouldn't that be fun? Like a slumber party," Abigail says, "And we wouldn't have to find parking that way!"

Laura murmurs something, but the door sweeps shut behind me, silencing her.

I don't go to the restroom. First, I go back to the front of the winery, to inspect your photo once more—to read the inscription below it, though it's of no consequence, just the normal *Madeline was loved and will be missed* bullshit every memorial ever says. At least they didn't put your name on a bench. I inspect it, as though it will give me some clue, but it's just a sepia-tone image of your smiling face.

When I turn to go toward the restroom, I catch a figure looking through the window, just as Laura had—hands pressed up, blocking the light to see through the tinted glass, to see inside. Their face is shadowed from the darkness, from their own hands. I go still, then duck behind the bar.

Wine splashes over the rim of my glass, soaking my hand, my wrist. I peer again, realizing they never caught sight of me. It's a man, and he's still looking in, this time having shifted off to one side.

A would-be customer, ensuring the winery really is closed?

Or the man who followed me earlier, trying to catch sight of me again?

I breathe out as he steps back from the window and disappears back down the sidewalk. Gwyn *had* gone so far as to have us gather in the back room, specifically so we wouldn't catch the attention of customers hoping the winery was open on a Monday evening. But my pulse is loud in my ears as I pace back and find the restroom to dump most of my wine out. I splash water on my face and take a slow, deep breath.

I need to be clearheaded for what I have planned next.

TWENTY-SIX

MADELINE

Four Years Ago

I bought Benji's wedding gift.

It was too soon—August was still months away, but as I strode through the halls, noting *crown molding* and *new door*, I decided it was perfect timing—I'd need some prep time to get it ready.

It was a *house*. A house we could grow our lives in. And even better, it was a house near Daddy's, alleviating my concern about leaving him alone all the time. Elena swore she'd help when I moved out, but I suspected it would slip her mind more often than not.

A huge window gave me a glimpse onto the bend of a road —right around which was Daddy's house. So he wouldn't be able to see us, but we would be close by if ever he needed help. It was perfect, everything I'd ever dreamed of. On the road I grew up on, the same view of the Puget Sound Daddy's house had, access to the beach, and instead of having neighbors on both sides, it had *woods* on one side. They backed right up to the yard, and it was like my own little getaway. Gwyn promised to help—redoing the bathrooms, changing the colors in the kitchen. No big renovations, but little stuff.

Daddy helped me with the down payment, but my trust fund covered the mortgage payments, plus when Benji and I combined our incomes, we'd have more than enough. I clasped my hands and strode from one room to the next, excitement bubbling over, but aware I'd made a big move without consulting Benji—buying a house! I hoped he wouldn't be mad I hadn't included him in the search. I wanted to. But I also wanted it to be a surprise. Besides, we had to have somewhere to live after we got married—his condo was too far from Daddy, and I didn't want to rent.

Our lives were going to be perfect. Heck, they already were.

Gwyn came with me when I looked at the house—this time with *the keys* in my hand.

"God, I can't imagine a more perfect home," she'd said.

I could hear the jealousy in her voice. Maybe we could introduce her to one of Benjamin's friends once she officially broke things off with Alex. "I can't believe this is going to be your life," she said after that, which seemed strange—the house was actually smaller than Daddy's, but it did have a better view.

We walked from one room to the next, me pointing out what I loved and what I wanted to change. "I hate the tile in this bathroom," I said. "Do you think we could do something with it?"

Gwyn nodded, scribbled something down in her notebook. "You sure? The tile looks like it's original. And it's gorgeous." Her fingers touched over the tiny tiles dating back older than me—older than Benji, for that matter.

"I'm sure."

We talked about fixing up the office for Benji, getting rid of ugly sliding doors and replacing them with French doors to

open up the space. We discussed colors in the kitchen, and
wood floors in the hallways, where currently, ugly carpet
promised god knows what kind of germs.

Afterward we sat out back with a bottle of champagne I'd
brought along to celebrate.

"I'm jealous," Gwyn said after we'd been sitting out there a
few minutes, staring at the Puget Sound. "I'm happy for you,
but I'm also jealous. Madeline Hughes, the girl who swore off
men, ending up engaged to Benjamin North. With this house.
Who would have ever guessed you'd be getting married before
me?" She leaned over, bumping my shoulder with hers compan-
ionably.

I bumped her back, smiled, but I didn't know what to say.

She was right—it really wasn't fair. But life was unfair. I
could barely even remember my mother, but she saw hers once
a week. That wasn't fair, either.

"You'll find the right guy for you," I said, because what else
could I say? Then a thought occurred to me. "Hey, do you like
Kip?"

Gwyn lowered her sunglasses and looked over at me. "Kip?"

"Yeah. He's cute, right? And he's kind. He's got that
accent."

Gwyn's lips turned up at the edges. "He is cute. And I do
like his accent." She frowned. "Honestly, I thought you kind of
had a thing for him. Walking off with him the other week. And
you're always texting with him."

My stomach wobbled at the implication behind her words.

"We're friends," I said. "We see each other almost every day
at work. He's like—" I shrug. "I don't know, a brother."

She snorted. "He is anything but a brother. But okay, if you
say so."

I opened my mouth but couldn't find the right words. So I
didn't say anything, just sat back and drank more champagne

and wondered if I was giving Kip the wrong idea. Or if Gwyn was just toying with me. She was a good friend, but I wouldn't put it past her, especially given the thread of jealousy in her voice.

I had no doubt, though. Benji was the man for me.

TWENTY-SEVEN
REBECCA

Now

Gwyn is busy entertaining Laura and Abigail with some story about her college days when I creep past the doorway and toward the back of the winery. A series of doors give way to the employee lounge, and beyond it, offices. I go in the last one. The largest one.

Benjamin's office.

It's dark, but I enter, flick on a low desk lamp in the corner.

A quick scan tells me it hasn't changed much since the last time I was here. And he seems to be using it, too, given the mess that is his desk. It's a change—after you bought that house and gave him the home office he always wanted, he used it primarily. His desk sits in the corner, giant and wood and way more than any single person needs. A leather rolling chair. A calendar that hasn't been flipped forward in two months. I pause long enough to listen to make sure in their tipsy state no one has noted my absence, then get to work.

Drawers are filled with pens and pads of paper and other office odds and ends—stapler, tape, rubber bands. Like someone went shopping and got him a bit of anything and everything a person might ever need in an office. Likely, Gwyn.

Next, I go through file cabinets. It seems strange he'd have them—they are a new addition since my last visit—and isn't everything digital now? But I find paper copies of tax forms, employee information, and more business stuff that in no way helps me prove what happened to you.

Then my gaze lands on the computer resting on the desktop. I hadn't noticed it at first because it sits beneath a fan of disorganized papers. But from this angle, I can just see it. It's the same laptop he had before—not that I was ever closely acquainted with his laptop. But he carried it around, and it has that same silver exterior.

My hands shake as I reach for it. Fear of being found out flashes, but then fades away, as I focus on the matter at hand. I pause and listen again. Cackling laughter comes down the hall, and they seem busy enough. I crouch behind the desk, snatch the laptop up, and huddle with it on the floor. Just hidden enough that if someone walks by and gives the office a casual glance, they won't notice me.

It opens easily, and when the password screen pops up, I enter the same number Benjamin programmed as a keyless entry to your house—and to my relief, I get right in.

Then I freeze. My heart beats against my rib cage, heavy *thump-thumps*, and I realize I'm biting my lip so hard I'm about to draw blood. I don't know where to start. But the web browser is open, and his email is right there, and so I start scrolling—he apparently never clears out his inbox. Two minutes later, it's clear I could scroll forever and find nothing. Down the hall, excited voices, high and dramatic with the effects of the wine. I scroll faster, then stop and put the cursor in the search box. At first, I plan to search for business loans or for life insurance— had he taken a policy out on you before you died? Although, maybe that was a normal thing to do before getting married.

Down the hall, Gwyn's voice rings out, cruel as though she is making fun of someone. I frown and instead type in:

Gwyneth Swanson

I hit enter, and no fewer than a hundred emails pop up. Then I see this is only page one of ten. That the emails go back even further. I start to scroll—everything from adding her to his auto insurance and combining bank accounts to her CC'd in business emails about the winery. Not helpful. They're all impersonal, or not even really between Benjamin and Gwyn, but addressed to all employees.

Instead of scrolling through, I navigate to the earliest page—to the very first email.

My breath comes up short when I see it's only a few months into your relationship with him. Before Benjamin hired Gwyn to help with the interior design, before they had any business exchanging personal emails.

The subject line reads *Important* and nothing else.

I click.

Dear Gwyn,

Benjamin North here. So sorry to send you a random email, but I don't have your phone number, and this was easy to find at your company's website.

I have a favor to ask you. I would like to get a camera for Madeline. If I ask her, I know she'll suspect why. Do you know anything about cameras? Has she talked about one she might like? I would greatly appreciate your help with this gift. Would you be able to meet me downtown sometime this week?

Thanks,

Benjamin

The email isn't anything but Benjamin being a good boyfriend. A part of me deflates a little. Another part of me could just about cry—it always seemed like he loved you more than anything else, and maybe he had. He'd reached out to your best friend for help buying the camera that then became part of his proposal.

But then why would he have killed you?

I read the email again, then exit out and scroll through more. My stomach feels queasy, rehashing the earliest words between the couple that's now set to marry. Knowing that when these words were written, you were still happily alive and by Benjamin's side. I blow out a breath and scroll faster because I'll be missed any second now.

Your engagement comes and goes—I read a thank-you email from him to her. And her response, full of exclamation points and compliments.

It ends with *"Madeline is such a lucky girl, that bitch LOL. If only I'd spotted you that night!"* There's a wink after that—making it a joke. But knowing Gwyn, it doesn't seem like one. Something inside me tenses, skimming her words again. Alex was her boyfriend then. Alex, who manipulated her and left her in tears more often than not. Gwyn always envied what you had, but about the time you got engaged was when the jealously started to really come through.

It's also when Gwyn and Benjamin started spending a lot of time together as Gwyn started working on the winery. I scroll down, finding emails exchanged almost daily. Sometimes more than once a day.

I click on one at random.

Hey, Ben,

I was thinking about the color palette, and it might be worth considering bolder colors. The way Seattle can be so gray—

I scroll, noting her casual use of *Ben*, something I've never heard anyone call him. You're the *only* person who used a diminutive with him.

It seems like an innocent enough email, until the very bottom.

Let me know if I can help you with your tux for the wedding. With your upper body, I'll bet you'll look good no matter what you wear.

It's enough to give me pause. To grip the edge of the desk a little harder. To remind myself to breathe. To make me reread the email and try to decide if it's meant to be flirtatious, or merely kind. Maybe I misread it.

But no. No, that's what it says.

I open another half dozen emails over the course of the following month, noticing a disturbing trend—Gwyn is definitely flirting. Benjamin is more being kind, but he's still responding, letting it happen.

And if that weren't enough, the timing changes. The emails are no longer sent at noon or at three in the afternoon. They are sent at nine at night. Five in the morning. Like they were emailing before bed and then carry on first thing in the morning. They both stop using *Benjamin* and *Gwyn* when they sign off, instead using initials. The emails become short, almost conversations back and forth like a text.

It's the email that's dated two months before your wedding that gives me pause.

From Benjamin: *Of course I'm looking forward to the wedding—save a dance for me!*

Benjamin's message puts my teeth on edge, but he was kind to all your friends. It doesn't quite cross the line, more toes it, along with the frequency of messages back and forth.

From Gwyn in response: *I'll save you two.*

Followed by a heart emoji.

And then another from Gwyn: *And hey, if you get cold feet, let me know. If Madeline were out of the picture, I'd leave Alex in a second.* She ends it with a laughing emoji, and then an upside-down smiley face—communicating it's a joke.

But it wasn't a joke. Because that's exactly what happened. She left Alex. And then you *were* out of the picture. Permanently.

And now, here they are. Engaged. Living together. Soon to be married.

Just like Gwyn wanted.

TWENTY-EIGHT

REBECCA

Now

I return the laptop to the desk with a trembling hand. I've been gone too long, and only the effects of the wine have kept them from looking for me. I want to leave the winery altogether— escape to run the Seattle streets and sort through what I know and what I think I know and what I've just uncovered.

Your best friend, suggesting what they might do if you were out of the picture. Perhaps hinting to Benjamin what he should do. What he did...

Not returning to my newfound friends would ruin everything, though. So I go back. I laugh and share a story about the worst patient I've ever had and the most difficult physician I've ever worked with, and they listen in awe, lapping it up.

Two hours later, we leave the winery. Abigail and Laura go one way, and Gwyn and I the other, down the cold street to the car.

Something *was* going on, and you knew it, too. You should have trusted yourself more than you trusted either of them. If you had, maybe things would have turned out differently.

I keep my mouth shut to keep myself from saying something to Gwyn that I'll regret. What I found simmers inside me, threatening to boil over. I take deep breaths, focus on the goal at hand. As we go outside and to the car, I look both ways for reporters and stalkers alike. I wait for Gwyn to sit in the passenger seat and buckle herself in before speaking. "Do you want to go somewhere for something stronger?"

I'm not sure if I'm asking because I hope she'll crack and tell me more about how she and Benjamin got their start, or because I want to take her somewhere in her state of inebriation and—I don't know—smack the shit out of her.

Maybe it wasn't Benjamin, after all. Maybe it was Gwyn. I stare at her, trying to picture her doing it—shoving you over the cliff. The vision comes to me more easily than I would have expected, and I suck in a breath, turn away, force myself to stay calm. To stay Rebecca.

They say *it's always the husband*—and that's what I've thought was likely true. But maybe Gwyn has been playing a long game this whole time. Maybe it really was her.

She opens her mouth and hesitates before responding. "I would actually love to, but I can't tonight." Her phone is in her hand, and she swipes at it. "I want to see Benjamin before he goes to bed. I don't think he's home yet—he's not answering my messages, so he must still be getting drinks with his business partners—but he should be soon."

"Next time, then."

If it was her, that means Benjamin is innocent. Which means he never stopped loving you.

Or—I halt all this *Benjamin is innocent* bullshit because there's no way he's totally innocent. He hooked up with your best friend, asked her to marry him, before you were even declared dead. Declared dead *early*, might I add. After three years, instead of waiting seven.

Or, they were in on it together. Maybe there was an affair.

Maybe he was an active participant, and then they decided they wanted to be together and your money was conveniently enticing and—

I cannot do this here, now. Not with Gwyn watching me.

I start the car, eyes peeled for dark forms wandering anywhere near the vehicle. We pull away from the curb. I swallow and try to come up with useful conversation. "Is he pretty torn up about... what was in the news?"

"He's—" Gwyn presses her lips together, looking down at her phone and it feels like, purposefully not at me. "He's funny about it. It was really hard for him when she went missing." Her throat moves as she swallows. I get the sense there's more—I *know* there's more—but I wish I could hear it from her perspective. "I don't really know how he's coping. He won't talk about it with me." She turns her head and stares out the window.

I bite back a sarcastic reply.

"He must be hurting then," I say. "You said he's your best friend, so if he won't talk to you about it—" She doesn't answer. I inhale oxygen, exhale rage, force myself to be kind. "Are you okay?"

Her fingers move over the phone screen, but it's locked—a nervous tic. A topic she doesn't like to discuss. Understandable, but...

"It's been a long day," she says and offers me a small smile. "I don't know if I'm okay, but I can't talk about it right now. Maybe another time."

My whole body is tensed, waiting for her to say something incriminating—but instead, she deflected. And I need to be sure I haven't pushed too hard.

"Sorry. I had a hard time talking about my husband after it happened, too."

Her face changes to sympathetic in the near darkness. I turn the wheel, wishing the winery were farther away—we're almost to her house already.

"Want me to drop you off at the beach? Or, I don't see any news vans?"

"Out front is fine. I just didn't want them following us earlier."

Following us. Maybe it was someone from the news at the front of the winery. That makes the most sense, come to think of it. I can't help my eyes flicking to the rearview mirror, watching for headlights right behind me, but there's only dark, damp street.

"Thanks for tonight. That was so fun," I say, the expected exchange from one new friend to another.

"Anytime. I'll text you tomorrow, let's run sometime this week." Gwyn disappears from my car and, clutching her purse tight to her, strides toward the garage door. I pull the car away, because my night's not over yet. But who knows how much longer hers will last, or if she and Benjamin will tuck themselves right into bed the moment he gets home, which she said should be soon. I round the corner, pull off in an alley, and cut the engine. I'm already in dark colors, so I just switch my flats for running shoes and pull a rain jacket over my top.

I want to know how they act when they're at home, unaware they've lit themselves up for the outdoor world. That anyone willing to creep through the dark damp forest beside their house can see right into their real world. I want to know if one of them cries, if neither of them so much as acknowledges the news that reported your body found. And if one of them tries to flee, concerned they will be found out and charged with murder, I want to stop them.

Because they will not get to continue walking free while you will never walk this earth again.

* * *

When I arrive at my spot in the forest, I see only Gwyn.

She has changed into white pajama bottoms with a lacy white nightgown top, and she wanders the kitchen, the living room, almost aimlessly. She stops at the back window, looking out over the dark Puget Sound. Her phone is in her hand, and she checks it every few seconds.

Nervous. She looks nervous.

I want to know where the hell Benjamin is. He's worked late as long as I've known him, the sort of thing that drove you crazy with loneliness, then crazy with jealousy when you thought he was cheating on you. The memory of the woman in the woods flits by—perhaps that's where I should have gone. Perhaps he's meeting her, whoever she is, or maybe he's the guilty party and his business meetings were a cover to leave town unnoticed by even his fiancée. By now he could be in Oregon. Northern California. Or if he went east, into Idaho. North, into British Columbia. But if he ran, I'll follow him.

Don't worry, Maddy—I'll finish this, no matter how long it takes.

My attention snaps back into focus when the crunch of leaves comes from off to my left, near the road. Another crunch —a constant pattern, signaling someone walking through the woods. Walking toward me.

Goosebumps prickle along my skin as I make a hasty retreat from my post, nearly tripping as I climb over rocks and duck around another thicket of pine trees. My retreat is noisy, but not as noisy as the person coming through the woods.

My stalker?

A homeless person looking for a place to make camp?

The dark shadow of a person is right where I just was, and they go still—listening.

I go still, too, pressing the length of my body against a pine tree, the bark rough beneath my palms. I inhale, exhale, try to slow my racing heart. A fight-or-flight instinct creeps in. I want to shut my eyes and pretend there's no way they can see me, but that won't help—so I stay perfectly still and, when the person makes noise again, peek around the edge of the broad trunk, a sticky sap clinging to my fingers.

What I expect is for someone to be searching the woods for me. But that's not even close.

A man sits on the rock I inhabited mere seconds ago. He wears dark clothes, gloves over his hands, a dark beanie on his head. But even with the cold weather clothing, there's no mistaking who he is or what he's doing.

It's Benjamin. And Benjamin is watching Gwyn.

TWENTY-NINE
MADELINE

Four Years Ago

I promised him I'd never be like his ex, but all of us have a line after which jealousy is appropriate. I *knew* his ex was jealous of everyone and everything, so I was trying—I really was.

But I think anyone would be jealous if their fiancé did what Benji did.

He called at 3 p.m. to cancel—again—and I took the news as well as I could. He didn't know it, but I was going to give him his wedding gift early. The house was almost ready, thanks to Gwyn's help, but it still needed a few finishing touches. And since it was going to be *our* home, I wanted him to weigh in on those decisions. So, I told him I had a surprise for *him*, and that I'd pick him up at his condo at six.

A catered dinner would await us in our new kitchen. His favorite bottle of chenin blanc would sit chilled either on the patio, or safely inside, both with a view of the Puget Sound sunset, depending on the weather. He'd ask me what the hell we were doing in this giant empty house—and I would tell him to close his eyes. I pictured this surprise over and over. Benji would ask why, or refuse to do it at first, because men are like that—but then he'd give in, because he always gives into me, and I'd press a key into his hand. He would open his eyes and—

I wasn't sure what he'd do then. Be delighted? Be shocked? A bit of both?

I'd pour him a glass of his favorite wine and take him on a tour of our new home. I was proud of our main bedroom, where I'd already had a new king-size bed delivered, so we could spend the night if we wanted. I'd show him the his-and-hers vanity with a knowing smile, because when I spent the night at his condo we always had to do battle for the sink in his tiny bathroom. I'd show him my closet, complete with a shoe rack where my red shoes that first caught his attention would go, and I'd show him the hall closet, where he could store all his random crap taking up space in his apartment.

After that, I'd take him to the office—*his* office. A common complaint in his condo was that there wasn't really a place for him to set up, and he wanted something closer than going all the way to the winery. He'd be thrilled.

I'd save the best for last—the view. The Puget Sound view with the Olympic mountain range rising up beyond it.

My heart raced, even thinking of the tour.

But instead, I sat in my brand-new kitchen alone, texting the caterer, directing them to donate the food instead, because I wasn't going to eat it all by myself.

Sorry, my delivery person is already almost there. She has two more stops after that.

A second later, the doorbell rang, and when I answered it, a young woman greeted me with a smile and an armload of food. I pointed her to the kitchen where she started to lay it out presentation-style.

"Oh, don't bother," I said. "Thank you." And I handed her a

sizable tip. Just because I was miserable didn't mean she had to be. Disappointment left a bitter smile on my face, a heaviness to my body. I found the wine opener and unscrewed the cork and drank straight from the bottle, wincing at the bright flavor so different than my own favorite. But I'd gotten what Benji liked because that's what people in love do—they make sacrifices.

I tried to bolster myself with the knowledge he was working hard not only for the winery, but for us. Sure, we'd have my trust fund to live off, and yes, I'd get an extra lump sum when we got married, because my mother was generous like that, not that I knew from firsthand experience. But Benji didn't want to depend on my family's money, and I could respect that.

But seriously, I'd told him I had a surprise for him. I planned the evening a week out. And he had to work late, caught up in whatever was happening up at the vineyard in Woodinville. Even with traffic, it was rarely more than an hour drive.

The food sat there, instructions on how to heat it up on a fancy piece of thin manilla paper. I touched my fingers to the smooth paper then picked up my phone and scrolled until I found the most recent group text.

Anyone want to come to the new house? I got dinner catered in, but Benji canceled.

Leah got right back to me: *Sorry, working evening shift tonight. Hugs.*

Natalie wrote: *On a date! So sorry. I wish I could. xoxo*

Gwyn sent a sad face emoji and added: *Sorry, behind measurements at the winery, I'll be here all night working at this rate. Lunch tomorrow?*

And then a fourth reply came through, and I realized I hadn't texted our regular group chat—I'd texted the one Kip was included in.

Kip: *Sure! Send me the address.*

I cursed under my breath, and seconds later, predictably, Gwyn privately sent me a laughing emoji. *Bet you didn't plan on that, huh?* I swiped away her message and scrubbed at my face, trying to decide if I should come up with an excuse, or simply say *Sorry, I didn't realize you were included!* What was worse was that all three of my friends knew I'd effectively set up to have Kip of all people over for a private dinner, just the two of us.

But once again, the wine made me bold, and I was tired of spending evenings alone. I sent him the address. I wasn't doing anything wrong. We worked together. We were *friends*. And I'd never cheat on Benji. This double standard that I wasn't supposed to even have male friends was ridiculous. Besides, Benji wasn't the jealous type. It wouldn't bother him I'd had dinner with Kip.

Kip arrived, and I gave him a tour of the house—a scaled down version of the one I wanted to give my fiancé—and we sat out back, watching the sunset, sharing the wine and dinner I'd gotten just for Benji. Kip's last day with Elena had been weeks prior, and we spent the time catching up. He told me about his latest residency block: "Pediatrics. The kids are cute. But I don't care for it. The parents are the worst, always worried there's something wrong with their perfectly normal kid, but they read it on the internet somewhere..." He continued, rehashing stories from medical school. Soon, I was laughing, and we drank more wine, and after a while the sun set. I found myself telling him about Benji, the winery, our plans for the future.

"So where is he tonight, then?" Kip motioned to the view. "Missing this? With you?"

"He just knew I wanted to do dinner with him. He didn't know—" I nodded back at the house. "About the surprise."

"Still." Kip paused and drained the remainder of the wine in his glass. "He cancel on you a lot?"

I thought about it. "Sometimes. He runs the business on his own, and he has vineyards up north. Plus the winery here. It's a lot."

A slow nod, but I could tell there was something that Kip wasn't saying.

"What is it?" I asked.

"Just—" He turned and gave me a quarter smile. "Be careful, okay? You're a nice girl. My friend. Don't let him hurt you."

I wasn't sure what to say, where his words had come from.

"Did Elena say something to you when you were working with her?" I asked after a beat. She'd been so supportive lately, but she was the only one who'd ever uttered a word against Benji.

"Of course not." But there was something in his voice that made me wonder.

And then the worst thing to happen to me in years came in the form of a phone call.

"Gwyn's calling." Kip pointed at my phone, resting between us on a wicker and glass table.

I answered, expecting to hear how she would *never* be able to finish the design on time, or her most recent complaint about Alex, or anything but—"Maddy, I'm coming over. I have to talk to you."

"Are you okay?" I sat up straight, alarm in my voice.

"I'm fine," she said, voice flat. "I'll be there in five."

Minutes later, she blew in like a storm, blonde hair flying around her face. She caught sight of Kip and immediately said, "He needs to leave."

My heart almost stopped. Gwyn would kick Kip out only if it was serious, and not just serious, but *sensitive*. Like if someone had died or, or... I couldn't even fathom what it might be.

"Maybe I can help," Kip said. "I can at least keep a secret."

He looked back and forth between us. "But I can also leave. I understand if you want me to."

More than anything, I wanted to know what she had to say.

"What is it?" I asked, ignoring Kip's presence altogether.

Gwyn hesitated, looking at him, at me, like we were up to something. Then she shook her head and stepped closer, lowering her voice as though someone might overhear.

"I was at the winery, taking measurements for the shelves Benjamin wanted for storage in the back—" She breathed again, like she'd sprinted over her. "And I heard someone come in the back entrance. The employee-only one. It's Monday, so of course that seemed strange to me."

The winery was closed Mondays, so it *was* strange.

"Did you see who it was?" I asked.

Gwyn looked at me, really looked at me, her gaze flicking back and forth between my eyes as if searching for an answer. "No. But I heard them."

"Could you tell who it was?" My phone was in my hand, my pulse starting to slow—a break-in or an employee grabbing a bottle of wine was something I could call the police for or simply text Benji about—it certainly wouldn't have required this level of concern.

But then she said, "Benjamin, Maddy. It was Benjamin. And he was there with a woman."

THIRTY

REBECCA

Now

I stay frozen behind my tree until I'm literally freezing—fingers numb, legs rigid as I try with all my might to not move, to not make a sound. Even my breath I try to quiet.

When I risk a glimpse, Benjamin is leaning forward, elbows on his knees. A glimmer of light from the windows casts his face a pale yellow, though he's otherwise cloaked in shadows, his form a mere outline. Other than one leg, which jiggles every now and then, he doesn't move, watching his fiancée through the window as she paces, makes herself a snack, lifts her phone to make a call.

The air practically vibrates around him with the intensity of his gaze. Like he's waiting for something—I wish I knew what. This isn't the fond watchfulness of someone in love. This is anticipation—like he's sure it's going to happen, whatever it is.

I lower myself into a crouch and watch Gwyn alongside him, but her actions are of no consequence. When he gives up—and from the way he shakes his head and sighs, it feels that's exactly what it is, *giving up*—he moves back down through the trees. It's then I realize it's no coincidence this tiny nook exists in the woods beside their house, a hidden trail leading to a relatively comfortable rock to sit on. I look around and see what I should have noticed the first time—the trampled leaves, the spot on the rock where no moss grows, because someone has often sat on it.

This isn't the first time he's sat here, watching her. But *why?* Maybe it's the same reason I'm watching them—lack of trust. Suspicion. He doesn't trust Gwyn. Which implies he knows something about her. Or suspects something about her. Maybe, that she wanted to take your place. Or maybe, he thinks she's having an affair.

It does seem as though *they* had an affair, after all.

Except, he had been with that woman in the woods, and that had to mean something.

I'm about to follow him—to rush to catch up, to see if he heads back to that spot in the park.

But he appears before me seconds later, in the house, and I sit down to watch the show. A thoughtful, concerned smile. Arms opened wide, enfolding Gwyn. A gentle kiss shared between them.

Oh, what a genius actor he is—even better than me.

I'm not sure if I should think Gwyn's getting what she deserves or be concerned Benjamin's going to steal away my opportunity for revenge. After all, he's lying to Gwyn the same way he lied to you. And things didn't turn out so well for you.

THIRTY-ONE

MADELINE

Four Years Ago

It was a strange week. I didn't feel right, didn't feel *normal*. Didn't feel like the Madeline who'd fallen for Benjamin, who flirted her way into calling him Benji, who'd been whisked off to Europe, who was proposed to on a boat in the Puget Sound, and who was now planning to marry him.

I tried to act normal. But it was impossible not to watch him, to read into his every action, his every text, his every *I'll be a little late getting home tonight.* Because my mind automatically jumped to the *why*—was he meeting with her? *Again?* It was entirely possible he'd lied to me before—that he in fact *had* planned to meet her, and I was an idiot to believe him when he said she was just a jealous ex in the past.

Gwyn overheard them meeting at the winery, when he was supposed to be in our new home with me, on a night we should have remembered for the rest of our lives.

But that wasn't the only thing that left me trying to sort out reality from my paranoia. When Gwyn rushed to meet me, she left the winery fast—afraid to be caught witnessing whatever was happening—she left so quickly, she hadn't heard anything other than those few words from Benjamin: "We really shouldn't be here." Gwyn had stared at me, wide-eyed, then added, "That's what he said. Except he said it in like a"—she blinked, searching for the right description—"flirtatious way. And then she giggled."

We really shouldn't be here.

First of all, who was we? And that meant they were up to something, I was sure of it. The fact she *giggled* suggested something inappropriate, but why would he take a woman to the winery? Why not take her to a hotel if he meant to sleep with her? Unless it did have to do with the business. Or... My gut filled with dread. Or, it was both. It could have been his ex.

My mind spun out with the possibilities while Gwyn rambled on. After Gwyn left, Kip turned to me.

"Can I say something totally crazy and have you not hate me?" he'd asked.

I could barely breathe. My whole world was evaporating before my eyes. Or maybe, going up in flames was a better way to put it. I was certain Benji had met with his ex. He'd taken her there to—I don't know what, show her around? Show her his success in the wake of their breakup? To make *her* jealous?

Did he shove her up against the stone walls and—I shut my eyes and pressed my palms against them to keep out the vision of them together.

"Madeline, listen to me." Kip nudged my shoulder with his.

"What?" I dropped to the ground because there was no furniture to sit on. Kip slid down beside me, and the two of us took turns taking swigs from the bottle of wine. I stared at the paint I'd picked out—yellow, because with the white trim and sunlight, it made the whole space look lit with sunshine. Was it all a waste? Would there be no wedding? Jesus, did I have to call it off now?

"Two things. One, you don't know anything. Gwyn left

before she saw Benjamin. She didn't even *hear* anything besides them laughing and chatting."

"Giggling," I said. "They were *giggling*. And he said they shouldn't be there."

"The woman giggled," Kip interjected. "Anyway, she could have been an employee or an old friend or—"

"His ex," I filled in.

"*Two*," Kip continued, "consider the source of your information."

My stomach flip-flopped, and in my wine-induced haze, I struggled to understand what he meant. "Are you saying she's lying?"

"No. But she could be. Or twisting the truth. It's clear she's jealous of you. Of Benjamin. Of—" A gesture at the house. "You have the life she wanted. I know she's your best friend. But Benjamin is the man you want to spend the rest of your life with."

I swallowed more wine.

"Weren't you just saying to be careful?" I asked.

"Yes. And I still say that—be careful about your fiancé, your friends, your own health—" With a quirked lip he pulled the bottle from my hands and set it out of reach before I could take another drink. "So *breathe*. Think it through. Ask Benjamin what he was up to tonight, see what he says. You can't deny Gwyn, good friend though she is, is also jealous."

I remembered what Gwyn was capable of when she saw something she wanted, so I could see what Kip meant. And Gwyn did tend to err on the side of the dramatic. She'd seen nothing. Heard only voices that, as Kip said, could have been anyone, even an employee who'd forgotten her purse.

My chest unclenched. I remembered how to breathe.

I would figure out if Benji was up to something—very carefully. And if he was, I'd squash it. Because we were perfect together. And I wasn't about to let the only man I've ever loved slip through my fingers.

THIRTY-TWO

REBECCA

Now

When I drove home last night, I circled my neighborhood three times—ensuring no one followed me. I closed blinds and curtains and double-checked locks on windows and doors. The vision of Benjamin watching Gwyn through the window stayed with me, and every time I shut my eyes, it came back.

The emails come back to mind. The slow flirtation between Benjamin and Gwyn. The suggestion of *if you were gone.* Before, I would have leaned toward Benjamin being the guilty one—the most to gain. The one who married you days before your death. But Gwyn had said—had *suggested*—*if Madeline were out of the picture...*

Maybe it was her. It would explain why Benjamin was watching her—was he suspicious?

For now I can't exclude anyone.

Guilty until proven innocent.

I roll over in bed and gaze at my phone. I need to get back into their house. Do a proper search. Look for the camera, the diary. Find *proof*. But before I can text her, a message beeps through from Gwyn.

> *Hey, sorry to bug you, but the news vans are back, and I'm out of coffee. Don't suppose you'd want to bring some over via the beach? I have fresh blueberry muffins.*

I reread the message to make sure I understand it correctly, and that she's asking *me* for coffee, as opposed to Laura or Abigail. Are we forging a connection, as I had hoped? Or is it that they both have jobs with a regular schedule, and she knows I didn't work last night? My lips twist in distaste—it's like Gwyn to expect others to do her bidding—but since it makes my life easier, I text back, *Sure, I can be there in twenty*, and pull on clothes, hashing out how I'll distract her long enough to go through Benjamin's things.

Coffee is easy—there's practically a coffee shop on every corner in Seattle, and once I've procured both to-go cups and a pound of coffee to restock her supply, because that's what friends do, I park in an alley and walk the short distance along the beach to her backyard. The tide is out this early in the morning, dark sand filled with tide pools and exposed rocks taking up the space between me and the water.

I think of how the water would make an icy-cold grave for anyone caught in its depths. I consider the chill of the water, and how long a person would last before they became hypothermic, before they slipped beneath the water, disappearing forever—

"Oh, thank god." Gwyn is beside me, jolting me from my reverie. She takes the cup I offer her. "Oh, and you brought coffee beans, too. Thank you, thank you, thank you." She's taking a long pull from the coffee already. "Come inside, it's freezing."

Her kitchen is lit up as brightly as before, and true to her word, on the stove are a dozen blueberry muffins, their scent filling the house.

"How'd you sleep?" I select a muffin and sidle up to the eat-in kitchen counter. She leans on the counter across from me with her own muffin, peeling the sticky wrapping from the bottom of it.

"I always sleep well," she says.

Her words feel cold at first—who sleeps well after their former best friend's body has been found?—but she flicks her gaze up at me and continues. "Sleeping pills. Anxiety meds. They work wonders."

"Me, too," I say. We make small talk about which meds we each take—and I'm pleased to hear it's the same one, meaning if I drug her with it, and for some reason she gets tested for toxins, it will only show up as her own prescription. I eye the hallway leading to their bedroom. The opposite hall leads to Benjamin's office.

Before I can bring up another topic—running or the winery or whatever else might get Gwyn talking—she presses her lips together. "We're friends, Rebecca. Right?"

My body tenses, but it's just a question, so I sip from my coffee, pretending her inquiry hasn't affected me in slightest. While my body is still, my mind races: What is she going to ask me? What favor does she want? Was coffee just a way to get her foot in the door?

"Of course. Hopefully, becoming good friends." I offer a tentative smile.

Gwyn smiles back and holds up the coffee cup. "You brought me coffee. That makes you a best friend in my world." But the light dims from her eyes and she takes a deep breath. I stare at her, anticipation vibrating through me. "I was hoping I could ask you for a favor. I would ask Abigail or Laura, but—" She bites her lip. "To be honest, this isn't something I feel comfortable sharing with them."

I lean toward her and mirror her body language—hands clutched around the still-hot coffee, muffins forgotten beside us. I tilt my head, to let her know I'm listening.

"Benjamin got home really late last night. And it's not the first time he's been home later than I expected. He also smelled funny."

I frown. "Funny how?" *Like the forest?*

"Like—" She shrugs. "I don't know. Not normal for him. Not like perfume necessarily, but not... not *him*."

I know what she's getting at. And a good friend would offer comfort—would reassure her. Offer explanations that involved him not doing what she's afraid he's doing.

"Didn't you say he was at a bar or something?"

"An associate's club," she replies.

I sip my coffee, think of comforting things to say. "Could it have been that? Like someone he sat near or if they smoked cigars or something. Is that his thing?"

Gwyn takes a moment to collect herself. "It could be, yes. But—" She looks up at me. "But I also noticed something else, and these things make me wonder if something's going on."

She doesn't mention that she's the one who first suggested to you that Benjamin might be cheating on her. And that if a man cheats on one woman, he'll likely cheat on another. Probably, she's come to that conclusion, though. Does she feel stupid, trusting him? I hope so.

"What else did you notice?" I ask.

Now she fidgets. "I looked at his phone. He left it on the bedside table when he took a shower."

"That's trusting of him if he's..."

"Having an affair," she finishes. I have to fight to not smile. To not gloat.

"Yes," I say, curious where she's going with this. "Did you find anything?"

Gwyn's hands move slowly, picking up and tearing the blueberry muffin into pieces. She takes a chunk and holds it like she's going to eat it, but she just stares into space.

"He's been texting someone. It goes back as far as his phone saves them, but that's only a month. It's just a number, there's no name."

"Who could it be? Anyone you can think of?"

Crumbles of the muffin fall from her fingertips. "The only person I can think of is... his ex. Before Madeline."

Alarm streaks through me like an electric shock. I let my own muffin fall to the countertop.

"Why do you think it's her? The ex? I thought you said it was just a number."

She pauses. "I'm... assuming, I guess."

Gwyn won't look up, won't meet my eyes. She takes a long draw off her coffee.

My mind races because I know of this mysterious ex thanks to you, but I block that information out. I don't understand why Gwyn would assume it's his ex. Unless there's something she's not telling me.

She might not trust me as much as she claims to by sharing this with me. Or—she wants something from me and looking helpless will only help her to get it. Benjamin was watching her for a reason.

Before my eyes, she changes—the way I see her changes. Is Gwyn your killer?

I cough to clear my throat—clear the emotions clogging up inside me. "What were they texting about?" I ask. Gwyn's face twists with grief, and my own stomach churns in response. That might be who Benjamin met with the other night in the forest, but I don't understand how him watching Gwyn factors in. You were concerned about Benjamin's ex, too, but it seemed that Benjamin and Gwyn were the ones who had something going on—unless maybe he was seeing more than one other woman besides the two of you.

I force my mind to stop circling and just listen.

"She asked him to meet her."

"Did he reply?"

"Not the most recent time, but—it wasn't the first time she'd asked that. And once, Benjamin asked her to meet him."

Gwyn's muffin is now pulp in one hand, destroyed under a tight fist.

"Did they actually meet? Could you tell?"

She nods yes.

"Is there any way it could have been..." I search for something normal to ask. "About past stuff? Like maybe they still had belongings of one another's? Or could you tell where they went?"

"No." The word comes out sharp. "They never say. It's always vague." Gwyn shakes her head. "I don't even know her name. It's just a phone number, and honestly, I'm assuming. But she talks about the past in some of the earlier texts."

"How can I help?" I thread compassion into my voice and reach out to take one of her hands, ignoring the smear of blueberry that instantly covers mine.

Gwyn looks at me with tears in her eyes. "I don't know how to ask you to do this, but could you follow him sometime?"

I blink at her, feigning hesitation.

This couldn't be more perfect.

"I don't know, Gwyn, I mean—"

"Please." She clutches my hand. "*Please,* Rebecca. I can't ask anyone else."

"I wouldn't even begin to know how to follow someone." I chew my lip, forcing myself not to internally fist-pump at my luck. "What if he sees me?"

"He won't. You're quiet. And you're a fast runner."

"Are you—are you sure you want me to spy on your husband?"

Gwyn nods, tears in her eyes.

"Okay. Maybe I could try." I put a thoughtful look on my face, like I'm considering it. Not leaping with joy that she would ask me to. "When?"

"Tonight?" she asks. "He goes for a run every Tuesday night, and sometimes other nights, too. It's so unusual, it just started one day, but he'll never run with me. He says he has to clear his mind, but—I mean, he told you the other day, he's not a runner."

"Of course." I wait a beat. "How was he last night? When he got home?"

Gwyn pushes away and waves a hand, as though dispelling this whole conversation. "He said he was tired. Showered and went straight to bed. We still haven't talked about Madeline. Or much else, for that matter."

The pain in her voice tells me to drop the topic. But that's answer enough. Neither of them seems terribly torn up about you. Both almost seem suspicious of one another—Benjamin watching Gwyn, Gwyn asking me to spy on Benjamin. Maybe they're both guilty, both afraid the other is going to expose them.

The appearance of his ex a second time leaves me wondering—and brings a potential accomplice into the mix. Or a jealous ex who wants Benjamin for herself.

The woman he met in the woods—it might be her. And tonight, I'm going to find out who she is. But first, I need to use Gwyn the way she's using me.

THIRTY-THREE

MADELINE

Four Years Ago

My plan was in full force. I didn't know if Benji was cheating on me, but if he was, he was good at it. I had Gwyn keeping an eye on him at the winery as she added a decoration or suggested more built-in storage, but her time at the winery was coming to a close. I'd started dropping in on him at work, taking him coffee, delivering it with a kiss, but he was always alone, working on this or that. When I could get my hands on it, I'd scour his phone, but I never saw a call or a text suggesting anything besides loyalty.

Sometimes he worked late, and sometimes he went on business trips, and more than once I went so far as to call him at the hotel. He'd answer the phone, and I'd say, "Isn't this fun? It's like what our parents did, landlines and everything!" as an excuse for my behavior. He chuckled, because he remembered using a landline growing up, whereas I'd never had one.

Benji bought it all. And it wasn't a lie—it's who I really was. A devoted, loving fiancée, who never thought she'd meet a man worth her time. And now that I'd found him, I was determined we would have a happy life. There was no reason we shouldn't.

Gwyn, of course, texted me updates every day: *He's selling some woman wine*, as though that were a crime, giving me reason to lean into Kip's reasoning that she was jealous, struggling through her own relationship. Kip, meanwhile, continued to hang out with the three of us, blending into girls' nights flawlessly.

Elena, who still hadn't hired a receptionist, figured out *something* was going on, maybe because we're sisters.

"What's up with you?" she asked one afternoon after the last patient left.

"What do you mean?" I shot her a look as I sorted forms into folders to be scanned into patient charts. The office wasn't the same without Kip, whose playful humor I missed. I wished he'd stayed longer, added an elective block to continue learning about plastics, but he was off in pediatrics. Couldn't say I blamed him—Elena, with her exacting standards, wore on people.

"I mean a few weeks ago you were happy as could be. Engaged. You bought the house. You couldn't stop smiling." She came up short of the hallway that led to her office and turned to face me directly. Her gaze softened. "You seemed... good. And now..." She stepped closer and pulled up the second chair. "Now you seem not so happy. Is everything okay?"

I shared eye contact with her, something we often avoided. My chest expanded, and for maybe the first time ever, I felt warmth in her presence. "Just... stressed. About wedding stuff." I couldn't tell her everything. And besides, it seemed more and more likely there was nothing to tell. Benji hadn't met with another woman so far as I could figure. When I'd asked him about that night, he freely admitted you had stopped by the winery to grab papers you'd left there, though he made no mention of a woman.

Elena's gaze lingered on me. "You sure?"

I gave her a tight nod, because if I said my biggest fears out loud, I'd cry. And at least on the surface, Benji was the perfect fiancé. He was attentive and mostly showed up on time and brought me little gifts and called just to say hello. He held my hand and opened doors and answered the phone when he was out of town or working late—if it hadn't been for Gwyn's report of him with another woman—*his ex?*—I'd have suspected nothing. I had zero evidence of him doing anything wrong. Which really meant this was my own problem, not his. Why couldn't I just relax? Clearly, Gwyn mistook whatever she heard.

"Listen, I'm only going to say this once." Elena took one of my hands, her cool palms and carefully filed nails smoothing over my skin. I stilled at the unexpected contact. "It's okay, if for any reason you decide you don't want to marry him. No one understood when things ended with *my* ex, but they also didn't know the inner workings of our relationship. Only that perfect exterior. And there's always more than meets the eye. So know that if there's something going on, I will support you, no matter what you do." She leaned in and hugged me—maybe the third hug we'd ever shared—then, in a very Elena-like fashion, left before I could reply, the amount of emotion compressed into those moments way too much for her stoic self.

My heart palpitated as I watched her walk away. Maybe I should have invited her to be my maid of honor instead of Gwyn. She *was* my sister, after all. But then she called back, "Make sure you get that scanning done before you leave," and that warm feeling dissipated.

She cared. I knew that. But she was still Elena, my demanding sister.

When it was time to leave for the day, I debated which house to go to—Daddy's, Benji's condo, or *our* house. I'd waited another two weeks to show it to him, making sure I saw no signs he was cheating on me.

"This is *our house*?" he'd asked and walked in a slow circle, admiring the front room, eyes catching on the crown molding Gwyn recommended to soften the lines. I took him on that magical tour I planned out, showing him each and every room, the view of the Puget Sound and his office the icing on the cake. Then we made love, just as I imagined we would, on the king-size bed in our room.

Afterward, we laid there, spooning, staring out the floor-to-ceiling windows that lined the back of the house. I could see a boat from where I lay clasped in his arms, his breath gentle on my neck.

"Are you still excited to marry me?" I asked, the honest words slipping out before I could contain them. Behind me, his body went still at the question, and I wished I could pull it back, have the perfection of the moment as it was before I spoiled it.

But he relaxed and whispered, "Of course. Are you having doubts?"

I shook my head because I couldn't form the words. And besides, I wasn't having doubts. We *were* getting married. I only wanted to know that he still wanted me, still needed me in his life.

"You're the only woman for me, Maddy. We fit each other perfectly in every way." Benji squeezed me tighter to his chest, as if to accentuate the point.

I breathed out, coming back to reality, shaking the memory of us in bed from my mind. Because in less than two months, we would be married. No one would get in our way. I'd make sure of it.

THIRTY-FOUR

REBECCA

Now

"We should look through Benjamin's things."

Gwyn pauses in the middle of refilling our to-go cups with fresh coffee from her own coffee maker. "What?"

"If he's cheating on you, there may be other evidence." I let my words sink in, pretend I'm not on the edge of my seat, hoping she says yes.

Gwyn takes a moment to process this, then resumes filling the cups.

"I don't know what I'll do if he's cheating on me," she says. "I mean, we just got engaged. I moved in with him. I quit my job at the company I used to work for and started my own business, but I'm not—I'm not making a ton of money at it yet."

I stay quiet to let her process, but this tells me one thing—she doesn't have a trust fund or a rich uncle to fall back on. *Maybe they both wanted your money.*

I watch her a moment, summoning every memory I have of her, gauging what her reaction to my next suggestion will be.

"Marry him," I say. "He's either not cheating on you, in

which case you'll be married to the man you love. Or, if he is cheating on you, we'll have evidence of it. You can divorce him, it can be his fault, you'll have proof, and you can take half of what's his."

In truth, I have no idea if this is how it would work under Washington law. But Gwyn doesn't know any more than I do, and it must sound good to her, because she nods, slowly.

"Do you want me to look through his things?" I murmur. "I understand if you don't want to do it." Put that way, it's like I'm doing her a favor.

"Okay," Gwyn says after a moment. "But I don't want to be here for it. It would feel too weird." She looks out at the Puget Sound, the sun now up, but the sky cloudy and gray, the wind sending ripples across the water. "I'm going to go for a run. I'll go up the beach and come back in... an hour or so." She swallows. "Is that enough time?"

My pulse pounds light and thready. I can't sound too eager. "It should be."

Gwyn disappears to change clothes. When she comes back wearing running tights and a long-sleeved shirt, I pull her in for a hug. "It's going to be okay, either way."

She leaves out the back door. My whole body feels light, adrenaline plunging through my veins at high speed, and I don't hesitate—I go straight to their bedroom, searching for the camera, the journal, or anything else that will give me a clue as to who's guilty. But there are no secrets in Benjamin's drawers. His closet holds only fancy shoes and shirts not bearing lipstick upon the collar. No journals or cameras are hidden between the suit jackets, in shoeboxes, or anywhere else I can find.

I do a quick sweep of the bedroom—in the bedside table, beneath the bed, the obvious places. I rush down the kitchen stairs to the basement and spend half an hour scouring every nook and cranny, peering in every storage tote, rifling through cardboard moving boxes.

But I find nothing. No sign of your last days. No sign Benjamin's cheating on Gwyn. No signs of something Gwyn might be up to that would lead to him watching her. I'd hoped to gain clarity as to if it really was Benjamin, or if the discoveries around Gwyn truly meant something. If she's guilty. Instead, I've learned nothing new, which throws me a bit. There should be evidence of something... right? My phone lights up, and it's a call from the hospital. I stare at it. This could be the phone call that ends it all. I inhale, exhale, and then answer, body buzzing with adrenaline.

"Hello?"

"Ms. Rebecca Johnson?"

I wet my lips as my heart rate increases. The voice is unfamiliar. Not Riley. Not another charge nurse. "This is she."

"This is Veronica Wells, the nurse manager. An anonymous complaint came in regarding patient care on your last shift with the patient in Room 119."

A pause. I absorb her words. Room 119 was Louise, who I took impeccable care of. Who had no family that visited, and who likely was still intubated and unable to make a complaint herself.

"Okay," I say the word cautiously, not sure what to say in response. I'm about to ask what the complaint says when Veronica continues.

"It's a bit odd, because it isn't specific." Papers rustle through the phone line. "I'll be honest, Rebecca, it only says *I am concerned about the nurse's ability to care for this patient.* But there are no details. Do you know what this is in regard to?"

I take a moment to breathe. Make sure the innocent, breathy voice that is Rebecca comes through. "I'm so sorry, I have no idea. I know exactly which patient you mean, and I take care of her every shift I work. As far as I know, everything has been going well." I bite my tongue before I can give more detail —less is usually more.

"You're working in the ICU. You're a traveler. You have previous experience working in an ICU?"

"Yes." I recite the ICU experience the real Rebecca had. Then the two travel assignments I did in Kansas City.

Eventually, Veronica heaves a sigh. "Well, I don't see any issues here. Please do come to me if you feel like you need additional training on any aspect of your job."

We disconnect.

My mind spins in overdrive, trying to connect dots. The only conclusion I can form is that Riley did this—and likely, suspects something. Even if she's not sure what. Fear flickers in my belly. This anonymous complaint couldn't have come from anyone else. The fact it lacked details leaves me hopeful she doesn't have enough to *do* anything—like she's throwing spaghetti at the wall to see what sticks—but it also means she's not leaving it alone.

I have to move quicker, Maddy. Before they realize what I've done and realize that I'm not Rebecca Johnson.

I tuck my phone away and keep searching.

When Gwyn returns, I tell her I found nothing—and remind her that's a good thing, that I'm glad, that I'll follow Benjamin tonight, just to make sure, if she can let me know when he gets home, when she thinks he's heading out.

And then I go home, taking the long way to drive by the front of Chris's house. I don't expect him to be out front, raking leaves, but there he is. His hands grip the handle of a rake, and his dog sits on the front porch, and it takes everything I've got not to stop and say hello as though we are friends. But it is good to see him during daylight. He looks up as I pass by and offers a smile, a wave—like neighbors do. I pretend not to notice. I can't be memorable, and in fact, probably shouldn't have driven by at all.

So why did I?

I exhale. Check my rearview mirror, and there's a black

sedan behind me. I memorize the contours of the car, the sunglassed occupant, the best I can with such a limited view of them. But they turn off on the next road, and then there's no one.

My phone chirps—a news update on you, and I realize why I drove by Chris's. Because on some level, I miss a real connection with someone. With no manipulation or twisting or using to my advantage or knowing I'm being used to their advantage. But the connection with Chris isn't real. Just the illusion of real.

A body found in Mount Rainier National Park is "consistent with the age, sex, and approximate size of Madeline Hughes," officials said at a press conference on Monday afternoon. Due to environmental elements, DNA results are still in processing.

It's not much of an update, but when I get home, I print it out and smooth it into my album. Then, I sleep, the combination of night shifts and flipping my schedule to days catching up to me. When I wake, it's late afternoon. I eat, search the internet for news on your case, then search for information on Benjamin's ex. But there's no mention of her, nor any sign of her on social media.

I'm already out on the streets when Gwyn texts. I'm leaning against a tree, watching Chris toss a ball for his dog, beer in his hand, talking to who I think is his mother via Bluetooth. My phone, tucked into my running tights, vibrates.

Gwyn: *He's home. He's changing to go for a run. I even asked him to stay because I haven't seen him all day—but he said he needs to clear his head.*

Chris laughs out loud, and it startles me. I watch a moment longer, then whisper a silent goodbye, stepping away from his fence line and into the alley. I cast a wary look one way, then the other—but no stalker has followed me today, so far as I can tell.

I'm coming, I write back.

A moment later, as I jog down the sidewalk and get caught in a frigid breeze, my phone vibrates again.

Gwyn: *I'm scared, Rebecca.*

She should be. If I find out she's your killer, it's over for her.

I wait until I'm within sight of her house to reply, this time staying across the street near a playground. I can't see inside their home, but I'll be able to see Benjamin when he leaves, regardless of which direction he goes. No news vans wait outside, probably off chasing the newest and flashiest murder story.

I tap out a bullshit message back to Gwyn and hit send.

It's okay to be scared. You love him. This matters.

The house is lit up as usual and I'm in no better position than I was a month ago, only now I have a small amount of time to get you your revenge. I keep thinking of the way Benji looked when you got engaged, and then on your wedding day—as though he loved you. But what if it was all a lie, an act, a ploy?

At what point did Gwyn stop being a real friend to you? Wish you were gone so she could take your place?

The real honeymoon was called off due to a hurricane—that couldn't have been a lie. Neither of them could have counted on that. Nor could they have counted on someone suggesting a backpacking trip instead. They couldn't have predicted that, three glasses of champagne in and riding the high of marrying the perfect man, you would have stupidly said yes.

I try to think back to that moment—Aaron had encouraged the idea. But I couldn't remember if Benjamin or Gwyn had said anything in support of it or against it. It was shocking

Gwyn had agreed to go, though. I linger on that detail, especially in combination with her desire to replace you.

Does he have anywhere else he keeps things? I text Gwyn. *Other places he could keep a secret or take a person?* I wince with these last words. But she texts back immediately.

The winery? The vineyards up north? He has an office both places. She adds a tearful emoji, and I almost feel bad for her.

Almost.

The sound of shoes slapping concrete draws my attention back to the matter at hand.

Benjamin, jogging down the street.

THIRTY-FIVE

MADELINE

Three Years Ago

I had a plan. We busily moved into our new house—no need to wait until after the wedding, we were adults, and it was the twenty-first century. Invitations were sent out months ago, RSVPs returned. We'd be married on a rooftop garden, a view of Mount Rainier in one direction, the Puget Sound and the Olympics in the other.

I crafted seating charts, found the perfect photographer, showed up for last-second fittings. The bridesmaids were ready to go, and we'd decided to treat them all to a few nights at the same resort we were staying at on our honeymoon, before spending another week on our own.

But that was the fun stuff.

I couldn't help but notice Gwyn continued to find reasons to work for Benji—spending more and more time in the winery, to the point he mentioned, "It's almost like she's another employee! She even helped sell wine the other day." It was a weeknight, and we were out to dinner, one of the few meals we'd caught together recently, considering how busy he was.

"She's mentioned freshening up the look of the vineyard in Woodinville, too. People go out there to do wine tasting, you know. It's an untapped piece of the pie. I mean, sure, we do tastings, and we have a little courtyard, but what if—" Benji kept telling me about Gwyn's ideas as I stuck a fork into my salad and took a bite. As I chewed, I wondered if Gwyn saw an opportunity—well, certainly she *did*, but was it more billable hours working for my fiancé? Or *was it* my fiancé?

In fact, I wondered if there even was a woman she overheard him with that night weeks ago. Or if, having told her the story about the winery employees talking about his ex, she'd decided to take it a step further for her own benefit. Two days after she told Kip and me what she heard—which I was realizing, was really not much—she and Alex called it quits. And just last night she'd said, "I miss the days when we were both single, Maddy. Remember how fun that was?"

But she's always been with someone, so I wasn't sure what she meant. I thought she was my best friend, but sometimes, I wondered if she was trying to get close to Benji. I wondered if she was trying to drive a wedge between us. Or maybe her words were sincere. Maybe she really did miss those brief college days before she stole Alex away from another woman. Or maybe she missed every other moment of our relationship up until I met Benji—when I was at her beck and call.

The buzz of a vibrating phone broke Benji's monologue on how great Gwyn's work was coming along, and my heart constricted as I wondered who was calling him at eight on a Wednesday night. He frowned down at the screen. "Unknown caller." He hit the red button to refuse the call, and momentary relief flushed over me, followed by debating if he'd purposefully had his ex call from a number that would show up unknown— was that a thing a person could do? Was there a star code for it? —so that he could pretend it was spam if I was around when she rang. Or was it Gwyn? Was Gwyn trying to throw me off her own trail—

No. I had to stop this. Benji was the perfect fiancé, and so far as I could tell, nothing was going on. That flash of shame anytime I felt jealousy—anytime I became like the ex he left behind. Except, she wasn't so very far behind, was she?

Benji excused himself to use the men's room. The timing wasn't lost on me. I checked my phone to find a message from Kip: *How's date night going? Let me know if you want to catch up soon, I'm taking off in a couple weeks for Oregon.*

Kip had become the fifth wheel to our girl gang. But even that, sadly, was coming to a close—he was headed to Oregon for his next residency block in mere weeks and wouldn't be able to make it back for the wedding.

I set my phone down without answering and looked for Benji's—he wasn't the sort to carry it everywhere with him—but it wasn't in his jacket pocket or on his side of the table, either. A twinge of worry shot through me, but I'd check it tonight, after he fell asleep. It had become my regular thing, which I hated.

When he strolled back a moment later, I caught sight of it in his hand. Who had he messaged? I couldn't exactly follow him to the restroom. He sat down beside me, a faraway look in his eyes.

"What is it?" I asked.

Beneath the table, his hand clutched mine. "No big deal, just... a blow. We lost an investor."

"What does that mean?" I could imagine, but I wanted to know what he was thinking.

Benji pulled his lips into a tight smile and met my eyes. "Nothing, Maddy. The business will be okay. We have enough in savings."

I realized then Benji couldn't be lying to me about his ex—because he was a terrible liar. Grasping that one fact made everything better, and I decided this was a gift from the universe.

"You're not worried at all?" I asked, to test my theory.

"Not at all." Benji's voice was all cocky self-assuredness, but his eyes stayed glued to his wineglass as he took a long sip from it.

I called Daddy as soon as I got home. I told him what Benji told me, and Daddy didn't hesitate.

"I'll take care of it, Maddy. The business will be okay."

And I knew Benji and I would be, too.

THIRTY-SIX

REBECCA

Now

The moon is out tonight, shifting clouds bringing short drizzles of rain. Water sits atop the streets and sidewalks, and every step Benjamin takes is louder than the one before—wet slaps of his sneakers disguising my own steps. I run on the opposite side of the street, always half a block back. I memorize his route as I go, because it's possible he takes the same route every time he plans a rendezvous with whoever this woman is. The phone in the waistband of my running tights vibrates once, twice. Likely Gwyn, asking for updates. I ignore it.

Benjamin stops after a mile. He's at a cliff overlooking the Puget Sound, the view of a ferry just beyond the beach. The giant boat is coming in, lit up as it docks against wood beams sticking out of the water. Within minutes, cars stream out from a ramp, and Benjamin watches the process.

I wonder if he's waiting for someone—almost expect a woman to walk off the ferry and head his way. Or if she's driving a car and if she picks him up, I won't be able to see what happens next, though him getting in a car with a woman would be incriminating enough. It would be helpful for Gwyn—not so helpful for me. But Benjamin waits just a moment longer before striding back into the night.

I'm so focused on following him—on staying close enough to see which way he turns without being so close he can turn around and see me, or for that matter hear me pacing behind him—that I almost don't notice we've wandered close to the Magnolia neighborhood. Which in and of itself is no consequence, but as he steps off the sidewalk for a wooded path, I recognize where he's headed.

He's going toward his boat. The same boat he used to take you out on, the one you got engaged on. Maybe that's where he's meeting the woman. Disgust roils through me, imagining he probably took Gwyn out there, too. His way of charming women. Maybe they're taking a romantic cruise out onto the Puget Sound.

The marina itself is mostly abandoned so late on a Tuesday night, only a single car parked in the lot. Lights illuminate the rows of boats. I stop at the edge of a building and watch as Benjamin walks down the plank to his boat. When he gets there, he takes a deep enough breath I can see his whole body move with it—an inhale, then his shoulders slowly lower as he exhales.

Then he gets on the boat and disappears from view.

It occurs to me he could have something hidden on the boat itself, unless Gwyn uses it often. Gwyn. I pull my phone out, but there are no messages from her—only texts from my job. Stuff I can ignore about working extra shifts, but still, it makes my gut twist and swirl with anxiety.

I move from one building to the next, hoping I can get a better look at him—but he's in the cabin, as I can't see him in either spot. It's another half hour before he emerges, winding his way off the boat and up the ramp, on the phone. I go still behind a tree, watching as he takes long strides up a staircase until he's back on the sidewalk, his steps quick, sharp. He gestures with one hand, and whatever it is they're discussing, he's not happy.

When he gets closer, I hear, "I don't have any money for you. I told you that. All that ended a long time ago. Stop calling."

I glance down at my phone and take a mental note of the time—9:02 p.m. Gwyn can check his phone when she has the opportunity and see who he spoke to. Maybe it was his ex, like she thought, but he was telling her he wasn't interested. But he mentioned *money*. Why money?

Benjamin hangs up and starts running again. Half an hour later, we've gone three more miles, and with each step, I grow more concerned with the direction in which we're headed.

When Benjamin turns a corner, I stop breathing. He comes to a sudden stop, and I know a second before he does it that he's going to turn around and check the sidewalk behind him. I duck behind a car, and when I dare to peer out again, he's striding up the grassy front of a house.

My house.

* * *

Instead of following Benjamin, I skirt the house next door, not giving a thought to whether someone might be home, that they might come sweeping out wondering what the hell I'm doing there. No, my focus is on Benjamin. I round the corner and watch as he does what I usually do—follow along the side of the house, pressing close to it in case someone should be watching out the window. I'm not home to see him, but he doesn't know that.

My insides feel as though they are vibrating, adrenaline spiking my heart rate, my senses. A broken spiderweb, fluttering in the breeze, flits over my skin, and it takes effort not to yank it away, to curse out loud. Someone has been following me, watching me—and that someone is Benjamin.

Watching me the way he's been watching Gwyn.

Is he onto me? Or perhaps he saw me that night, following him.

Benjamin North. Winery and vineyard owner. And now, man stalking through the night, looking through windows, watching women. Maybe it's nothing new. A vision of him watching you fills my body with revulsion.

Why didn't you listen? When you first thought something was wrong, you should have ended it. You should have run.

My fingers grip the rough bark of the tree I've stepped behind as Benjamin moves from the window to the back door. I hadn't considered the possibility he'd try to get in—my breath comes up short, and I try desperately to remember if I hid my album of photos and articles about you. I can't recall.

But he tests the back door—a gentle jiggle of the doorknob— and about that time, a motion sensor light flashes on, lighting up his face, which creases with panic. I'd forgotten the motion sensor light in the back. The front one doesn't work, and I rarely have reason to go out on the tiny back porch, where the paint is peeling and nails stick up at odd angles.

Still, *he followed me. He's trying to* break into *my house.*

People don't break into houses for good reasons, only bad ones.

He's lying to Gwyn. Watching her from afar.

Dread builds in my gut, imagining his reasons, his plans. If I'd been home alone, unsuspecting, he would have watched me from a sliver in the curtain. Given me that same intense stare he gave Gwyn. I can't quite take a full inhale, imagining his plans for me. For Gwyn. This man is dangerous.

A piece of me wants to approach him, question him, knock him off balance. If I do that though, he'll know he's been caught. It will change our interaction, my ability to worm my way into their lives. Moreover, if he means to harm me physically, which I wouldn't put beyond him, he'd beat me hand to hand. And I have no idea if there's a weapon tucked away somewhere. It's not worth it. So, I continue watching.

A new idea occurs to me: maybe I haven't fooled him. Maybe he did recognize me. Fear flutters through me, leaving me cold and on edge.

Benjamin goes down the stairs on the balls of his feet, tucks himself back around the side of the house. When no one comes to the back door, he eases over the lawn back to the window where the curtain doesn't completely hide the inside—I know what he must be looking at. An unmade bed. A laptop on the side table. A pile of clothes in a corner. Nothing interesting.

Not unless he knows who I really am.

Gwyn might know, too. They might be playing me.

I swallow down a lump of fear. Probably, I'm just paranoid. I've changed so much—filler and Botox, surgery and a change in my body, the way I move—there's no way they know. Right? Surely I'd have noticed the flicker of recognition in their eyes. I exhale.

Benjamin's hand moves, and the screen of his phone illuminates his face for a moment before he answers it. He listens for a moment then growls, "What?" A pause. "I know they found the body. I know what that means." And then a pause and, "Don't forget who you're talking to. I'm not afraid to do whatever I have to," and I can't miss the threat of violence threaded through his voice.

When he leaves, jogging away at a fast clip, I don't follow. I stay right where I am against the tree, sorting through what just happened, wondering what he knows—or if he makes a habit of following Gwyn's friends. Did he follow yours? Or is this a symptom of him knowing who I am?

Jesus, who is Benjamin North, anyway? The Benjamin I knew before would have never done anything like this—at least,

I wouldn't have guessed he would. But if I've learned anything over these past years, it's that people don't necessarily show you who they really are. They show you the version of themselves they want you to see.

His form fades as he turns a corner, and I sag against the tree, relieved. I'm not sure what to think. Sure, Gwyn has her secrets. She certainly had motive. And it's possible they're working together. But Benjamin isn't acting like an innocent man. If anything, he's acting like one with something to hide. Or, who's suspicious.

Eventually, I work my way inside and shut the house up tight. Unease winds its way through me, until I can't sit still, can't relax. I'm checking my computer for news, I'm debating running a background check on Benjamin to see if he has any history of crime or violence, I'm steering clear of the windows, but can't resist peeking through the curtains every now and then just to make sure he's not out there, watching me.

I text Gwyn, *I lost him after a while, but he didn't meet anyone that I saw.*

And she replies, *I think he came straight home. He got here about five minutes ago.*

I spare a thought to wonder if she's safe. If I am. It's nearly two in the morning when I fall asleep, a creeping feeling telling me I'm getting close to finding your murderer.

THIRTY-SEVEN

MADELINE

Three Years Ago

When Benji called to tell me we were going to have to cancel the honeymoon, I was crushed. I sat in my hotel suite with Gwyn powdering her nose on one side of me, Natalie trying to show me which eyeshadow I absolutely *had* to use, and Leah picking her way through a veggie tray. Music played in the background, Destiny's Child, I think. Fizzy champagne was flowing already, because we had our rehearsal and rehearsal dinner in half an hour.

But Benji and I were connected via phone, and the news knocked the wind from my sails.

"I'm sorry, Maddy. We knew we were taking a risk with hurricane season, but the storm is getting stronger. I don't think we can in good conscience fly out there—the two of us or taking all our friends."

It had sounded like the perfect combination of fun and romance, but now, we weren't going on a honeymoon at all. My thoughts annoyingly switched to the three bikinis I bought just for the occasion. Of all the things to be concerned about.

"Okay..." I held up a hand to stop Natalie, who wouldn't give up on trying to help me with my makeup. "So, what do we do?"

A voice in the background stopped him. Whoever it was sounded mad, and also—

"One sec." Benji muted his phone, but I *heard* it. And he was supposed to be at his condo with his brother, Aaron, and no one else.

For the first time in months my heart began pounding in my chest.

"What's wrong?" Natalie whispered, another brush in her hand. This time I didn't thwart her efforts, and she dabbed at my face with god knows what.

"I heard a woman," I whispered.

"A woman?" Gwyn's ears all but perked up and she swung around. "Who are you talking to?"

Natalie tossed an annoyed glance Gwyn's way but continued attempting to swipe mascara on me.

"Benjamin."

Now all three of them looked at me. A knock at the door interrupted us.

"Who else are we expecting?" Leah stood to answer it.

"Elena. She got caught at work." I was still sitting there, phone pressed to my ear, considering hanging up on him. I wasn't sure if I was more upset by the canceled honeymoon or the fact I definitely heard a woman in his condo. My mind raced with possibilities—a delivery? Then I considered Benji's best man, his brother—"You think it could be a stripper?" I asked Gwyn.

She just looked at me—that same look she'd given me when I told her I trusted Benji, that I didn't think he was fooling around on me. It said something like *Come on, girl, be smarter.* I could have given her the same look in response—she wasn't going to the wedding alone. No, she'd jumped right back into the dating pool. Kip hadn't planned on coming because he had a big test coming up, but Gwyn called and begged—and he somehow made it work.

I'm so sad I'm going to miss your wedding! And a day later, *Gwyn invited me as her plus-one. Is that weird? I think I'm going to say yes. My boss is letting me reschedule the test.*

It was weird, but I wasn't going to tell him that, and besides, if it meant he'd be there, that's all that mattered to me. And heck, if he was at the wedding with Gwyn, maybe it would put to rest the rumors something was happening between us.

"It's Kip," Leah hissed. "Are we letting him in?"

"Just for a second," Gwyn said. "We're all decent."

Leah stepped back, the door opened wider, Kip shouldering through, giving us a wave. His hair was mussed, like he'd driven straight here.

That same moment, Benji came back over the phone. "Sorry about that. Where were we?"

"The honeymoon," I murmured.

"Oh, right. So I looked into going to Hawaii instead, but the issue with that is—"

He rambled on.

"Benji, was there a woman in your condo a second ago?" I asked, unable to stop myself. Kip's eyebrows shot up, and my friends went still, staring at me.

A long pause. Blood thrummed in my veins, the pulsating reaching my fingertips until they vibrated. I wanted to say, *Please tell me you're not fucking around on me the day of our wedding, please, please, please.*

Benji cleared his voice. "I'm not going to lie to you, Maddy. There *was* a woman here. She was a stripper. I didn't touch her. Someone knocked on the door right after I called you, and Aaron let her in. I put you on hold to ask her to leave. He swears he didn't send her. She didn't give me a name. I think it was someone's idea of a joke or—a gift or—something."

I listened for the lie in his voice, but I couldn't hear it. Did I need to see him in person to be able to tell if he was lying? I wasn't sure.

"Okay," I said, and my inflection must have told everyone else everything was okay, because they went back to primping, and Gwyn dug through her purse to find a spare invitation I'd wrangled for Kip. Given the status of my family, security would be present, and only those with an invitation would get in.

"Let me see what else I can come up with," Benji murmured, his voice that low comforting tone he used when I was upset. "We *will* do something wonderful for our honeymoon."

It was like wrapping myself in a sweater. I just wished some asshole friend of his hadn't sent a stripper in at exactly the wrong time.

We hung up, and I hugged Kip. "I'm so glad you could make it."

Another knock at the door, and Elena came sweeping in. "I'm here, I'm here." She froze when she saw Kip. "What are you doing here?"

"He's my date," Gwyn said with a hint of pride.

Something flashed on Elena's face—jealousy?—but she'd had her chance and made it clear from day one she wanted nothing to do with him.

"Is that a good idea?" Elena murmured when she got close enough only I could hear her.

"Is what a good idea?" I'd wrestled the brush away from Natalie and was busily swiping on my own makeup.

"You have a guy in here. You're getting ready for your wedding."

I looked at her. "It's just Kip. He's our friend. And Gwyn's date. It's not like we're in our underwear."

It had to be jealousy—a venom in her tone I wasn't familiar with left me second-guessing my own choices, but moments later Kip called, "See you at the ceremony," and took his leave. I watched him go and turned back to Natalie, who waited with lip oil in one hand and blush in the other.

She smiled. "Let's get you ready to marry the man of your dreams."

The man of my dreams.

I forced myself to smile back and ignore the tightness in my chest. This was my wedding day. Everything would be fine.

THIRTY-EIGHT

REBECCA

Now

When Gwyn calls the next morning, I answer immediately, even though I've just taken a bite of toast and have coffee in my other hand.

"Hello?"

"How did last night go? I know you said nothing happened, but... I was hoping you could tell me a little more. Where he went, how far he ran." A pause. "Anything." That last word is said with a note of desperation—a woman, scared of what's happening with her fiancé. I try to feel bad for her—to be Rebecca, her friend. But it's like pulling teeth.

"He ran maybe five miles," I say. "He stopped near the marina. Does that mean anything to you?"

Gwyn sighs. "He has a boat there. He's been talking about taking it out. After Madeline disappeared—he stopped. Like, I don't think he's used it more than once or twice since then. I've never even been on it with him. Maybe that body being found—maybe he's thinking about her."

Or maybe he's hiding something. Maybe he's spent a lot of time on that boat, and you just don't know about it.

"He got two phone calls," I say. "If you can get his phone again, see who it was—maybe it was his ex, maybe it was someone else. It might have been two different people."

"Could you hear what they said?" she asks.

"The first call he said he didn't have money for someone. That he'd told them that before, that..." I try to recall his exact phrasing. "That something was over, I think? Do you know what that would be about?"

Gwyn takes a second to answer "I don't know. I don't know of anyone he owes money to. He has investors for the winery, of course, but the winery is turning a good profit, so... I don't know."

But I had overheard that call about closing the Woodinville location. Maybe he was keeping things from her. Maybe she was lying.

"The second call sounded like he was threatening some-body. Then he said—" I hesitate again. "He mentioned he knew the body had been found."

A gasp over the line. I wait for her to say something—we all know a body was found that is likely yours—but she seems to be reading something else into this.

"Gwyn? Does that mean something to you?"

"No, I just—" She hesitates. I get the feeling she's holding something back. "Of course he knows. We all know. All of freaking Seattle knows thanks to the news. It just sounds so jarring that he'd say that over the phone to someone else. The media was so crazy after it happened, we made a decision to only talk to one another about it. We didn't need Madeline's death becoming entertainment."

A beat passes, her words echoing my own thoughts, my own abhorrence of the dozens of podcasts that speculated about your life, your friends, your family, your secrets. The worst thing to

NEVER TRUST THE HUSBAND

ever happen to you became forty-five minutes of entertainment for someone to listen to on their way to pick their kids up from school.

"Thanks for following him. Would you be willing to..." She exhales. "I understand if you don't want to do it again."

"Of course, I will. I'm... worried," I say. Not a lie.

"I know. I love him. I don't want to lose him."

"Will you tell me if you recognize the phone numbers from the calls?" I ask. "And send them to me? Maybe I can figure out who they belong to. Maybe—" *We're friends. She's worried her future husband is cheating on her. She wants reassurance.* "Maybe it's all work related."

"Sure, of course," Gwyn agrees, and we disconnect.

The next thing I do is call in sick to work, almost against my better judgment. But I want to see them tonight. Want to watch what happens. I don't know what's going on between them, but it's not normal, and I plan to see it firsthand.

THIRTY-NINE

MADELINE

Three Years Ago

Our wedding day arrived, and I was officially a Mrs.—though, I hadn't decided whether I was going to take Benji's name. *Madeline Hughes. Madeline North.* I scribbled them both half a dozen times, even trying the hyphenated *Madeline Hughes-North*, but that was too long. I leaned toward taking Benji's name, not because of any old-fashioned BS, but because with the winery, I loved the idea of hearing *Hello, Mr. North! Hello, Mrs. North!* as we strolled in to check on things. And as much social standing as my own last name gave me, there was a certain ring to *Madeline North* that I liked.

Speaking of, I tried so hard not to photograph every moment of our special day—we hired professionals for that—but I still took a couple hundred photos. Of the rooftop venue, of the winery, decorated for our reception, of my bridesmaids, of his groomsmen—even of Benji. I wasn't worried about bad luck seeing the groom, or any such nonsense. Getting to see Benji before the wedding was what helped me feel good about going through with it.

Not that I was seriously doubting it. I know Aaron well enough to know he'd hire a stripper and deny it—and then admit years later, laughing about the look on Benji's face, disregarding the fact it left me in tears wondering what the hell was going on. In fact, that might have been *why* he'd done it—as much as he mostly played brother-in-law without complaining, he still dropped jabs every now and then about how I'd taken Benji away from him. *Domesticated him*, were his actual words.

Anyway, I saw Benji, and he positively *glowed* with happiness. Benjamin North, happy he was about to marry Madeline Hughes. That the two of us, people who might have never married anyone if we hadn't met one another, were about to join our lives forever. The minister went on and on about how the ring represented eternal love and how there was no ending and *blah blah blah*. Benji winked at me. He squeezed my hands, and we shared a smile, and it almost turned into laughter—but my eyes welled with tears in that moment, because it was true. I loved him as though I loved no one else, how I presumed I would never love anyone.

After the first round of greetings and congratulations, we followed the minister into the shelter of a tent to shield us from the breeze blowing in off the Sound.

"I have the paperwork here." He pointed to a piece of paper. "That's your license. You'll both need to sign, and we'll need witnesses, too."

I knew it was supposed to be an honor to sign someone's marriage license—but Elena was nowhere to be seen, and Daddy was already drinking a Scotch. Kip and Gwyn were closest, so I called them over to act as witnesses. In seconds, we were married—both in front of our friends and family, but also legally, our names scribbled on the document. Beverages were passed around—the reception wouldn't start for another couple hours, near sunset, so the party could extend into the evening.

I made the rounds, my heart full as I shook hands and

offered hugs and embraced people whose names I struggled to remember, but they were happy for us, and that's what mattered.

Eventually, Benji wrested himself free of our friends and family, and came over, but he wasn't smiling.

"I thought Kip couldn't make it?" he asked, voice low, frowning across the room.

I shot a glance in his direction, then met Benji's eyes. "Gwyn invited him as her plus-one. What's wrong?"

"I just—" Benji pressed his lips together, shook his head. "Nothing, never mind."

"What?" I pressed.

"I've never been crazy about how much time you've spent with him. I thought he left. I thought this"—Benjamin waffled his hand back and forth, to indicate my friendship with Kip— "was over, since he left town."

I frowned. "Seriously?"

For all his complaints about a jealous ex-girlfriend, *he* was apparently the jealous one. But he had nothing to be jealous of. Unless...

Unless Gwyn set this up. Unless Gwyn, who he'd been spending time with at the winery, who'd been trying to convince *me* that *he* was cheating on me, suggested there might be something to be concerned about. Gwyn, trying to drive a wedge between us.

"Did Gwyn say something?" I asked before I could stop myself.

"What?" Now he looked confused.

Crap.

But before the conversation could continue, Daddy was there, hugging us both, and a burst of light as the photographer caught the moment.

Daddy pulled away, and I looked up to find Kip in the

crowd again. His eyes were on me. Not Gwyn, though she did stand nearby, shamelessly flirting with another man.

"I'm..." Benji sighed. Pressed a kiss to my temple. "I'm sorry. I'm being ridiculous."

"Benjamin, come try this Scotch," Daddy called, holding up a bottle from the nearest bar, and Benji wandered off, pressing a gentle squeeze to my shoulder as if to continue his apology.

Kip met my eyes across the crowd and waved, a shy smile on his face.

A cavern opened up inside me—of realization, of dread—was *I* the one acting inappropriately? Was I the one giving Benjamin reason to think I was screwing around on him? But no. It couldn't be. He'd met Kip, invited him to our new house for a barbecue months ago. He knew we were just friends. But then why had he questioned me about him at our wedding of all places?

My gaze slid to Gwyn again, but then Benji returned, champagne in hand. We toasted. And then we toasted our friends—including Kip, who Benji greeted with a "Good to see you." Eventually, we took posed photos, first on the rooftop where we got married, and then in the winery. The wedding party, the friends, the family.

The official reception began, a DJ queuing up typical wedding songs. Benji danced with me. I danced with everyone —by nine we were a bumbling mess of tipsy twenty- and thirtysomethings, and it was perfect. Like everything else about us.

It was then that Kip pulled us aside. "So what's the deal with your honeymoon? Did you figure anything out?"

I looked at Benji. We hadn't spoken about it all day—I'd forced it to the back of my mind, too busy with getting dressed and meeting with the makeup artist, the hairstylist. From the way his mouth opened, then closed, a resigned look in his eyes, I suspected I knew the answer to that question—there would be no honeymoon. Or at least, nothing like what we'd planned.

"Hurricane season," Benji said. "It's ruining everything." Then he added, "I mean, it's worse for the people who live there, of course. Their lives are in danger."

Gwyn sighed. "Too bad, I was excited to check out the Caymans. I've never been. You two will have to go when the weather clears up."

Benji frowned. "Maybe we could do something local so we could still do something with our friends." He met my gaze, took my hand. "Any ideas?"

I shrugged—I had no ideas outside of renting a house up north in the San Juans, but we did that all the time. And while it was a fun trip, there was nothing warm and beachy about it that compared to the Caymans or Hawaii.

"Do you like to backpack?" Kip asked. "I was hoping to do the Wonderland Trail before I left Washington, but I never got enough time off at once. You might be able to get a walk-up permit."

My teeth clenched, but I kept my thoughts to myself—I wasn't crazy about hiking. The dirt, the bugs, the inability to take a shower. I had no idea how long the Wonderland Trail was, but the way Kip was talking about it, it sounded as though it would take a few days, at least.

"Oh, totally," Aaron piped up. "Me, too." He looked at Benji. "You in? The views of Mount Rainier are *amazing*. You can literally see the glaciers." His eyes flicked to me, as if just now remembering this was supposed to be *my* honeymoon, too. "The most romantic sunsets, too. Pink and purple." He pulled his phone out and seconds later thrust it at me. A panoramic shot of Mount Rainier, a brilliant hot pink and purple sunset behind it, reflected in a lake that sat just in front of it. He swiped through a couple photos, and the next shot was of a mountain meadow, wildflowers carpeting it like something out of one of Gwyn's design magazines, the perfect exterior of a house, except there was only an old log cabin.

I was about to say, "Are you kidding me?" But then I looked at Benji, his gaze transfixed on the photo. He wasn't an avid outdoorsman—but he loved getting out in the mountains, something he rarely had time for these days. He'd shown me photos of when he was a Boy Scout growing up camping in the Sierra Nevadas. And I could see, from the look in his eyes, this appealed to him.

"Okay," I said hesitantly. "Tell me more."

FORTY

REBECCA

Now

I leave my house in the late afternoon, wandering through Seattle on a six-mile run before circling back and rounding the block twice to make sure no one—particularly Benjamin—has followed me to where I plan to spend the evening. It occurs to me he's either been following me since I first met him, or maybe since I first met Gwyn. Or—and I shudder at this possibility—he saw me that first night in the park, when he met the woman. In fact, maybe the reason he hasn't met her again is that he knows he's being followed.

I'm four miles in when I hear, "Rebecca! Rebecca!" and the steady beat of running shoes. I turn, too fast, paranoid because someone's been following me, Benjamin has been to my house, and Riley suspects I'm not who I say I am—but it's only Abigail. She can't contain her grin, and she throws her arms around me in a quick hug. She's in pink short-shorts, a baby-blue top with white reflective stripes, and the same high ponytail as before.

"So good to see you! How many miles do you have left?"

"Oh—um—I'm headed home."

I need to get to their house, but I have no doubt Abigail will ask if I want to run with her. And as soon as the thought occurs to me, she chirps, "Oh, I'm running ten. Do you mind if I run your last little bit? I'm *so* bored. I was listening to a podcast, but then my headphones died, even though I just charged them—" She's still talking, about a mile a minute, energized from the run, I suppose.

Around us, the sun is setting. I have enough time to pretend to go home, then run back to Benjamin and Gwyn's.

I meet her smiling face. "I'd love to."

We continue the route, taking a left turn instead of the right I'd need to go to my real destination. Abigail is talking about her husband, his job, their plans for the future, the summer vacation they're considering—

When it occurs to me this run could be useful.

"Is Gwyn doing okay?" I ask when she stops talking to take a breath.

"What do you mean?" Abigail lopes along beside me like a deer, smooth and effortless.

"She seems down. Do you know if something's been bugging her?"

Abigail's face twitches, that telltale sign of someone who knows something they aren't supposed to share, unless she thinks that I already know. That this isn't a secret.

"I'm just afraid I'm saying the wrong thing sometimes. I mentioned my best friend back home, and she got quiet. I saw the sign in the winery about Madeline Hughes, and I—I heard the news."

Abigail's pace slows, a thoughtful look on her face. She shoves blonde bangs back and blows out a sigh. "Yeah, I mean, I think she's sad, you know? She didn't want to do it. But it seemed like the only way it could be right."

A second passes as I try to understand what part of the conversation I missed. I have no idea what she's talking about.

"Get married?" I ask finally, a tentative note in my voice.

"What? No. Of course she wanted to get married. That's why she insisted Benjamin have her declared legally dead. I mean, she couldn't marry him if his first wife was still technically alive, right? Unless he divorced her. And can you imagine doing that? Divorcing someone who's been missing this whole time?"

The puzzle pieces align in my head, and a chill goes through my body.

"Gwyn insisted Madeline was declared dead?"

"Yeah, so they could get married. I think she feels shitty about it. Benjamin had held out hope for so long. They both did. But it's been three years, you know?"

We run a few minutes in silence before I work up the courage to pry more. "So I guess they got engaged kind of fast, then. If they hoped she was still alive. They must have not started dating until recently."

Abigail wrinkles her nose. "I'm not sure. I know they've been together at least a year. They celebrated some sort of anniversary last August."

You got married in August. You took a long fall over a cliff in August, too.

"Why do you ask?" Abigail turns a big smile and big blue eyes on me.

"Oh, I—I thought maybe they got together in September. Since their wedding is in September. That's what my husband and I did. We got married the same day we got together." I swallow. I haven't always lied so quickly, so easily. "Anyway, I'm just glad they found each other, you know? After they've been through so much loss. I hope they can be happy together."

"Me, too." Another bright smile. Another mile.

And a growing sense inside me that Gwyn couldn't wait to be rid of you.

FORTY-ONE
REBECCA

Now

I slip into my hiding place just as Benjamin's Tesla pulls into the garage. At least I know he's not watching me from afar. Unless someone else is following me, too. The thought makes my skin prickle, and I run my hands over my arms, pushing the paranoia away.

Night has fallen, and the neighborhood is a glittering display of fancy lighting. Even from where I wait on the rock, I can see through the trees and across the street to where a family sits in front of a window at their dining room table. Eating in full display of anyone who goes by. My attention shifts to the window in front of me as Benjamin comes into view and Gwyn meets him halfway—they embrace, kiss, before he so much as sets his briefcase down.

Benjamin disappears for several minutes, and Gwyn putters around the kitchen, pulling a long serving plate from the refrigerator. She wears a simple ruby-red dress. Her hair is straightened around her shoulders, and I'll bet she put on makeup, too.

Almost like the little lady awaiting her husband's return at the end of the day. Putting on a show for him.

When he returns, now in jeans and a T-shirt, they kiss again, and Benjamin says something that makes her laugh as he reaches for wineglasses. The evening is almost an exact repeat of the first night I watched them. Benjamin lights the heat lamps outside, and a gas fireplace flickers to life. Soon they sit on the back patio, warm as they watch the distant waves of the Puget Sound. The long tray sits between them on a table, and they eat the finger food between sips of wine. I can even hear their words, carried by the breeze.

"Great new employee at the winery," he says. "Moved down from Woodinville and wanted something closer." They talk about it at length, about future hires, and I would agree with Gwyn—it doesn't sound like he's hurting for money.

Gwyn murmurs something about the news vans I don't quite catch, and Benjamin shakes his head in disgust.

Moments later he says, "More wine?" and she replies, "I got it, honey," and takes their glasses inside. My first thought is why not bring the bottle out with them?—but I see immediately why —and suspect she left it inside on purpose. Gwyn brushes her hair behind one ear and casts a glance back at Benjamin, but he's leaning back in his wicker chair, feet propped on the table, eyes closed. Relaxing after a busy day thinking his dead wife's body had washed up to shore.

Gwyn, meanwhile, types rapidly at his phone, trying to gain access. She smacks her palm down on the counter—frustrated— and tries again. Then a third time. She looks back at Benjamin once more, and I lean forward, heart frantic as I wonder if she'll be texting me phone numbers in seconds—but she shakes her head, mutters something under her breath, and grabs the bottle of wine to pour.

A minute later, I get a message from her: *He changed his password on his phone. Guilty.*

I stare at her message. More likely, he doesn't trust her. And I don't blame him. But I don't say that, instead texting back, *You don't know that. Why don't you ask to use it? Say you left yours in the other room?*

But she's already back outside, handing him his fresh wine with a loving smile. They spend the next half hour engaged in a conversation that has them leaning toward one another, talking with not only their mouths, but their hands. Debating opening a second winery south, in Olympia or Tacoma, and then which city would be a better place to live should they ever want to move out of Seattle. Eventually, they run out of wine and retire to their bedroom, far from my view. Not a word about you or your potential dead body. I wait another half hour in case Benjamin heads out on another run, or if they planned to come back out and watch a movie. But neither reappears. Gwyn doesn't text back with phone numbers, either.

I watch another twenty minutes before slipping away, and I'm headed to Chris's when she finally messages me.

Gwyn: *He's not acting right. Something's definitely going on.*

I peer at the text.

Not acting right, how? I hit send.

She replies immediately. *He's spent the whole night looking at his phone. He keeps saying it's for work, but I don't believe him. He was distant at dinner. Barely said a word to me. Left the table the second he was finished to go work in his office.*

The three dots indicating she's still typing ripple over the screen, but I ignore them, staring at her words.

I just watched as they shared a romantic meal where they lingered with wine for half an hour afterward, discussing anything and everything. Benjamin's phone—per my own view—was left in the kitchen for the entirety of the interaction.

Gwyn's playing up the facts to make whatever Benjamin *is* up to look worse.

Which means she's lying to me.

FORTY-TWO
MADELINE

Three Years Ago

We decided to go for it.

The last thing in the world I thought we'd do for our honeymoon, but it was happening. Our wedding ended, and Benji and I went to our honeymoon suite. We opted for water instead of champagne—we'd had more than enough already—and took a bubble bath together in the giant tub overlooking Seattle. I laid back, my body against his in the steamy water.

"Are you sure about a backpacking trip? I know this isn't your... thing," he said.

"I'm not sure about it. But it does look beautiful. And we can't leave for a proper honeymoon for another couple weeks. We already took the time off. So... why not?"

"You're really something, you know that?" Benji squeezed me tight and pressed a kiss to my hair.

I smiled and settled back, his arms folding over my stomach, one of his hands catching mine.

"I just can't believe we talked *everyone* into going."

"I know." I looked up, catching his eyes. "I can't wait to see Gwyn realizing she has to squat behind a tree to pee."

We both laughed, but mine stopped abruptly when the overhead lights caught the glint of our platinum bands, the sparkle of my engagement ring. We were *married*.

"I can't believe we did it." I nodded at the rings. He lifted his hand from the water, and I brought mine up beside it, water and bubbles dripping from our fingers, the bands on our fourth fingers.

"We did it," Benji whispered.

"Do you feel different?"

"Happier," he said.

"Why happier?"

"Because." Benji let his hand fall in the water and clasp around me tightly again. "It means I get to be with you forever."

* * *

The next morning we met our friends at the local outdoors store up the hill from Pike Place. An hour later, we were outfitted with backpacks, sleeping pads and bags, and other little necessities a saleswoman sold us on—silicon sporks, compasses, quick-dry clothing, freeze-dried meals, backpacking stoves. Aaron already had equipment, so he headed to the park to see if he could get a walk-up permit for our group.

By the next evening, we were putting it all to use. We parked three cars at a place called Mowich Lake, an almost two-hour drive from Seattle. When we piled out, pulled on boots, hoisted up backpacks, I felt my first flutter of *oh shit, what did I agree to?*—the air felt like opening the freezer door, a blast of cold. I couldn't see more than twenty feet in front of me, a thick fog covering the mountainside. But my hesitation disappeared once we got on the trail, seven of us in a line, chatting, cracking jokes, occasionally singing out of tune. In the end, it was Benji and me, Gwyn and Kip, Aaron, and Natalie and Leah. Elena begged off—"*Sorry, it's just not for me*"—and part of me was relieved she'd decided to stay home, and not just because that meant Daddy had someone to call for help.

The trail wound around the side of one mountain, and then up, until we broke through the clouds and found ourselves in a place called Spray Park—the same meadow Aaron showed us photos of. Wildflowers dotted bright green grass. White boulders stuck out of the ground like something from another world. A flash of wildlife, and Benji grabbed my hand, pointed. "That's a marmot. Cute, right?"

It wasn't the honeymoon I expected, but I got busy with my camera—photographing everything, including us, as we stopped to eat lunch and boil water for mid-hike coffee. The air was cool, but as long as we kept moving, we never felt cold. If anything, after spending so much time downtown, it felt like opening my eyes, breathing fresh air. Realizing the next morning as I woke and peered out of our tent, I couldn't hear the highway.

It wasn't all perfection—whenever I paused to write in my journal, my hands turned to icicles, the cold damp air setting in. My socks never totally dried from one night to the next, and going to the bathroom required a hike to a pit toilet, one the whole campground shared. Natalie and Leah shared a tent and by day two had already ripped a hole in it—not that it mattered. There were surprisingly almost no bugs out there. Kip and Gwyn were off on side adventures every time we stopped, and I wondered if maybe they might end up together. But rain was coming that night. I dreaded it, watching the dark clouds swirl in, but Benji swore our tent would keep us dry.

I had come to one conclusion—I'd rather be backpacking with Benji than doing anything with anyone else. So while I wouldn't be proposing we go backpacking for our anniversary next year, or, well, ever again, I decided to make the most of it.

Tomorrow night, after the rain, Aaron said we'd be at the perfect location to see shooting stars. I was going to photograph the night sky and have it printed to put over our bed. There was a time-lapse setting on the Nikon Benji gave me, and I'd brought a small folding tripod—so I could set it up and step away, let the camera do its thing, taking photos every so often, then blending them together into one gorgeous streak of light remembering our imperfectly perfect honeymoon that turned out to be just right. Mostly, because I was there with my husband. It would be my gift to him, and we could hang it in our home, and be reminded of our first adventure together as husband and wife.

FORTY-THREE
REBECCA

Now

The run home after they go to bed leaves me breathless and gutted. I know better than to let anyone in. At no point had I truly considered Gwyn a friend, but it seemed maybe she considered *me*, Rebecca, one. But she was just using me—maybe like she used you.

Stopping at Chris's on the way home only makes that feeling more acute, as I watch for him for twenty minutes, but he never shows. He's almost always home. Probably, he's on a date, meeting the woman who one day will share a beer with him in his backyard.

I ease away, still turning Gwyn's actions over in my head. Maybe she knows Benjamin's watching her. Maybe she's scared, so she's trying to play up what's happening, to keep me close, to keep someone who can help her close. But why not tell me the whole story, then?

The better question is why am I making excuses for her? She looks as guilty—if not guiltier—than Benjamin does.

I glance over my own shoulder. Only dark alleyway as I trot away from Chris's and toward my own house. My own street is lit up with the shine of a full moon, freshly out from behind a clump of clouds. The rain has cleared, and I take the steps up to my front door two at a time. Inside, I pull off damp clothing and go straight for the shower, letting hot water wash away the anger boiling inside me that Gwyn hasn't been honest with me.

Of course, I haven't been honest with her. That makes me stop, consider why I feel this way. I can come to only one conclusion—I got too close. For a second there, I let someone in. And the worst person, too. Someone who hurt you.

When I get out of the shower, I feel no better. My phone chirps, a news alert. I wrap a towel around my body and pick it up, squinting through the steamy room to read the headline.

DNA Results Inconclusive in Madeline Hughes Case

I hurry to my laptop, not bothering to dress, and pull the article up, skimming for details. In short, DNA testing is not infallible. Further testing will be required, the article reads, and a detective on the case is quoted as saying, "This doesn't mean we have not found Ms. Hughes' body. It means further testing is required to verify it. We hope to have results in two to three days."

I print the article, wondering if news vans have already arrived at Gwyn and Benjamin's house. Will she text me again tomorrow, asking for coffee or lunch or something else she can't easily leave the house to obtain without people following her? I glance through the window out of habit. But Benjamin is tucked safely in bed beside Gwyn, so he shouldn't be creeping through the streets. If he was, she'd surely text me, wanting me to do more of her bidding.

A breeze flutters the curtain in the bedroom window, as if in response to my thoughts, and my gaze fixes on it, a tingle of fear radiating through my veins. I shut that window before I left. I shut *all* the windows before I left. The memory of doing so pulls up easily, but was it from this morning? Or last night? Had I opened it in between?

I get to my feet and close it, lock it. Consider finding a dowel rod to secure it shut from the inside. But the paper on the printer grabs my attention, and I pull it from the tray and head to the living room to add the article about inconclusive DNA to your album.

My scissors sit on the coffee table next to the mug I'd used that morning for my first cup of coffee. Remnants of lunch sit on a plate beside it, where I'd sat and pored through the articles for the billionth time, rereading a podcast transcript, trying to let the pieces form a complete puzzle in my head. But when I reach beneath the sofa to pull the book from its hiding place, my hand catches only air. I reach around, sure I've shoved it one direction or the other. A lick of anxiety streaks through me as I drop to hands and knees and peek beneath the sofa, sure I'll see it shoved farther back than I can reach. But there's no album, only my medical books. I look a second time, then beneath the table.

I get to my feet and turn a slow circle, taking a deep breath, forcing my heart rate to stay steady. I've moved the book a couple times in the last days, even taking it to bed to go through yesterday. It must still be in the bedroom. But I could swear I looked at it this afternoon. I hurry to the bedroom, but it's not beneath the bed, tucked into my dresser, or even in the closet, where I never keep it. My eyes fall on the window that had been open.

The vision of Benjamin creeping around my house echoes in my mind.

But Benjamin had been home tonight, and I'd been home until half an hour before he arrived at his house.

I bite my lip hard, then race through the house, searching every nook and cranny a second time, sure I've missed it, that the book with three years of articles and media and photos about you is here *somewhere*.

But it's not.

FORTY-FOUR

MADELINE

Three Years Ago

Okay, so maybe it wasn't an imperfectly perfect honeymoon—Gwyn rolled her ankle, Natalie got stung by a bee, Benji slid into a lake and soaked his boots while he was filtering water, and we took the wrong trail and ended up almost doubling our mileage for the day.

But we all survived and finally arrived at our campsite. I helped Benji set up the tent and inflate our sleeping pads. Our sleeping bags kept us from snuggling at night, yet there was something intimate about sharing that tiny space inside the tent that I could get used to. Maybe after this we could get a two-person sleeping bag—Aaron said they make them as he gave us a lewd wink—but maybe we *could* go camping. Occasionally. Close to the car.

It was night now, and everyone else was asleep in their tents. I had waited for the sky to get dark, so I could sneak out, so I could go to the gorgeous cliff we watched the sunset from and photograph the stars streaking across the sky. Benji was asleep beside me—handsome as always.

It was my chance to surprise him, to capture the mountains and stars, and I couldn't wait to show him the resulting photograph.

Pushing my sleeping bag away, I grabbed my camera, unzipped the tent flap, and escaped into the night. Cold air nipped at me, and I took one last look back at Benji, curled up in our tent—I would get this photo, then return to my husband's warm, safe side. I still couldn't quite get over the fact I got to call him my husband.

I blew him a kiss and stepped away from the tent. With my headlamp flicked on, I strode away from camp, up a foot trail that curved around a bank of trees, and another hundred feet to the cliffside. A narrow extension of rocky outcrop, anchored by tall pine trees. A gust of wind blew through, the scent of rain already heavy on it, but above me, I could see for miles—so many miles. I flicked off my headlamp and stood utterly still, letting my eyes adjust to the pitch black.

Overhead, stars emerged, the pattern of the Milky Way taking shape. A shooting star streaked across the sky, then seconds later, another one. The trees rustled like someone had accompanied me from camp, but I knew it was only the wind. I could even see the dim yellow light of Seattle, far off in the distance.

I breathed out and went about setting up my tripod, securing it to my camera, adjusting the settings. I stepped to the side, pressed the button, and crossed my arms against the chill. All I had to do now was wait. The camera would do the rest. It would take a while, and my journal was tucked under my jacket. When I got bored—if I got bored, the stars were so incredible—I'd plunk down and write a little by the dim light of my headlamp. But until then, I'd enjoy the night sky. I stepped to the edge of the cliff, just out the camera's field of view, and peered over—I knew this cliff emptied out to the river formed by a glacier. That during the day, I could see the hundreds of feet a person might plummet if they went over.

Another rush of wind fluttered through my hair, and I could swear I heard the whisper of a boot over the gravelly rock behind me, the breath of someone close—but before I could whip around, a firm hand landed square between my shoulder blades, and I could do nothing to stop the inevitable.

The force of that shove sent me plunging over the cliff and into the infinite darkness.

FORTY-FIVE
REBECCA

Now

Someone's been following me. Someone's been in my home.

I repeat the words to myself and turn in a slow circle, looking for other signs a stranger has been here. Anything else that might be missing. But the laptop is there on my bed, the only other item I own of value.

I have to sit down as I try to sort through what this means. My biggest takeaway is that someone knows I've been following your case closely—obsessively, even. And then it hits me—if someone's followed me to my home, it's possible they've followed me to Gwyn and Benjamin's home. And they know I'm watching them.

Or... they *are* them.

I've been watching Benjamin and Gwyn, presuming they don't know who I am. But maybe they do. I go to the bathroom, look in the mirror, gaze at myself.

I've become Rebecca. Through changing my body, but my face, too. I'd gone under the knife, had Botox and fillers. I'd become someone entirely different.

How many actresses swear they haven't had plastic surgery performed, a before-and-after photo makes it clear they have, and yet they still look like themselves?

What I realized is that these people don't *want* to look like someone else. They want to look like a better version of the same person.

So when I went under the knife, I made it clear—make me someone new. And they had.

There's no way Benjamin and Gwyn know it's me. I turn my face, run fingers over my skin. No way at all. Which means someone else is after me.

In one motion, I'm out the bathroom door. I grab a bag and shove the basics in. I grab my car keys, my phone charger, my laptop, and clothes. I sweep toiletries from the tiny shelf in the kitchen into the bag, and then I'm out the front door, not bothering to lock it, because there's nothing of value inside, anyway.

But as soon as I start the engine to my car and crank up the heat, I realize I have a decision to make. A hotel—or, the choice to keep my friends close, and my enemies closer. It's almost eleven, but she owes me, right? I followed her husband for her. Brought her coffee when news vans kept her from wanting to leave.

I take a breath and dial Gwyn.

"Rebecca?" A drowsy voice. "You okay?"

I clear my throat, gather my thoughts. "A water pipe broke in my house. I'm sorry to call so late, but would it be too much of an inconvenience for me to spend a night or two at your house?"

She hesitates, but then her voice turns sugary sweet. "Of course. Just park outside and come to the front door. I'll get the guest room ready."

* * *

It's midnight when Gwyn presses a cup of peppermint tea into my hands and bids me good night. The guest room is thankfully on the opposite end of the house from the main bedroom, tucked at the end of the long hallway that also leads to Benjamin's office. The one space I hadn't been able to search when Gwyn let me snoop through his things before.

Benjamin slept through my appearance at their door, Gwyn's gentle questioning, "What happened?" and, "You poor thing. You can stay here as long as you need to." She'd offered me fresh bakery cookies and tea, offered to stay up with me awhile until I got tired, but I politely declined.

"I appreciate it. I'm just ready for sleep, though. Such a shock, getting home and seeing..." I had to remind myself it wasn't a burst pipe—it was a missing album of a dead woman. Of you. "Seeing the house like that."

"Well, let me know if you've forgotten anything. We have spare toothbrushes, I can loan you clothes, whatever."

I sit alone in the guest room now, watching a clock that sits over the door tick slowly to 12:05 a.m., then 12:07 a.m., and so on. At 12:25 I decide it's been long enough, and I open the door to my room. It creaks, so I stop it just wide enough I can squeeze through. The restroom is in the hall, so I have a perfectly good reason for opening the door, but still, I stop and wait, listen.

The house echoes with silence. How can they stand such a large space being so quiet? I've become accustomed to the small sounds of my small home—the thin walls that keep me apprised when someone walks a dog down the street, the collar jangling, or a car speeds by. I'd forgotten that in addition to being lit up like a dollhouse, homes like this have the privilege of utter silence.

Suddenly, the ticking of that clock over my bedroom door sounds loud—like my own heart in my chest, as I ease down the hallway in bare feet.

I go past the bathroom.

If Benjamin took my album about you, maybe he hid it in his office—the one place I haven't searched. Or maybe, it's on his boat. Or at the winery. So many places left to look.

Paned French doors stand between me and a large office space, a window on the back wall offering a view of the deep murky waters beyond the house. I press fingertips to the doorknob and turn it—both doors open inward, and neither of them creak, much to my relief. When they open wide, I pause, listen for that infinite silence again.

The only sound I hear is that ticking—the clock. Or maybe, my heart. I should be nervous, going in here, knowing the two people I've come so far to watch are a mere hallway away. But I'm not. Somehow, I feel calm as I step inside and smooth my fingers over the antique wood desk. The one Gwyn picked out for him. The room is almost too dark to make anything out, and I don't dare turn on the desk lamp. My phone in my hand, I use its minimal illumination to slide open drawers, finding only miscellaneous office supplies—spare printer paper, an ink cartridge, pens, a spiral notebook that says *Business Plan* over the front of it, something that must date back to Benjamin's early days running the winery.

A bookshelf sits behind the desk, and I do a quick scan, but there's no stolen album there that I recognize, nor the camera or journal for that matter, not like I expected him to have it on display. A closet is built into one corner of the room, and I cross over, easing open the door.

An even deeper darkness within the closet's depths.

I risk a glance down the hall again, but it's silent.

This time I turn on the flashlight on my phone to get a good look at what turns out to be shelves of storage—both business and nonbusiness related. Books from an MBA program, books on wineries in English and French and Italian, and a myriad of shoeboxes.

Shoeboxes? In an office closet?

It doesn't make sense, but maybe it makes for easy organizing. I open one and find bills from years ago, when you were still the woman of the house. The next shoebox has receipts. There's a third shoebox, behind the first two, a stack of books set atop it. I pull it out, expecting more superfluous paper of some variety.

My heart about drops into my gut when I see what's contained inside.

A Nikon camera.

FORTY-SIX

REBECCA

Now

I almost fall to my knees, the cool black exterior of the camera smooth and heavy in my hands. I have to remember to breathe. I turn it over in my hands once, twice, studying it by the light of my phone. For a moment, I wonder if it's really yours—but then I see the inscription Benjamin had etched on it: *For Madeline, my love.*

You treasured this camera and loved telling the story of how he tricked you into photographing your own engagement—a feat you were sure no man before your fiancé thought to do.

As I look at it now, this long sought-after object capable of capturing images—a murderer's image, maybe—I'm almost surprised by how it looks like literally every other camera in the world.

I carefully set it on the edge of the desk and take one last look in the closet, hoping your journal, your own recordings of the days leading up to your death, will make a miraculous appearance as well. But there's no such luck, so I close the door and force myself to tiptoe back to the guest room, camera in hand.

My fingers shake as I acquaint myself with the buttons and controls—but it's easy enough to figure out, and I press the button to turn it on, heart hammering in my chest in anticipation.

I'm about to see your last photos. What might be the last moments of your life.

Nothing happens. The screen remains dark. I push it again, then turn the camera this way and that, sure I'm missing something. I flip open a small black latch where the battery goes and a gray rectangular battery falls onto the bed.

It must be dead. And it's not a battery I can just go out and purchase new—it's specific to the camera. I squeeze my hand into a fist, debating my options, wanting so badly to see what's on the memory card—assuming it's still there.

I find the memory card slot, open it, and—cool relief washes over me. It's there, intact. Another thought occurs to me, and I check my laptop, but there's no slot for it to be directly inserted into the computer. So I'll have to wait until I can buy a new battery or a charger for this one to see the images. Or find another way to view whatever's on the card.

Well, one goal achieved, but that doesn't mean all is well. Someone still knows more than they should about me, still has my album on you. The ticking of the clock draws my attention back to the door. I'm in their home. I could spend the whole night sorting through their belongings, trying to find both the journal and the album. Or... I can wait until tomorrow and ask Gwyn where else Benjamin might be hiding evidence he's cheating on her. I can play into her own game... after all, following her text telling me how awful this evening was, how will she refuse my offer to help her?

I wrap the camera in a pair of sweats I brought and tuck it into my duffel, which I shove under the bed. Then I crawl beneath cool sheets, realizing the downside of being close to my enemy is that I'm literally in their home—and that if they want to hurt me, I've just made it easier.

The covers melt away as I sit up and use all my strength to drag the dresser until it blocks the door. At least now, if someone barges in, I'll have a second to wake up before they can do me any harm.

* * *

Sunshine streams through gauzy curtains when I open my eyes the next morning. The ceiling, a matte gray, leaves me disoriented until I remember where I am.

Soft noises come through the door—a door opening and shutting, a sink turning on. Morning noises. I listen for a few minutes. I imagine Gwyn is in the kitchen making coffee. It's after eight, so Benjamin has likely left for work already. Knowing I won't run into him when I leave this room makes me eager for coffee, and I sit up slowly, inspecting the room again in the yellow light of a rare sunny Seattle fall morning. The room is an abnormal shape—more of a pentagon than a square, the last room at the end of a long hall, three of its windows creating a semicircle against the edge of the house. I know that outside those windows will be a partial view of the lawn, the road, the neighbor's house. Exposed to the outside world.

Part of me wants to pull back the curtain, make sure no one's standing just outside the window. My skin prickles with the desire, but I force myself to get up and pull on clothes for the day. I squash the anxiety and turn my mind to the matter at hand. Gwyn. The need to continue searching Benjamin's things. I need to find the damn book someone swiped from my house—without it, and the ability to flip through and see every detail of your case, I find myself feeling naked, like a piece of me is missing.

Maybe that's a sign I've become too involved, too focused on avenging you. But I'm so close I can taste it. It's too late to stop now. And anyway, I have the camera. I just need to be able to see what's on it.

I'm about to go greet Gwyn when my phone pings with an unfamiliar sound—an email. I created an account under Rebecca's name when I started working under her name, but only the travel nursing agency I work for, and the hospital, have it. It's a strange enough occurrence I stop short in the hallway and check it.

When the sender's name pops up, I curse under my breath —Veronica Wells, nurse manager. The woman who called before.

My heart beats a little faster in my chest, and I tap it open— but it's not a notification I'm fired. Not a notice that they've figured out I have a falsified Social Security card and ID. No, it's a request.

Please have your travel agency verify your Washington State nursing license with us. We've found an inconsistency... please verify within five business days.

Five business days.

There's no inconsistency, and *that's* the problem. I'm using the real Rebecca Johnson's information. But Riley's raised the alarm. Asked them to look into me. Which means this job is coming to an end, and fast. I thank the universe I didn't use my little house's address on the hospital forms—rather, the address of the Airbnb I was staying at while I looked for housing.

If they don't know yet, they will soon. And what will they do then? I'm not sure. I mean, there's no proof of anything. I look like the real Rebecca Johnson.

I exhale. Close the email, tuck the phone away. A problem

for later. But a big problem, nonetheless. Because I have to be *somebody*.

Gwyn's voice floats down the hallway, issuing orders to her phone—"Remind me to pick up wine," and "Set an alarm to call the Wilson family." When I arrive in the kitchen, she greets me with a chipper smile. "Morning. Coffee?"

"Please." I force a smile to my face. With any luck, I won't have to be Rebecca much longer. Besides, Rebecca will almost certainly be a killer by the time this is all over. I suppose I'll have needed a new identity either way.

Gwyn pours a cup and sets it at the breakfast bar nook off the kitchen counter. She pulls up a second stool and pats it, and we sit next to one another.

Best friends, I tell myself.

"Thanks so much for letting me stay here." I offer a tentative smile. "Can I make you dinner tonight to say thank you?"

Gwyn waves her hand. "Girl, you don't have to thank me. We're friends, right?"

She's *asking* me. The same way she asked me the other day before asking for my help with Benjamin. This time, it feels manipulative. Like the sales technique where someone asks you to say yes to something small so you're more likely to say yes to something big—a foot in the door and all. I play into it.

"Of course, we are. And I'm so glad for that." She's about to speak, but I continue, "It sounds like last night was really rough. Are you okay?"

Gwyn gathers her thoughts before she answers, I presume because she has to recall what lies she told me. "I really miss the way we used to be," she finally says. "Before he was so distant." Her fingers play over the handle of her coffee mug. She looks down at it, avoiding my eyes. "He said he was going to go running again tonight. I don't suppose—" Her gaze slowly raises to mine, her lips twisting in a sad pout.

"I'll follow him again, of course," I say. "I was thinking—"

And now I do my own act, hesitating. "I realized yesterday I never checked his office the other day when I looked for signs he was, you know—cheating on you." My eyes flick to the French windows down the hall, just viewable from where we sit in the kitchen.

Gwyn frowns. "His office?"

I nod at it, and she turns to follow my gaze.

"Oh, he hasn't used that as his office since I've been with him. It's my office now."

I blink, taking in her words.

"Yours?" I ask.

"Yes. I run my interior design company from home. He cleared his stuff out and moved it to the winery. Other than a handful of old books, everything in there is mine."

FORTY-SEVEN
REBECCA

Now

"Rebecca? Are you okay?"

It's Gwyn's office.

The words roll through my mind over and over.

I let my gaze slide from the floor back to her, somehow arrange my face to normalcy and say, "Yes, sorry. I'm just tired. Long night."

Gwyn clucks and slides off her stool. "I'll make you some toast. Food will help."

I mentally reframe what I learned in the last forty-eight hours. She suggested they get together if you were magically out of the picture, and apparently is the one who wanted you declared dead sooner than later. Benjamin was *watching* her. Gwyn asked me to follow Benjamin, then lied about their evening together. And now this.

Gwyn is guilty.

But I *saw* Benjamin at my house. Which leads me to the conclusion they could be in on it together.

Except... Benjamin has been spying on Gwyn.

My head spins, trying to keep it all straight. I sip my coffee, thinking. If Gwyn played a role in your death, if she knows I know, then I'm a danger to her, and her to me—which means drinking coffee she made could be a hazard to my health.

A plate of toast is in front of me in the next moment, and Gwyn sits down again. I swallow, searching her eyes for signs she's a murderer. She only smiles in response, and frustration unfurls inside of me. It might be her. It might be Benjamin. It might be both of them. I've nearly been found out as not being the real Rebecca, the clock is ticking, and I'm no closer to sorting out who's ultimately guilty than I was a few days ago.

Am I going to have to kill them both?

I squeeze my hand around the scalding coffee mug, not minding the burn, just wishing I could make sense of all of it. Of *them*. As far as Gwyn knows, you're dead, your body currently undergoing a second round of DNA testing, and she is *smiling*.

I force my mind into action, my lips to form words. "Any luck with the phone numbers?"

"No. He changed his password." Her eyes grow wider. "Can you believe that? Cardinal sign he's cheating on me. Do you really think I should marry him either way?"

I don't. Not anymore. I don't think anyone should get married, ever, because it's becoming clear the only person you can trust is yourself. But I say something encouraging, and her eyes gloss over with tears or lies or god knows what.

"Anyway, I have to be off—I have an appointment with a potential client, but I'll be back around ten. Want to go for a run?"

"I can't," I say without thinking. "I have a work meeting. But I'll make dinner tonight, okay? Hopefully my landlord can get everything straightened out, and I'll be back in my house soon."

Gwyn's hand clasps my forearm. I'm sure she means it to be

comforting, but I want to yank it back, imagining that same hand shoving you to your doom. "Stay as long as you need to, Rebecca. We have the space."

When I've watched her gather her purse and portfolio, when I've heard her vehicle grumble from the garage, I finally breathe again. And then I grab my own car keys and my duffel bag and head out because I need to find a way to see what's on the camera's memory card.

* * *

In the end, I take a risk.

The pharmacy has a computer where photos can be printed, and it accepts the same memory card the camera has. I pull it from the camera and act as though I've done this dozens of times—pressing the touch screen to activate the program, following the directions to create an account. When the machine asks how I'd like to add photos, I select *storage card*, and when it asks for me to insert it, I do.

My fists clench into nervous balls at my side, waiting as the machine reads the card. Seconds tick by, customers line up near the registers, and I can't help but eye the security cameras. I have nothing to hide, and yet, it makes me wonder when else I've been watched, caught unawares. I glance back toward the sliding glass doors, paranoid I've been followed here, as well. I'm fully aware how easy it is to watch an unsuspecting person.

The screen flickers, and I tear my gaze away from the doors back to the screen. Photos populate it in rows and columns, small thumbnail versions. Instructions pop up: *Scroll and select the photos you would like to use today.*

I inhale, fingers clearing the menu and flicking the thumbnails up and down, eyes narrowed as I inspect the photos.

Looking at them is like a gut punch, and I reach for the flimsy stool the pharmacy staff has placed nearby for use at the machine. Hundreds of photos of you—of your friends. Of the days leading up to your wedding. My fingers skip over one photo, enlarging it by accident, and there you are—your smile lighting up the room, the people around you staring at you with anticipatory smiles, but never anticipating days later you'd be dead. These were the photos you took for yourself, for your social media. Photos you never had the chance to post.

I skim through them, careful not to enlarge another one—seeing you up close and personal will make this too hard, the memories too vivid, the loss too real. The photos change from day to night, the rehearsal, the rehearsal dinner, a moment someone else picked up the camera and captured you and Benjamin pressed together in a private moment, staring into one another's eyes.

Jesus.

And now he's engaged to your best friend. In fact, Gwyn comes up in the next photo, hugging you tight, her teeth bared in a bright *I'm so happy for you* smile the photographer caught. Nausea stirs inside me. My old face shows up in photo after photo, and I flick the screen faster, trying to get past all this personal crap. I don't have the time nor the emotional bandwidth to see the people who should have loved and protected you in the days before one of them betrayed you.

Finally, I'm past the wedding photos, past the handful of photos you took at the reception and that night, your wedding party wandering Seattle, celebrating in the bars and clubs that had become second homes. And then everything changes. There are no more buildings or straight lines. Instead, the photos are populated by trees and distant mountains and giant rocks. The wedding party, but no longer wearing dresses and tuxes—instead, in backpacking gear, shiny new backpacks and boots and hiking poles.

I scroll faster, because I'm almost there, I can tell from the date and time stamp—I'm *almost* at that final series of images, where I'll finally know what happened. If you were shooting the cliffside against the starry background, you were likely taking a long exposure, or maybe multiple photos as a time lapse, either of which you would have set up with a tripod. Which meant surely the killer had been caught somewhere in there.

More photos. Even more, as the world took on that yellow golden glow Washington always does half an hour before sunset. The world fades around me as I scroll. In seconds, I'll know who did it. Surely, the camera caught it.

One more flick of a finger, and then—

Nothing. No more photos. Panic rushes through me like a tidal wave.

I exhale a breath I'd been keeping tight in my lungs, realize my palms are laced with sweat, and that it's made the touch screen malfunction.

I grab at my shirt, wipe my palms and fingers, then brush them down my jeans for good measure. I take another slow, deep breath, shut my eyes, open them, stare at the photos of the wedding party gathered around the fire in those final moments before you were gone forever.

I press my fingers to the screen once more, but again, nothing happens.

And that's when I realize it's not scrolling because there are no more photos.

FORTY-EIGHT

REBECCA

Now

I arrive back at the house and key in the code at the side door to find it empty. Gwyn's purse rests on the kitchen counter, so I presume she's out on a run. Benjamin should be gone all day. The sleek house rises up around me. I turn in a slow circle, eyes catching on something you chose—a particular wallpaper—followed by something Benjamin or Gwyn must have done—hanging shelves, books stacked amid decorative succulents I'm not sure are even real.

Is anything real?

I take another look around, remnants of you reminding me why I'm here—and this time, I don't head for Benjamin's closet. I head for Gwyn's. Her closet is twice the size of his and filled to the brim. Dry-cleaned clothes still in plastic hang in one corner, and everything else is categorized by use and color—running clothes to casual to business. Shoeboxes sit on racks up high, and I search them one by one, finding only heels.

But then I open a shiny black box and go still. Shoes I would recognize anywhere.

Your red ones, the ones that first caught the attention of Benjamin.

I can't help checking the size, stroking a finger down the smooth exterior—making sure I'm right. Sure enough, they are your size. And a peek at Gwyn's shoes tells me she could never wear them.

Why keep these?

I try to frame it as something a best friend would do, but it feels off. The shoes go back in the box, back in their place on the shelf, and I leave the closet to go to the office I searched last night. Maybe I'll find something different in the light of day.

The sun breaks through the dense clouds outside, as it often does midmorning. A ray of light shines through the paned windows of the office, casting a golden glow over the wood desk, the white pad of legal paper lying on its surface, reflecting off a gold and green banker's lamp. In the daylight, I can see where Gwyn's touches are—the plants in the windowsill, the abstract paintings on the wall. Very Gwyn. Very not Benjamin.

I do a second search, even going back to the box I found the camera in, but nothing new appears. By the time midafternoon hits, Gwyn has returned from her run and left again, and I realize if I'm going to cook dinner, I need to go shopping—and cooking dinner myself is the only way I'll eat it here in this house ever again. Something isn't right. Someone knows my secret, I'm sure of it. But a day of searching has not turned up your journal, nor the album of articles I collected on you.

Although, maybe it's a moot point. Maybe they're both guilty, and both afraid of being found out—maybe they're in the process of turning on one another, suspicious the other will cast them in a poor light and point their finger at them.

I turn this idea over in my head as I select fresh salmon and salad greens and choose wine from a different state entirely—the idea of drinking anything made in Washington leaves my stomach lurching.

The market is busy for a weekday afternoon in autumn—
tourist season is at a high in summer, when the rain holds off.
But now, people walk with coffee cups clutched in hands,
perusing the market stalls—eyes lingering on flower arrange-
ments, local honey, chocolate-flavored pasta, the fish market
where fishmongers toss giant slabs of fish for the crowd's amusement. For a moment, I step back in a corner and enjoy the
anonymity of it. But I have work to do.

Back at Gwyn and Benjamin's, I get to work cutting potatoes and prepping the salmon.

When Gwyn walks in twenty minutes later, dripping sweat
from her second run of the day—for endurance, she's informed
me—I greet her with a "Hey! How was your run?"

She holds up one finger, pulls earbuds from her ears, and
grins. "Great. I was only supposed to do six, but it was such a
beautiful day. I ended up running ten." A grimace. "Don't tell
my run coach." That flash of conspiratorial grin all too familiar
to me from years ago, the one that made me want to leave when
I hung out with your group of friends, because I didn't want to
be involved in her twentysomething bullshit.

"Great job. And my lips are sealed." I shake greens from a
wax-lined paper bag into a bowl. "I'm making dinner for you
guys. I got the *best* fish from the market today."

Gwyn's gaze darts away, then back to me. "Oh yeah?"

"I always feel like such a tourist going there. But I guess I
kind of am." A self-deprecating grin.

She gives me an obligatory smile and slides closer. "Did
you..." Her voice drops in volume, though I know Benjamin isn't
home. "Find anything today? Did you look?"

She means on Benjamin. I search her gaze and consider
making something up—but decide against it.

"Wine," I say. "We need wine. Red or white?"

I turn, racking my brain for something that might make her
worry. Might make her lose her cool.

"Let's do a red."

I pour a pinot noir, pass her a glass, press my lips to the rim of my own glass, and pretend to take a long sip.

"I didn't find anything," I say. "But I did see him out and about."

Her eyebrows raise a notch. "Oh?"

"He was close to the police station," I say. "Talking to someone. A woman. But it didn't seem... overly familiar."

It's bullshit, but I want to see the look on her face. They don't trust each other, and one—or both—may be responsible for your death. I'm hoping she will think he's ratting her out, but she just frowns.

"Oh."

Nothing. She gives away nothing. Or maybe, there's nothing *to* give away.

Benjamin comes through the garage door at that moment.

"Gwyn—" He starts. He sees me and breaks his words off. He must have missed my car, parked around the side of the garage. It occurs to me he didn't know I was even here last night. "Rebecca, nice to see you. Gwyn putting you to work?" It's a good recovery, but the flash of surprise in his eyes makes me think he knows more.

Benjamin and Gwyn look at one another, and the tension there is palpable. But *where* is that tension coming from is what I want to know.

"Pinot noir?" I ask Benjamin. "It's from California," I add, a note of apology in my voice.

"That sounds great." His voice brightens again, and I'm reminded they are both excellent actors. I just wish I knew what script they are reading from. With wine in their hands, both excuse themselves after more polite chitchat, this time to shower and change clothes. Benjamin leaves his phone locked and on the counter.

I watch them go, kitchen knife in my hand.

FORTY-NINE

REBECCA

Now

When Gwyn enters again, her hair tied up in a wet bun, her face free of makeup, wearing jeans and a T-shirt, she ignores his phone all together—which makes me wonder. Is she really concerned about him cheating? Before I can suggest she check his phone, Benjamin joins us. He's in running clothes, dark shorts, a long-sleeved athletic shirt, and white running socks.

"Thought you weren't much of a runner," I say with a smile. "More wine?"

Benjamin eyes me, as though I'm an opponent, not his wife's friend. Or maybe I'm just reading into it. "No, thanks. I am going to get out for a run after dinner." He pats a nonexistent gut. "Gotta stay in shape."

We sit at the dining room table, a spread of salmon and salad and roasted potatoes before us. "How long do we have the pleasure of your company?" Benjamin asks as he passes the plate of salmon.

"Oh, just another day, I think. My landlord had someone come by today. They said they could have it fixed tomorrow."

Benjamin nods. "Fast work. Last time I had a busted pipe it took a week."

I should have looked up the average time it takes to fix something like that. "His brother works in the industry," I say. "I guess he's getting faster service."

"Nice to know people," Benjamin says, and I can't tell if he bought my story or knows he backed me into a corner. Suddenly, I feel like *I'm* the one being played instead of the other way around.

Gwyn clears her throat. "How was your day, sweetheart?"

I barely keep the cringe off my face. Benjamin spears a potato with his fork and winks at her. "Great. I was invited to participate in a local wine walk this summer. Should be good for business."

"Oh, which one? I've heard the West Seattle one is fantastic. I can design your booth!"

They make lovey-dovey eyes at each other. Such good liars, both of them.

We clean up after dinner, and Benjamin makes a show of stretching.

"I don't know how you run after you eat," Gwyn says. "Rebecca, I'll be catching up on paperwork in my office if you need me. Make yourself at home."

I excuse myself to the guest room to change and wait for Benjamin to take off into the night so I can follow.

* * *

Benjamin runs fast tonight. Fast enough it feels as though someone is chasing him. Which I am. Houses and trees and cars fly by as we drop below an eight-minute-mile, something I'm capable of, but not for long. He's headed in the direction I'd hoped, so I do my best, and just like last time, he ducks into the cover of the woods.

This time, I don't follow him. I've familiarized myself enough with these trails I hop on a different one, one that circles around and lets me watch from a different angle. Tonight is colder, the wind harsher, and while it's blocked here in the forest, the forest never gets as warm, so I shiver as I find my spot. This trail intersects where Benjamin met the woman last time.

And sure enough, within minutes, he arrives. He balls his fist in the sleeve of his shirt and wipes sweat from his brow. The person he's meeting—and from this angle, I can tell it is a woman—arrives two minutes after that. I wrap my arms tightly around myself and edge closer on the trail, because I'm far enough away I can't hear them. But the wind through the trees rustles what leaves are left there, and within seconds, their conversation is over. He turns abruptly—angrily?—and when she reaches out to grab his arm, shakes her off. He takes off at a clip again, fast enough I know I'll lose him if I go around again—so instead, I launch into a fast pace toward them, like I'm just another runner out for a jog through the woods.

The woman is right in front of me, tall, slim with a slight build, hair in a ponytail.

It's only a second too late, right as I'm about to pass her, that I recognize her.

FIFTY

REBECCA

Now

If I wasn't sprinting already, I would be now. Did she see me? Notice anything about me? I force myself to breathe—likely, not. I look so different now, and besides, the night is dark, as most nights are here with no moon and no stars. And it was a moment—a flash of time so fast, I'm surprised I recognized her. In fact, now that I replay the moment in my head, am I even sure it was her?

I'm not. But... It could have been.

I race after Benjamin. When I reach the clearing, where the trail opens wide into a grassy area overlooking a Puget Sound beach, he's gone. My steps are slow, and I take a long look around. That's when I hear footsteps—behind me.

I should have kept running. Pretended I'd only stopped to look which way I need to go. But footsteps crunch behind me, and something about not trusting a stranger—or a person I suspect might be a murderer—leaves my instincts on overdrive. I whip around.

Benjamin stands three feet from me, his breath coming in

rapid exhalations after his sprint from the woods. My breath matches his, and for a long moment, we stare at one another—he, I suspect, realizing I've been following him. But because I've gotten good at lying, I say, "Oh. It's you."

His smile stretches across his face, thin. "Surprised to see me?" His head tilts, and he takes a half step forward.

My hands ball into fists, but I force my body to stay loose. To not step backward.

"Yes. You said you're not much of a runner. It's—" I beckon at the woods. "Dangerous in there at night."

"Dangerous, really?" Something in his tone makes me think he's baiting me.

"Yeah. It's a trail system. Have you ever seen it in the light? Roots sticking out of the ground, rocks, fallen logs." I shrug. "I can't resist it, though. I feel like I'm—" I laugh and hope it sounds real. "I don't know, a wild animal or something. It's... freeing."

Benjamin nods but says nothing. He's not buying it, which means I need to change my tune.

"So, listen," I start. "I know I'm new in your lives. And I don't know Gwyn super well, but... I actually was hoping to talk to you about something."

"Oh?" A cold wind lashes at us, but he doesn't look cold. He looks utterly relaxed. Which disturbs me more than anything else. Who can look so calm after angrily pulling away from someone, after running through dark woods, after finding someone following them? Especially when it's so cold my fingers have gone numb?

"I think something's bothering her. She seems..." I pause. "Preoccupied, a lot."

"What do you mean?"

"I think something's wrong. I just don't know what."

Benjamin watches me, and again, I think he's trying to figure me out. But then, he's been looking in the windows of my house. Which means *he* has followed *me* at some point. Maybe he has gone so far as to consider I suspect him.

"I think something's bothering her, too," he says. "I can't figure it out, though. I've tried talking to her. Encouraged her to see a therapist. It might be—" He sighs, and his whole body takes on a different posture—more relaxed. "Has she told you about Madeline?"

Hearing your name on his lips sends steel through my spine.

"Not really," I say. "She did mention a friend." I keep it vague so he'll hopefully say more.

"Her friend died. Who was my first wife. A body was found. It might—" He stops short, pulls a phone from a pocket, frowns at it. "Excuse me," he says and swipes to answer. Benjamin holds the phone to his ear and turns, putting his back to me, effectively removing me from the interaction. But I can hear every word.

"I see," he says. "You're sure? There's no way it could be a— a false... negative?"

A second later, my own phone buzzes—a news update.

I pull it out and know instantly what the call is about.

Police confirm human remains found are not of missing Seattle woman.

The words swim in my vision. When Benjamin finally turns around, his body folded in defeat and grief, it is clear this is news to him. He falls to his knees in the cold wet grass, shoulders shaking as he absorbs the news—that his dead wife's body has not been found, that he cannot lay you to rest.

I watch, trying to summon an emotion—trying to think of what the friend of his fiancée would do to comfort him—but I can't figure it out. I play dumb.

"Are you okay?" Kneeling beside him, I put a hand on his shoulder. His body shakes beneath my touch, and this does draw a lick of emotion out—sympathy, because I know what it's like to lose someone.

It's possible he's crying with relief—that the body isn't yours, that DNA evidence can't tie him to your death. But I don't think so. I think Benjamin is truly grieving you, Maddy.

FIFTY-ONE
REBECCA

Now

So much emotion leaves a person weak. Benjamin sobs on the ground as the wind whips around us. I don't think he could stand up if he wanted to, one hand pressed into the icy grass, the other held up to his face. I simultaneously try to understand if his emotions are real—and if they are relief or grief—and if I should do something to help him.

If he weren't Benjamin, if Gwyn wasn't who she is, I'd call her—I'd call his fiancée and say, "He needs you," and I'd have her come pick him up. In fact, as I kneel beside him and murmur, "Benjamin?" I suspect *he* would do the same if he felt like he could. Which only further fuels my suspicion he doesn't trust her.

"Is it Madeline?" I ask. It feels like it's a risk to say your name aloud—to say it to him. His whole body goes still when your name rolls off my tongue.

Benjamin nods. "The body wasn't hers." No further explanation.

I want to say more or ask a question or—*something,*

anything, to get him to say more. Vulnerable moments like this are when people's brains shut off, when they say things they might not say any other time.

But half a second later, Benjamin gets to his feet. Red-rimmed, tear-filled eyes lock on me.

"Did she hire you?" he asks.

"Hire me?"

"I know she's up to something. Does she know I know?"

His words make sense but leave giant gaps, and my brain hurries to fill in the spaces. Except, it's not that simple. He thinks Gwyn is up to something. He's concerned Gwyn knows that he knows, whatever that is. Which must be why he followed me the other night.

What's more—*It's not an act. They don't trust each other*.

And he wasn't concerned about her mental health. He's *concerned about her*. But I don't know why.

"I'm not working for Gwyn," I say. "We're friends."

He wipes a hand over his face, scrubbing away the grief the best he can. He shakes his head and takes a couple deep breaths until he almost looks normal—almost.

"I gotta go," he says, and without waiting for a response, takes off down the trail.

This time, I don't follow. His form grows distant, and I can tell he's not headed home—if I had to guess, he's headed for the marina. My legs almost ache to break into a run, to follow, to watch. But before I can, a voice startles me out of the moment.

"I hope you don't believe that little act he put on."

Her voice says it all. It's not the voice of a person talking to a random stranger in the dark.

I turn and fix my eyes on her form as she strolls from the forest trail. She hasn't changed a bit—tall, lithe, her discerning gaze taking in the fine details only someone with her skills would notice.

She stands right before me, inspecting my face, my body.

She reaches out a hand to grasp one of mine in hers, and she squeezes it tightly.

"It's really you?" she whispers, her voice wavering.

I swallow, because I didn't want anyone to know—even her.

"Hi, Elena," I say.

She pulls me into a hug. "I've missed you, Madeline."

FIFTY-TWO

REBECCA

Now

"I've been watching them for months." A server sets down our drinks, and Elena pushes mine toward me, eyes glued on my face. "I've suspected something since it happened. I knew Benjamin was—up to *something*. I could tell from the way you acted before the wedding. And then Gwyn just popped back into his life after you—" She stops short, as if realizing something. "How are you alive? How—" Her eyes search my face—the face of someone new, someone not her little sister.

"Someone pushed me." I look down at the drink in my hand and take a slow sip. I haven't talked about this in a long time. "I was taking photos. Doing a long exposure. My camera was set up on the tripod, so I was looking at the stars while it was doing its thing, and—" My heart thrums in my chest as I remember the moment before I was shoved—catching sight of a falling star, wishing Benjamin were there to see it with me. "It happened so suddenly. I couldn't even think. I was just over the ledge, the ground rushing at me. Then... darkness."

Elena leans across the table and clasps my hand in hers.

I try to remember more, but the details are foggy, moments lost from that night. "I hit something. Like an outcropping of rock. I must have lost consciousness for a second or a minute or —I don't know how long. I hit my head. But then I opened my eyes and realized someone had tried to kill me. So I pulled myself as close to the side of the cliff as I could. When I looked up, I couldn't see anything. It was too dark, and I was in like a little hole in the cliffside. I was..." I almost laugh. "Safe? I guess. But I wasn't okay. I kept losing consciousness. I was bleeding. It was too dark to see, and then it started raining, and I don't know if it was blood or rain, but it was so slick."

"Then what?" she whispers. Her other hand clasps her drink, but it's forgotten as I tell her what happened. As I share with her how someone tried to kill me.

How I survived.

"I crawled out. I nearly died doing it. But I didn't know who wanted me dead, only that it had to be someone who was backpacking with us. Someone in the group. And I had no idea who, so I couldn't stay there. Couldn't trust anyone." I exhale. The pain hadn't begun until much later—when the adrenaline wore off. But thankfully, I'd gotten to safety by then, my only goal survival.

"Did you—" Elena blinks. "Did you try to get help?"

I look down at my hands. "No. Benjamin had been strange in the days before the wedding—the months before, really. Something was going on. Maybe with his ex. Or maybe with Gwyn. Probably both. And Gwyn wanted my life. It wasn't like I could just walk into camp and hope whoever tried to kill me didn't see me. Didn't try again. Or worse, pretend I could trust them until they got the opportunity." I look at her. "Someone wanted me dead, Elena."

She frowns, holds out her hand and presses it over mine. "Why didn't you come to me? I would have helped you."

I clear my throat, because maybe I should have gone to

Elena—maybe I should have asked her for help. But if I was in danger, would I be endangering her by going to her? She knew and trusted the same people I did. Besides, we weren't close. Even now, as we sit across from one another at a dark, hole-in-the-wall Seattle bar, I'm aware it's only the belief I was dead that allows her to show so much emotion in this moment.

"I couldn't put you in danger by doing that." I look up, meet her eyes. "I had no idea who had it out for me or why—I..." I let out a heavy sigh. "I couldn't go to anyone they might expect me to. Because it could have put us *both* in danger."

Elena's gaze softens, and she nods, understanding. "What happened next?"

"I remembered some of your contacts from working at your office," I say, and it's only a partial lie, only skipping a few steps. "I didn't know who to trust, so I decided I had to disappear, you know? If anyone knew I was alive, they might try to kill me again. So I went to Mexico. I found plastic surgeons in Mexico who would..." I motion to my face. "Fix me."

I don't mention the shattered bones. The pain I thought would never go away. The days spent in a hospital. The fact that even if I'd *wanted* to look like me, like Madeline, I never would again. So I'd said, "Make me someone new," and they had.

I leave Daddy out of it, too. Daddy, who died two months after I married Benjamin, but who financed the trip to Mexico. Who tried to figure out who wanted me dead, but died before he could. Who helped me become Rebecca. Who made sure I had money to live off that first year, and who I knew would never tell another soul my secret, even Elena. It was he who told me we couldn't go to her for help, that it would only endanger her. And he who told me to go somewhere else—to start a new life. That in the meantime, he'd try to figure out who was behind it. But when I saw the article in the paper saying that he'd died of a heart attack, I knew my new life was it. Unless I did something about it.

I bite my lip and finally sip the wine—it's cool, smooth, expensive tasting, and I realize I've had it before. It's the same wine Benjamin and I served at our wedding, one of North Winery's reserve vintages. Elena ordered it while I went to the bathroom to splash water on my face to remove the sheen of sweat—the pallor of shock at seeing my sister for the first time in three years.

"How did you know it was me?" I ask after I swallow it down, knowing it should taste sweet, but it's bitter to me.

"Well, I've been living in Daddy's house since he died."

A tremor runs through me. I should have known that, should have checked. Of course, she was. She still had her plastic surgery practice in town—and this whole time, she'd been living five houses up the road from Gwyn and Benjamin.

"I followed you one night. I saw you running with Gwyn, who I was suspicious of, and I wondered who her new friend was. And then I saw you watching them, and that's when I followed you to your house." She tilts her head, narrows her eyes. "I didn't know what to make of a stranger doing these things, but I never guessed—" A halting, humorless laugh. "I never guessed I'd come face to face with my—" Her words catch in her throat. She presses a finely manicured hand over her mouth. "Sorry, I—I just thought I'd never see you again. My *sister*." She dabs at her eyes with a napkin. "I found the album with the newspaper articles. When I saw it was about you, I nabbed it, thinking—well, I'm not sure what I thought."

My whole body relaxes, knowing it wasn't Benjamin who took it. That means he has no reason to think I'm anyone other than Gwyn's friend. Though he is suspicious of me for some reason—that much is clear from the fact he went to my house. That he asked if Gwyn hired me.

"But then I saw you dash after him, and honestly, I wasn't

sure until I saw you near the beach. Until I heard your strange voice—all—*breathy*," she imitates it with a smile. "And when I got closer, I could tell you'd had work done." She inspects my face. "It's good work. But I can tell." She pauses. "You know, you actually look a little like me now. I don't think anyone else would notice. And then you said my name, and I knew it was you. Madeline."

The name no longer resonates with me.

"Madeline is dead," I say. "I'm Rebecca."

Elena's eyes widen, but she nods—I think understanding what I am telling her.

"One of them tried to kill you," she says after a beat. "I'm pretty sure it was Gwyn." She digs into her purse and slides something across it to me. "The album you had is at my house. But I had this in my car."

"My journal," I say. My hands smooth over the purple exterior. The pages, a creamy yellow, are still streaked with my slanted cursive, and flipping through a page or two, I immediately see the name *Benji* and *in love* and *we're getting married!*

I slam it shut. Press my lips together. "Where did you find this?"

"I still see them every now and then. I took them an engagement gift. Pretended to be happy for them. Gwyn left me alone when she went to help Benjamin unload groceries one night. I found it in her office."

The same place I found the camera.

My breath comes out in stuttered exhalations.

"I'm not shocked," Elena says. "But I wouldn't have guessed she'd be capable of it if you'd asked me three years ago."

"Me neither," I say. But that's not entirely true. How many times was it obvious she wanted what I had? How many people told me she was jealous of my life and warned me to be careful of her?

But I would have never dreamed she'd be capable of

murder. I gaze at my sister, who was sometimes the big sister, sometimes the overbearing mom. Who always looked out for me, even when it annoyed me, which was often. And I realize I'm not so alone in this world. This whole time, she was trying to figure out who killed me. Which also means we can do the rest of this together—we can figure out who did it, and we can get revenge.

This time, I squeeze her hand.

"You said not to believe Benjamin." I tuck the journal into my lap. I don't ask Elena if she read it—I'm certain she did. And she should have if she thought I was dead. It might have given her a clue as to who was behind my near murder.

"I think Gwyn is the one who pushed you," Elena says. "But I'm not entirely sure she acted alone. What do you think?"

I look down at the table and sigh. "He is acting strangely." I share everything I've found out—about his potential financial issues, how he's been running at night, watching Gwyn, hiding something from her. How I caught him trying to break into my house.

Her eyes go wide. "Maddy—so you think they're in on it together? They're both guilty?"

I open my mouth but don't say anything as I think through it. "I mean, maybe?"

"Jesus." She exhales a hiss, nods. "Okay."

"And the fact he's marrying Gwyn. I mean—isn't that strange?"

Elena nods. "You're right. You're absolutely right. Okay, so they're in on it together."

I feel my confidence bolstered. I've wondered all this time, and Elena, who's smart as a whip, can see it, too. Can connect the dots and sees how the puzzle pieces fit together. "He had me declared dead after only three years." I blink through tears this time. "*Three years.* He proposed to her before it even happened."

"It's okay." Elena reaches out, clutches my hand. The physical contact feels good. Solid. "You're right. What kind of man proposes to another woman before his current wife is declared dead?"

I squeeze my eyes shut, remembering Benjamin on the ground, racked with grief; images flash through my mind—his hands curled into fists, tears streaming down his face. Maybe it wasn't grief.

Maybe it was relief—no body, no evidence that could prove what he'd done.

I meet her gaze across the table. "A guilty one."

FIFTY-THREE

REBECCA

Now

We stay at the bar nearly two hours. Elena details her life the last several years. "Growing my practice, hiring two more doctors, dealing with Daddy's estate, and trying to figure out what happened to you. They suggested you'd had too much to drink, that you simply fell. But that never sat right with me." She holds her second drink of the night. "Anyway, I was never very good at being family to you and Daddy, but then you were both gone."

In a way, Elena and I have been living parallel lives. Going forward alone but trapped in the past. While I wanted to keep her out of it, wanted to keep her safe, going forward with her now is better than being alone. Having someone who knows who I am. Having my sister back. And it feels different now, too. Like we've figuratively moved out of the house and grown up a little and as adults can come together as friends again. As allies, in this.

"I was sad I couldn't be there for Daddy's funeral," I say. "I read the articles about it."

Elena nods. "I get that. But don't be sad. You were around when it mattered. When he was actually alive. I just wish he'd known you were okay. It tore him up."

I almost tell her everything then and there—how I had help from Daddy to become Rebecca. But it's something he withheld from her. It's the sort of thing that might upset her, make her feel left out, as she so often did before. I don't want any of that emotion in our relationship now. I've been on my own for so long, the idea of having a partner to figure out what happens next... I don't want to go back to being alone. To facing this alone.

I watch her across the table, the only person who knows my secret, but even then, someone I won't tell everything. Will it always be like this?

"I'm staying at their house right now," I say. "I'll probably go home tomorrow, though. Especially now that I know it was you who broke in. Anything I should look for with my last night there?"

Elena shrugs. "As far as I'm concerned, they're both guilty. I can't see either of them being innocent."

"Where was the journal again?" I press my fingertips to the edges of the pages, thinking of all the time and emotion the former me had poured into writing it. Entries I thought maybe someday I'd even read aloud to Benjamin—probably blushing at how hard I'd fallen for him, how fast. Maybe on an anniversary, or if we managed a romantic getaway far into the future, after we had kids. We'd laugh at how he'd somehow convinced me I could love a man enough so I'd followed him all the way to *Europe*, the sort of thing even now sounds crazy to me.

God, what had I been thinking?

Love. I was in love.

A trailing flicker of that emotion fills me now, thinking of my last moments with Benjamin—around the fire, sharing a cup filled with spiked cocoa, finding myself again somewhere I never thought I'd be: out in the mountains, about to sleep under the stars. Then tucking in beside him, waiting until he fell asleep to sneak out and photograph the sky.

If only I'd stayed with him that night instead of venturing out for photos.

Except... he might have been the one to follow me and push me. Hypothetically, what if he—or whoever—hadn't had the opportunity that night? What if, instead, they'd killed me at home, and succeeded? Then I wouldn't be here, talking to Elena.

The flicker of emotion fades away. Emptiness sits in its wake, the sort that makes me think I might not feel a bit of emotion avenging what would have been my death.

"The journal was in Gwyn's closet," Elena answers.

I wait for a flicker of something—anger or grief, maybe. Instead, I'm just numb.

"They didn't notice you took it?"

Elena shrugs. "Never asked me about it."

Maybe that's one of the reasons they suspect one another—maybe they both think the other took it, holding it as evidence in case the other considered leaving or letting them take the blame for what they did. Hell, maybe that's why Gwyn wants me to follow Benjamin, why Benjamin is watching Gwyn.

"Why would they want me dead?" I murmur. I'm not really asking Elena for an answer, but she replies, anyway.

"Best I can figure, Gwyn wanted your life. Your man. Your money. Benjamin probably just wanted your money. The winery almost closed right after the wedding—he got an infusion of cash from somewhere, but he'd had too many investors pull out."

Benjamin *had* been having money issues—I remember it. Maybe still was. And if Daddy died before he could solve the problems, fix it, as he'd promised to, it would make sense North Winery almost went under.

"But he'd have had the money by marrying me. I would have given it to him."

Elena shrugs. "Maybe they wanted to be together *and* have the money. Weren't you concerned they were having an affair?"

She knows I was if she read the journal. I didn't really think they *were*—but I knew what kind of person Gwyn was when she was desperate and sad and alone. I knew Benjamin worked long hours, often with her, as they got the winery up and running. I knew it was a possibility. I just thought I was wrong. That I was paranoid, because for the first time ever, I felt happy.

Pain creeps into the edges of my periphery—the sharp burn of betrayal. Thinking someone had cared for me, when really, they only wanted to use me.

"Let me tell you everything I've found," I say. And I tell her about ruling out that it could have been Alex or Aaron, Leah or Natalie. I share the emails I found, how Gwyn suggested if I were no longer in the picture, she'd end it with Alex—which she did—and how they flirted back and forth for months. How fast they got together, got engaged. I tell her about the possibility Benjamin is having financial issues with his company, how he *had* had problems in the past, how Daddy bailed him out, but maybe it wasn't enough. How Gwyn pushed him to have me declared *dead in absentia* after only three years, and how he had. How he'd gotten everything. I tell her how they don't trust each other, how he watches Gwyn, how she has me following him. When I've whispered it all across the table, I'm breathless. "But none of that is really proof."

Elena's bottom lip comes up in a pout. She reaches out. "Maddy—sorry, Rebecca—you have a kind soul. You've always wanted to see the best in everyone. But isn't it obvious?"

"What do you mean?"

"He needed money. They were certainly having an affair given everything you've found out. That they're together now. That they had you declared dead so soon. And that they are both waiting for the other to betray them." She pauses. Looks at me with love and concern and empathy.

I blink at her, pretending there are not tears in my eyes. She's right. *We're* right. They're guilty.

We talk another twenty minutes before a question comes to mind. "Why did you meet Benjamin in the woods?"

She tilts her head. "I'd already gotten a call that the body wasn't yours. I wanted to tell him in person, watch his reaction, see if he'd crack. Gwyn isn't a fan of me, so"—she shrugs—"I asked him to meet me." She pauses. "I wanted to see what he did. What he said. As it was, he was stoic. Eerily so."

All I can think of is the look on Benjamin's face when he answered his phone—the shock. Benjamin hadn't known until that moment, I'm almost certain of it. Unless... unless it was all a show for me. A show for whoever was on the phone. Or maybe it was a delayed response. Either way, it fits with how he's been this whole time—putting on an act. For me. For Gwyn.

"What about the other time?" I ask.

Elena's forehead wrinkles. "What do you mean?"

"You—did you meet him there another time?"

"No. He suggested it. Which was strange, by the way. Why couldn't he just meet me at a bar?" She gestures at our dim surroundings.

I don't have an answer for that, but it does give me more questions—who else would he have met in the dark woods?

"I should get back," I say. "It's getting late."

"What's your number?" Elena asks. "So we can stay in touch."

I tell her, and she keys it into her phone. "And you know where I live," I say. "I'll be back there tomorrow."

We get to our feet, and Elena wraps me in a tight hug. "Good to see you, sis." She presses a kiss into my hair, a maternal action that now leaves me warm on the inside—when was the last time anyone hugged me, much less cared enough to kiss me?

Outside, we go our separate ways. Elena back toward the park at a brisk walk, likely where she left a car parked on the side of the road. The alcohol sits heavy in my stomach. I tuck the journal, now wrapped in a plastic bag, beneath one arm and begin to run again. It's not time to go back to Benjamin and Gwyn's, though, not yet—instead, I run until I get to Chris's alleyway, where I slow to a walk and find my way down the alley.

The bouncing of the ball is audible, even from several houses down. The scamper of the dog's feet over pine needles and grass. The husky laughter of Chris.

I go still before I reach the fence line. I close my eyes and listen, for five minutes, ten minutes, maybe twenty. Long enough my toes go numb, and my whole body stiffens from the cold wind. Eventually, footsteps clomp over the wood of the back porch. The gentle whoosh of a sliding door. A dog collar, jangling as the dog trots obediently inside. Another whoosh as the door shuts. A click, as he locks it. I—*Madeline*—should have married someone like Chris. Someone who's happy to spend the evening with his dog on the nights he's not busy saving lives. Who truly believes in the good of people, and who is a good person himself.

Instead, I—*Madeline*—ended up with Benjamin. A friend like Gwyn, who illustrates the line *With friends like you, who needs enemies?*

I swallow down what feels like a sob rising in my throat. I don't have Benjamin. I don't have Gwyn. I don't even have Chris, who might as well be an illusion as much as the other people I watch and make up storylines for—he doesn't even know I exist, not in any tangible way.

But I do have Elena. And that's something.

I skirt the edge of Chris's fence line, crossing through his neighbor's lawn, to get one last glimpse of him. I've decided it will be better if I stop coming here, so tonight will be the last night I ever do. He's just one more person tying me to my past.

A stump sits next to where I stand, and I rest the journal on it to press myself closer to the fence and get a better angle of him through his living room window. He sits on the couch, staring off in one direction—not toward his television, I note. Maybe at a wall, deep in thought. Chris stands, comes to the window, and his eyes scan the darkness until they rest somewhere near me.

My heart practically climbs into my throat as I stay still, hoping he's lost in thought again, because his eyes are right on me—*right on me*.

And I can't move, can't run, because if I do, he'll see the movement. I just have to wait.

But then Chris presses a hand to the glass. Just a tic, I tell myself. How many times have I touched my hand to the cool glass and enjoyed the way it felt beneath my palm? No big deal.

But then, Chris smiles. He raises his hand. He waves at me.

FIFTY-FOUR

REBECCA

Now

I stay still, hoping I'm wrong—hoping he will move or look down at his dog, or I'll realize there's someone else out here who he's clearly waving a greeting to. But there's no one. Only me.

And then Chris holds up a finger, telling me *one sec*, and leaves the room—but there's no way I'm waiting. What is there to wait for? There's a reason I've been visiting in secret.

I bolt. Back through the lawn and past his fence line to the alley. A right turn, toward my house, but I'm staying with Gwyn and Benjamin tonight. I turn left as the alley ends, sprinting through the night.

Behind me, footsteps clomp over damp leaves and gravel. His voice calling out—"Wait, wait!"

He grows fainter as I put distance between us.

I could wait. I could talk to him. But he doesn't know it's me. And with what I think Elena and I have planned, it's better not to involve him. It's the least I can do. I don't slow until Benjamin and Gwyn's house is in sight.

I stride up the walkway to the side entrance Gwyn has

instructed me to use. I tap in a code they use in place of a key. I wait as the electronic slide flashes green, then moves to one side, and the door unlocks. Entering is like stepping back in time—it's only been a few hours, but a few hours ago, my situation felt very different. Very alone.

"Benjamin?" Gwyn's feet pad across the floor, and I stuff the journal into my jacket. Gwyn smiles when she sees me. "Oh. He's not home yet." She drops her voice as though someone might overhear. She beckons to me, pulling me into the kitchen with her. The clock tells me it's almost eleven—late enough he should be back. I was with Elena for at least two hours before I went to Chris's.

"You followed him?" Gwyn reaches for a kettle and fills it with water. I pull my jacket off, carefully folding it with the journal inside, and take a seat at the bar. I take a deep breath, sorting through the last few hours, which now spin in my head. So much happened.

She's half the reason Madeline Hughes is a featured missing persons case, now declared dead.

"Did you see the news?" I change the topic.

"News?" A half turn as she reaches for a higher mug, one with a jack-o'-lantern painted on the front.

"The body."

She stills. When she finally turns, her eyes are wide. The mugs are forgotten in the cabinet.

"Is it her?" she asks. And like last time, I can't figure her out. She's dead serious—earnest, even. Tears fill her eyes yet again. "Is it Maddy?"

Just like Benjamin. Real grief.

But also, this is Gwyn. Gwyn, who could do drama like no other. Who flirted shamelessly with *Benji*, who probably planned my death in advance from the moment she met him. *Take her man, take her money.* She'd done it before, and she'd do it again.

"No, it wasn't."

Gwyn melts against the nearest counter, not quite sinking to the ground. She stares down at her hands. Hands she killed with? When she looks up, her skin has gone blotchy, tears streaking it. "I don't know whether to be relieved or sad. Part of me wanted to be able to lay her to rest. Part of me still hopes—I mean, I know they declared her dead, but that was just to get it over with. Benjamin—" Her voice breaks off. I stay silent, hoping she'll continue whatever thought she just cut off.

A flicker through the window catches my attention, but it's gone as soon as I look, and I have to wonder if it's Benjamin.

He's watching us.

They've both shown genuine grief—or at least a good display of acting it. But Elena is sure, and so am I. They are the only ones who had something to gain by my death.

I force myself to continue playing Rebecca, the concerned friend. "It's a hard situation. There's no right way to act." I move in and hug her. After a moment, I urge her to sit down, and take over making tea.

"Benjamin went on a run. He didn't see anyone or do anything out of the ordinary," I say. "He did get a phone call, though—from what I could hear, I think it was about... about your friend. He was really sad. I lost him on the trail in the woods, but maybe that's why he hasn't come home yet." I can't help but look back out the window to where he's likely hidden among the trees.

"Gwyn?" I slide a mug of tea to her, and she cups her hands around it, not looking up. "I hope you don't mind me asking this, but... what do you think happened to your friend?"

"I don't know. The authorities thought she probably fell when she was taking photos. She'd been drinking, but not very much. They never found her camera."

Lies. Lies. Lies.

I have to take a moment, so I don't lash out at her. All this

time, holding it in and now I'm so close. Tension thrums
through me. I tighten my hands around my own mug until it's so
hot it burns.

"Was anything else missing?"

Her hands splay. "I don't think so."

*Another lie. Both the camera and the journal, found in
Gwyn's office. Elena's right.*

"Did they ever suspect foul play?"

"I know there was an investigation. She had just married
Benjamin, and—she had a lot of money. But he had no interest
in it. I mean, it eventually went to him, because they'd gotten
married. She refused to sign a prenup. Her dad didn't like that,
but her dad—" Gwyn pauses, takes a deep breath. "Her dad was
with a lot of women, and he always set up all these precondi-
tions, and Maddy hated that about him. It was like he knew
from the start he'd divorce them. She swore she'd be nothing
like that. Don't get me wrong, she loved her father, she just—she
wanted a different life."

The words are on the tip of my tongue: *Do* you *think
Benjamin was involved?*

I can't ask that directly, though. So I ask again, watching for
any trace of emotion or hesitation on her face, "So, what do you
think happened?"

Gwyn shakes her head, her blonde hair now limp around
her face. The steam has made her blotchy skin go completely
pink, and she wipes at her nose with the back of her hand. "I
think she fell. I think she got swept into the river. I went back,
months later, to look where they thought she'd probably fallen
from—this cliff, up the hill from the campsite. I don't know how
anyone would survive a fall like that. And the river wasn't deep.
I really thought the body was probably hers."

Emotion stirs me, almost against my will. "You went back to
where she fell?"

Gwyn nods. "I had to see it for myself. The next morning,

when we woke up and realized she was gone, it's all a haze. Like I'm sure I walked up there—and we'd all been there the night before, watching the sunset. But I had to get it right in my memory. I'd stay up late at night, thinking about it, wondering what happened to her. Hoping maybe, somehow, she was still alive."

I squeeze my hands into fists, resisting emotion. They always say criminals return to the scene of the crime.

Gwyn sips her tea. "Sometimes, I think I was a shitty friend to her."

A snide comment snaps into my thoughts: *Sometimes?*

"We were best friends since... college? We were roommates and all that. But I was in a bad place in my life. Shitty boyfriend. He cheated on me constantly. I was finally confident enough to leave him. And she was always there, always around to help me. She didn't date much. She thought she was too good for all the men we knew, and you know what? She was right. She really was." A faint smile traces her mouth. Warmth flushes through me, but I ignore it. "I was jealous she could be so confident on her own. But then she met Benji—that's what she called him—only someone like Maddy would have gotten away with calling him that—and everything changed. Anyway, I was jealous."

My emotions flip-flop between resentment and gratitude at her kind words. Resentment and betrayal win out. Of course she was jealous, everyone is sometimes. But she didn't just feel envy like every other person sometimes does—she did something about it. Just like she stole Alex, she stole Benjamin. She just had to clear the way for it to happen first.

I'm about to ask another question, but the door opens in the foyer, distracting us both. It occurs to me Benjamin might acknowledge we saw one another tonight—that I obviously followed him, that he's suspicious of me.

But when he comes in the room, he offers us a soft smile.

"Sorry I was out so long, babe. You see the news?" He comes closer, presses a kiss to her head—casts a wary gaze my way, but says nothing.

"I saw," she says. "Are you okay?"

"Not really," he says. "I was hoping..." A shrug. "For closure, I suppose."

"Me, too."

And the lie continues, I think to myself. Both of them pretending to trust one another.

But now, I know the truth.

FIFTY-FIVE
REBECCA

Now

When Benjamin and Gwyn retire to bed, I picture them sleeping back-to-back—both wide awake as they pretend to lovingly tuck in together. Both wondering if tomorrow is the day the other will crack, if the truth will come out, if their lives will be over. If left alone, maybe they would out one another. Maybe they'd admit guilt or frame the other person or... something. I don't have patience for that, though. Nor could I wait if I wanted to—my time as Rebecca is coming to a close. There is no way to verify my nursing license. I've ignored emails and voice-mails, reminding me the hospital needs that documentation. I have mere days before the hospital realizes something is truly wrong and launches an investigation. I need to be gone by then.

Which means they need to be dead by then. A jail term isn't long enough for what they took from Madeline.

I lie in my own bed, door blocked by the dresser again, staring at the ceiling, the fanciful crown molding and heavy curtains and walls painted a color Madeline never would have chosen. Elena pulses in my mind, and for a moment it is a dream—reunited with her after all of this. Having her on my side. I roll over and reach for my phone, and as if we are on the same wavelength, a text comes through.

It's E. You awake? How did the rest of the night go?

I shift and type back. *They're both pretending to be sad.*
I'll bet they're good actors, too, she replies. *Gwyn always did have a flair for the dramatic.*

I stare at her words and try to come up with something to say, but I'm distracted.

Have you thought about coming forward? Elena continues. *Take back your life?*

Once upon a time, I had.

You could get your money back, I'm almost sure of it. And your part of Daddy's estate. I would help.

The three bubbles appear, indicating she's typing more, but I'm not interested in this line of conversation. After a life-time of the limelight, society, Daddy's peers and friends and the incestuous families of upper-class Seattle, I can't imagine dipping my toes back in. Especially with the sort of attention I would get. I can imagine the headlines—*Dead Girl Alive!* —and far worse. Besides, our plan is to exact revenge on Gwyn and Benjamin. The last thing we need is someone looking our way.

I must have drifted off. I wake, sunlight streaming through the curtains.

The rest of the house is silent, and when I slip from the bed, pack my belongings, and step out into the hallway, it's clear Benjamin and Gwyn have cleared out—gone to work or running or wherever they escaped today. I let out a breath, feeling some of the tightness in my chest melt away. I stroll through the house one more time, looking for a reason to investigate a room, to search a drawer, but there's nothing left to solve, not really.

They are guilty. In one way or the other.

So I pack my bag into my car and drive away, this time relieved to never again have to step foot in the house that was once Madeline's. Once mine. It's been so long that I can't even think of myself as Madeline. That person is dead.

The morning is cloudy, those brief rays of sunshine quickly covered by mist and a slow drizzle of rain. The temperature hovers in the fifties, but it's a damp fifty, and I crank up the heat in my little car. My phone rings—the hospital—and I hit ignore.

Arriving at my house leaves me with mixed feelings. Relieved to be "home," but it doesn't feel like home. And it won't be for much longer, anyway. Maybe it would be better to stay with Elena.

I park my car and get out, taking a long look around me. I've also lost the vague sense of normalcy I'd built with a job, a house, regular neighbors I like to look in on. People know who I am—or at least, know I'm not who I'm pretending to be. Too many people asking questions. And I can't see Chris again after last night.

The world wobbles for a moment, and I feel myself start to spiral—but I'm close. So close. And once this is over, I'll be free. I can do whatever I want. And I'll have Elena to call my sister again. Maybe I'll finally find my sense of belonging.

FIFTY-SIX

REBECCA

Now

I get inside, but my phone is buzzing before I can so much as set my things down.

"Hello?" I answer without looking at the contact.

"Hey, girl, sorry I had to leave early. A client was in a panic over a party she's having and she needs everything delivered sooner than expected and—" Gwyn breaks off in a laugh, last night's grief gone entirely. "Anyway, hi, how are you?"

"Good," I say. "I'm so glad you called. I wanted to check on you."

"Oh, gosh. I'm sorry. I'd had too much to drink and worrying about Benjamin and—" She breaks off. "I'm okay. I wanted to ask before I plan dinner, do we get to enjoy your company again tonight?"

"Not tonight—I have to work. But I was thinking maybe we could do something fun soon. I know it's been a rough couple weeks."

"Sure. What were you thinking?"

I don't know why I suggest it—it's just the first thing that comes to mind.

"Don't you have a boat? Want to take it out?"

A moment of silence. "We do. Benjamin hasn't wanted to take it out in a while. But I could ask... hmmm." Another pause.

"Is it too cold?" I ask. Because it definitely is, but a plan is forming, one Elena will like. The boat will be helpful.

"It is cold, but we have an indoor cabin, so it wouldn't be a big deal. That and some blankets get you pretty far. It's that the boat reminds Benjamin of her... of Madeline. But... maybe it would be good in a way. Who knows if we'll ever have real closure, you know? So maybe we could like—I don't know, have our own closure."

"Are you sure?" I ask. "Would you want me there for that?"

"Sure," Gwyn says easily. "She would have liked you, you know."

I'm sure. I fight the desire to roll my eyes.

"I'll call you back," she says. "Maybe we can do it this weekend."

We disconnect, and I make a mental note to see if Elena can get herself invited. After all, if it's closure they're seeking, it would make sense to invite along Madeline's sister.

I make myself coffee and find a box of toaster pastries and sit down in the living room—then look up, staring at the rain and clouds. If I can see out, someone can see in. I press the journal down on the couch and get up, pulling blinds and curtains until I'm entirely alone in the small room. The sense of claustrophobia creeps in immediately—my heart beats faster, my pulse thrumming at my wrists, my throat—but it's better than risking someone else's eyes.

I text Elena: *Can I stay with you?* and return to the couch.

With the journal in my hands, I settle back into the cushions and shut my eyes, smoothing my hands over the cover, recalling the hours I spent poring over this book—writing about my own experiences before Benjamin, then with him, realizing it was a way to deal with the things I couldn't talk to him about. *Like him cheating. Lying.* Which perhaps should have been the first sign something was wrong.

It's not normal to worry whether one's fiancé is cheating on them leading up to the wedding. Or to imagine him off dallying with an ex or considering an affair with their own best friend. But I was young, and I was dumb. I was in love, and more than anything, I wanted that illusion of perfection. The belief anything was possible, so long as we were together.

It hadn't worked out that way. I'd become a true crime podcast, an ongoing story in the paper, an unsolved case for the police, and then one more person declared *dead in absentia* by a supposedly grieving spouse. I'd become a memory.

I flip through the pages, through the moments of the relationship that led to *Rebecca* returning to Seattle to exact revenge on Gwyn and Benjamin for killing me. No, not me, I remind myself. Because she is dead. They tried to kill *Madeline*.

My phone chimes, and it's Elena: *Oh, I would love to have you stay here, but I don't think it's a good idea. Not until we expose them. But I can help you get a hotel nearby. I'll book you a room, okay?*

I stare at her text too long, already in a dark place mentally. And now, my sister, the one person I can depend on, doesn't want me in her home. I bite my lip hard, hoping to taste blood, to remember the moment I realized I could trust no one. But she texts again: *If Benjamin sees you come here, he'll figure it out, you know? We need to keep this up just a little longer.* And it eases my mind the tiniest bit—she's right. It could screw this up.

I understand, and yes, thank you. I hit send, but before I can set my phone down, a message from Gwyn comes in.

Does tomorrow work to take the boat out? Benjamin actually sounded really into it!

Let's do it, I reply to Gwyn.

And then to Elena: *I have a plan.*

FIFTY-SEVEN

REBECCA

Now

Everything I own packs easily into my car. The furniture belongs to the house, as do the plates, the cutlery, the coffee machine—the personal belongings most people collect I rent as part of the place I live. I take one last look at the house, then turn and leave. And to think, I'd briefly thought it felt a little like home.

I reach the hotel minutes later—it's only a couple miles away, relatively close to the marina where Benjamin keeps the boat. I check in to find Elena booked me a nice room on the top floor, a view of the Puget Sound, which tonight is gray and still. The room is a suite—a small couch and office area on one side, where I set up my laptop, then a bed and a table opposite.

Elena messages *Just picked up dinner, be there in ten minutes.* I take the opportunity to gaze out the window at the water, knowing I'll miss it. Because once this is done tomorrow, I'm leaving again. I thought maybe I'd stick around for Elena—but that really isn't fair. It would put her at risk, and she's done enough for me. Besides, as she said, it's not as though I can live at her house.

I can't help but think about tomorrow. I don't know how I'll do it. I'm not a murderer. I recall talking pills with Gwyn—the same anxiolytic I have a prescription for. That combined with a sleeping pill and ground into beer or wine—or *something*—might make things easier. But do I want it to be easy? Or do I want them to be afraid, like Madeline was, freezing and bloody on a tiny outcropping over a certain fall to her death? The meds would, if anything, relax them. But so would a good dose of alcohol, and I've been on that boat with both of them before—neither go light on the drinking.

I fidget and look over at my suitcase. Prescription bottles sit in plastic baggies in the zipper pocket. Prints won't be an issue. Rebecca was once Madeline, and the boat was once Madeline's. If a print is found, they'll assume it's leftover from her, a dead girl.

A knock at the door interrupts my furious thoughts. When Elena comes in, she gives me a hug, a peck on my cheek.

"I brought your favorite," she says, lifting a plastic bag tied at the top. It's Thai, I can tell from the smell, from the packaging, as it wakes a memory inside me of a restaurant on a corner I used to frequent. But she's wrong—it's not my favorite, because I am not Madeline. Not anymore.

I don't tell her that, though. It was nice of her to put in the effort.

I pull out plastic forks and paper napkins and help her arrange the tiny table. We sit across from one another, and gazing at her over the table, I realize my earlier thought is true—we do actually look more alike now, with my contacts in, my different hair, my heart-shaped face.

"Your eyes are different than yesterday." Elena's brows furrow.

I blink. "I forgot my contacts." It's okay, though. A spare pair sit in my bag, waiting. I need to be more careful. So much is happening right now, it's easy to get distracted. But if anyone else had walked in that door—if I'd met up with Gwyn or happened upon Benjamin—a mistake like that could have brought down everything.

"Did it hurt?" she asks, motioning at my face.

"Yes." I twist noodles in my fork and look down.

"You okay?"

"Just thinking about tomorrow." I tell her about the boat. About the plan.

"I'll be there," she promises. "I'll see if I can hide on board before it leaves."

"You don't think Benjamin would let you go with us?"

She gives me a half-hearted smile. "No. I think he wants closure, and I'm not closure. I'm a reminder of you. Of what he did."

We eat in silence. Elena wipes her mouth with a napkin. "The boat idea is good. We'll wait until we're somewhere deserted on the Puget Sound. And then we'll push them over-board." She points a finger at me. "Don't drink too much, but get them drinking, if you can."

"I was thinking about drugging their drinks," I say.

Elena nods. "I like where your head is at. Do it if you can. I'll hide somewhere on board. It's a big boat—it shouldn't be too hard if I get there ahead of time. We'll leave them out there in the water. Stranded. The water temperature is probably only forty or fifty degrees. They won't last more than an hour if they've been drinking. I think we can handle Gwyn, but I'll try to take Benjamin by surprise so he can't fight back." She meets my gaze, a combination of compassion, love, and anger. "They left you to die. And now we leave them to die. Then, you can do whatever you want. You can stay as Rebecca. I'll help you however I can. Or if you change your mind and want to be you again, we'll figure it out."

I agree easily—but I know already that my bags will stay packed and in my car. And once they are dead, I'll move on. My only regret will be leaving my sister behind. Hopefully, she will understand.

FIFTY-EIGHT

REBECCA

Now

I barely sleep that night. I can't stop myself from rolling over, picking up Madeline's journal, reading every entry from start to finish. The entries before Benjamin came around—when she was still a twenty-seven-year-old with big dreams, a huge Instagram following, and more money than she knew what to do with. No direction, no purpose. A spoiled little girl just waiting for something in her life to give her direction. She thought it was Benjamin—*dumb, dumb, dumb*—and she locked onto that. With each entry it becomes more obvious to me now—the warning signs she felt, she saw, she ignored. All in the name of being a good girlfriend. Of not upsetting him by reminding him of his ex.

His *ex*. At least he hadn't ended up with her. Not that Gwyn was any better. I linger over that, wondering who she was. Did she ever suspect what he was capable of?

Was Madeline—was *I* the only one so naïve? I ignored the people who suggested I be careful, including Elena, who hadn't liked him to begin with. Who slowly accepted him. And then who told me it would be okay if I didn't marry him.

Her. She. Madeline. Not me. I'm not dead. Madeline is.

Elena was the only person to really show Madeline kindness the whole time. Sure, we weren't always the closest of sisters—but she's been there for me when it matters. Which is more than anyone else in my life can say.

I pick up a pen tucked into the hotel nightstand and press ink to paper. My writing is one thing that hasn't changed—that slightly slanted script, something my private school still taught in place of relying on printed letters and computers alone.

Benjamin and Gwyn tried to kill me—I start, and then pause, realizing it's only the second time I've written his full name out in this journal.

"Benji," I whisper, trying the nickname on for size, but it's all wrong now. I can't call someone I hate by a sweet name that reminds me of a favorite movie growing up. *How to Lose a Guy in Ten Days* was before my time, but Elena had it on once, and I never laughed so much—one of the few positive memories we shared.

Words won't come. I want to write about how much I hate him and hate her. I wonder if the original plan had been for it to happen out of country on a tropical honeymoon. I press the pen against the paper until it punctures it, trying to figure out what the original plan would have been had the hurricane not ruined his master plan.

I slap the journal shut, shove it in the drawer with the pen, and roll over, squeezing my eyes shut.

Eventually, sleep comes.

FIFTY-NINE

REBECCA

Now

I arrive at the marina half an hour early. The parking lot has only three other cars, but none of them is Elena's, and she's nowhere to be found. Hopefully, that means she's already aboard, and I'm not left stranded to do this alone. Though I could, if I had to. Throwing someone overboard into the icy-cold waters of the Puget Sound has never been on my bucket list, but through the years, I've known it might come to this. And finally, it has.

I can see the headline already: *Couple Found Dead in Puget Sound, Believed to Have Overdosed on Benzos and Alcohol.*

I run my fingers over the packet of ground-up meds in my pocket. Benjamin may be on guard—between Gwyn, who he clearly doesn't trust, and me, who he believes to be working with her.

Mist gathers over the marina, creating silhouettes of sail-boats and motorboats. A golden edge to the horizon shows where the sun should come through the clouds but doesn't quite make it. I hug my down jacket tighter around me, fighting the shiver snaking its way through my body. The water is still, reflecting the boats, even in the dimness of a cloudy Seattle morning. It's beautiful, and if I were still Madeline, I'd grab my camera and take a photo.

As it is, I'm left wondering how many bodies have floated in these waters, eventually descending into the Puget Sound's depths, never to be seen again. The image of Gwyn's blonde hair floating through the murky water leaves my chest tight. The mental picture of Benjamin's bloated face leaves me straight-up nauseated.

For the first time, I'm not sure I can do this.

But that's why Elena is here.

Gwyn and Benjamin arrive minutes later in his Tesla, the sleek black car tucking easily into a compact parking spot. Gwyn greets me with a wave, a grin, as though we're headed out for a fun day instead of what is supposed to help them put Madeline's memory to rest. Benjamin doesn't acknowledge me, doesn't even look at me, as he swings out of the car and pulls a gym bag from the back.

"Prepped the boat last night," he says, "so we should be good to go. Fueled up and everything."

"There's a heater on board, too," Gwyn says, rubbing her arms against the chill. "It's pretty comfy."

I follow them down the slope of the parking lot to the dock, my own bag tucked under my arm. We cross through a gate, then out on a walkway surrounded by water on either side, to a slip all the way at the end of the dock. Dozens of boats are lined up on either side of us, big white ones with sails, smaller ones with motors, a few bigger boats, like the one I know we're walking toward. When we get there, Benjamin climbs aboard first. He's wearing tan hiking pants, a heavy knit sweater in navy blue, a beanie. He holds out a hand, and Gwyn takes it, climbs on after him.

I smile and take his hand once she's on board, and he

doesn't say a word to me—his eyes catch mine, and there's no mistaking the mistrust there. Even the old me, the part that was Madeline, can't quite fathom what the look means, but I do wonder why he agreed to this. I wonder if he and Gwyn know more than I think they do—if today they plan to kill me just as I plan to kill them. I hadn't expected getting them to take me on the boat to be so easy, to happen so fast. I was expecting to need to cook up a Plan B, and maybe a Plan C, too.

My heart speeds. Maybe they've set me up as much as I've set them up. Pretending as though nothing is wrong, I brush by him and find Gwyn inside the cabin.

"Wow. Great boat." I take in the small kitchen, painting adoration over my face—pretending to see it for the first time. A booth seating area. Windows are on every side, giving us a view of the other boats, the Puget Sound. Benjamin comes in after me, tosses his bag in one booth, and starts messing with the boat controls, which are set inside, just behind the kitchen. A narrow set of stairs are to the left of it, and they lead down to one of two sleeping spaces inside the boat. I wonder which one Elena is hiding in.

"Yeah... it came with Benjamin." Gwyn tosses an appreciate glance his way, but he doesn't acknowledge her. "It was Madeline's favorite. They got engaged here, actually." She points a finger toward the back of the boat, where we came on board. "Right out there. He tricked her into taking her own engagement photo," she adds with a laugh. But then the smile fades. "Sorry. I'm just being weird now."

"No, you're not," I assure her. They're simply pretending everything is normal, which is what I intend to do, too.

Gwyn steps outside to assist Benjamin with the lines holding it to the slip. I watch them work together to get the boat free of the slip, and when their backs are turned, I call down to the master stateroom, the edge of the bed visible from where I stand. "Elena?"

No response.

I check that Benjamin and Gwyn are still busy with the boat, and stride toward the aft stateroom at the other end. "Elena?" This time, she answers.

"I'm here. Be quiet."

And with that established, realizing the plan is go, I pull the crushed meds from my pocket.

"I know it's early, but do you mind if I open a bottle of wine?" I call out the door.

Gwyn laughs. "Never too early out on the boat. Go for it. Maybe a red?"

Benjamin spares a glance back at me. "The red blend is supposed to be good. It's from a California winery we're in talks to acquire. I just put it in the fridge to chill for a couple minutes before we came. Open that one."

I almost snort—red wine is supposed to be served around sixty degrees, which is below the often-assumed room temperature, which is usually closer to seventy. Typical Benjamin. Three bottles rest in the mini-fridge, and I grab the red. Which I'm not mad about. It will hide the taste of the meds better than a white.

I pour myself a glass, then add half of what's ground up in the baggy to the bottle, swirl it, then swirl again, because speckles of it are visible through the glass. When it seems to have mostly dissolved, I pour two more glasses, careful to keep them separate from my own.

Gwyn wanders in and pulls off her pink rain jacket to show the fitted flannel below. She flashes a grin my way. "I'm so glad we're doing this."

Me, too, I think. And even though every bit of this is deserved, a stab of guilt winds its way through me. But then I think of the camera, the journal, that she must have grabbed Madeline's belongings after shoving her, or watching her be shoved, or knowing Benjamin had done the deed—and it just slips out. "It's so gorgeous out here. I brought a camera," I murmur. "To remember the good times."

Gwyn doesn't flinch. "Great idea."

The enthusiasm in her voice is matched only by Benjamin's call from outside, "And we're off!"

SIXTY

REBECCA

Now

Gwyn and I watch from the warmth of the cabin as the boat slices easily through the Puget Sound. I try to think of what to say as we sip our wine—how a friend would interact on a day like today, but all I can think of is that in a few hours, she will cease to breathe, her heart will stop beating. Gwyn will effectively be gone.

"It's supposed to warm up," she says. "It'll probably be windy out here, but hopefully we can spend a little time outside. There's nothing like it. Summers are the best. Especially in August, when we actually get some warm weather." Her lips tilt up at the edges, her eyes with a faraway look in them. She's remembering something, I think. I wish I knew what.

"Is that what Madeline liked?" I ask.

She shrugs. "Madeline liked the boat, period. Didn't matter the weather. Everyone thought she was this soft spoiled rich girl, and"—Gwyn scrunches her nose—"I guess in some ways she was. But she was also tough. She could help me sort through anything with my ex. And she'd stay out in any weather to be on this boat. Hell, she agreed to go backpacking when her honeymoon got canceled. That takes guts. I only said yes because she had, otherwise... backpacking? Sleeping outside on the ground? No thanks." She sighs out. "I miss that girl."

I examine her face, the longing written over her features. "You didn't want to go backpacking?"

Gwyn raises her glass to take a sip, but it hits the edge of the table, and a second later the glass is on the ground, the blood-red wine spilled over the carpeting. It's water resistant and pools to one side. I'm sure I can see the flecks of ground-up medication, but Gwyn just curses and reaches for a towel. "I felt like I had to. We were supposed to go on this fancy honeymoon that got canceled. She was my best friend. It was more fun than I thought it would be, but then she went missing..." Her voice trails off.

I'm again struck by the warmth with which she talks about her. Me. I can imagine Elena below, listening in—probably rolling her eyes. Thinking *good acting* again.

"Let me pour you some more wine." I stand, but Gwyn waves me off.

"Don't bother. I'm going to try one of the whites. This feels too heavy for early in the day."

I open my mouth to object—but she's an adult, and she wants a different kind of wine. I should have thought of this— should have opened one of each and added half the medicine to each one. Gwyn only took a sip or two of the red, which means she likely won't feel the effects at all. I glance around, as though I'll discover another way to disable her, but she's already across from me again, this time sipping a white with bubbles.

The Puget Sound goes by around us as I try to mentally adjust my plan—the swirling, dark waters, an occasional seal popping its head out. We cross close to land, but it's not inhabited—an island with a rocky edge, thick woods, a narrow beach piled high with driftwood. And after a while, we're far out in the water, not a thing in sight with all the fog.

I shiver; it reminds me of a horror movie more than an afternoon with friends.

Eventually, the boat slows, and Gwyn steps to the edge, peering through the window at the steering column overhead. "Oh, he's stopped. We usually find a good spot with a nice view and let the boat just float for a bit."

I look again, but with the fog, all I can see is water. We've been on the move for maybe forty-five minutes, at a conservative pace considering we can't quite see where we're going. I'd guess we're a handful of miles out—not far, but maybe far enough, especially for a day like today with such minimal visibility.

Benjamin ducks in the cabin, glass in hand, and melts into a seat. We all sit there a long moment, the boat rocking in the water.

"Refill?" Gwyn asks. She gets to her feet and takes a couple steps as though she's stretching her legs.

"I'm good." I fake a smile. Benjamin ducks inside and refills his own glass from the red bottle. He leans in, gives Gwyn a peck on the cheek, then finds a place on the nearest couch. I watch Benjamin as he splays out. Something's off about him, but I can't put my finger on what it is.

Gwyn peers out one window, then another, before coming to sit next to me.

"So, what do you think?" she asks.

I murmur something about how lovely it is. The moment is coming—the moment when they both will die. My stomach swims, thinking about it.

"Figured we could stop here for a few minutes," Benjamin says, breaking me from dark thoughts. "No one else out on the water today, not out here, anyway. Probably was a good morning for fishing back by the shore, though." Benjamin's eyes cut back the way we came. "Seals are bobbing around. Come outside, take a look."

He ducks out the door. Gwyn sighs, but a smile edges her face, and I try to parse out what her real feelings are—if she loves him, if she trusts him—but we pull on jackets and step out into a chilly, damp wind, the smell of the salty ocean thick in the air.

Benjamin stands at the back, hands pressed to the rails that line the entire edge. It's an open-air spot, only a cover over the top keeping the gentle fall of moisture from reaching him. Gwyn and I shuffle out, and Gwyn takes a seat on a chair to one side. She pats the spot beside her, and I fall into the cushioned seat. She's unaffected from the sips of wine she had, and Benjamin isn't showing symptoms of the drugs yet, but it shouldn't be long. If anything, the alcohol is masking the effect.

But then Benjamin turns—and the look on his face makes me tense. Makes me realize something is not right, and it doesn't have to do with the fact I want revenge and Elena is waiting below board to help with it. His eyes, usually alight with kindness, narrow. His forehead creases, and his hands clench.

"I want the truth," he grinds out.

"What?" Gwyn looks up, startled, confused. "Are you okay?"

He ignores her to glare at me. My heart palpitates in my chest, but I don't hesitate—I frown. "What do you mean?" Playing the part. Being Rebecca.

Benjamin looks at Gwyn now. "Something's up with you. And with her." He points at me.

Gwyn goes still—utterly still, in that way that says more than words can.

SIXTY-ONE
REBECCA

Now

"I think—" Benjamin stops short, turns in a swift circle, hands finding the railing again. He squeezes it until his hands turn white with the effort. "Gwyn, did you have something to do with what happened to Madeline?"

He can't even look at her as he says it. Can't imagine a world where his now-fiancée played a part in his then-fiancée's —*wife's*—death. My chest squeezes tight, and I glance at her for her reaction, but other than her eyes, a little wide, she has almost no expression.

I'm shocked by his actions. He couldn't have known what my plans were. But maybe he did and maybe he's trying to get ahead of it and pin it on Gwyn.

"Of course not." Gwyn's voice comes out in a gasp, and she shoots to her feet. "I loved Madeline."

"Then what the fuck is going on?" Benjamin rarely curses—even with the years between when he was Benji in my mind, and now, I'm startled at the harsh word on his lips. I stand, too, and take a half step back, my muscles tightening as though I'm going to go somewhere. But we're on a boat. There is no escape.

Besides, if anyone will be leaving this boat—it's him. And Gwyn. Permanently.

Of course, as much as I have them trapped on this boat, they have me trapped, too. My pulse picks up a notch, and I reach for the nearest surface to hold on to—to ground myself, more figuratively than literally.

Anger radiates off Benjamin as he looks back and forth between us.

Some tiny voice inside me wants to call out to him—*It's me, Benji*—but I squash it, because that little girl is dead, and the woman I am now doesn't like being spoken to like this.

"Gwyn has a friend who supports her," I find myself saying. "Who helps her when she suspects something's going on. Which she does." I force myself to advance on him. To press a finger toward his chest. "You have nowhere to speak on this topic."

Gwyn flashes surprised eyes at me. Benjamin's face twists in annoyance.

"We know you've been watching her," I say.

"You've been watching me?" Her voice goes shrill. "What is she talking about?"

A moment of silence, the two of them looking at one another, realizing, I think, that neither trusts the other. But it's too early to do this. Benjamin isn't weaving or unsteady on his feet in the slightest. Maybe the meds sank to the bottom of the wine bottle faster than I realized. Maybe he barely got any in his glass.

Maybe—

"Of course I've been watching you." Benjamin's voice drops an octave, cold, but calm in an eerie way that freezes me in my spot. "You practically threw yourself at me after she disappeared, when I could barely breathe I was so... so sad." He inhales. Exhales. His whole body rises and falls with the motion, and as his words stop, I can see how defeated he is. That urge to rush forward and wrap my arms around him, to cry out, "Benji, it's me," hits hard again.

And again, I tamp it back down. Guilty people deny their guilt. Make up stories. Find excuses.

"And it took me until I put a ring on your finger to realize it. I *do* care about you. But Jesus Christ, Gwyn"—he waves a hand at me—"then you have her following me when I just need some breathing space. Some time to process what's happening. When I think my wife's body has been found, when I think finally, after all this, we'll have answers. That maybe, we can put a body beneath her gravestone. It's like you don't trust me."

Gwyn opens her mouth, but he holds up a hand. "And I found the camera. The journal. Where did you get them? Did you—" He tilts his head, eyes wide as he gazes at her. Confusion flushes his face. "Where did you get them, Gwyn?"

A hard knot forms in my chest as a different tale unweaves itself. Is it possible Gwyn is behind all of this? She *had* invited Kip to the wedding. She had wanted something as perfect as Benjamin and Madeline had. And the camera and the journal—how else could she have gotten them?

Maybe Benjamin is innocent? I've had so many reasons to suspect him, reasons to hate him, but... is that clouding my judgment? Is it not him, and I've been trying to will it to be him? My heart about drops through my chest to my stomach, wrangling with the possibility and what it could mean.

"I don't know what you're talking about," Gwyn says.

Instant denial.

Instant guilt.

She holds up her hands. "I thought those things went missing. They said—they said she probably had them when she fell, I thought?" She looks at Benjamin. At me. "I don't have them."

"Then why were they in your office? Don't lie to me. I

found them there, months ago, hidden away in the closet." He stares at her with a penetrating gaze. "You moved in and suddenly, Maddy's missing things appear. What was I supposed to think?" His throat moves, his face gone blotchy, like he might cry. "I've had to wonder this whole time if you hurt her. So *why* were they in your office, Gwyn?"

The wind whips around us, frigid and penetrating. I put my back to the cabin of the boat and clutch my jacket tighter as we wait for Gwyn's answer. I want to know the same thing.

"They're not in my office. Where would I put them in my office? How would I even get them to put in my office?" She sputters as she talks, livid.

They stare at each other, Gwyn's arms crossed tightly over her chest, Benjamin's whole body heaving with angry breaths. I want to melt away—to let them destroy one another first. A malicious joy spreads through me, alien in the way it twists and writhes in my body—guilt chases after it.

I love these people.

Loved. Past tense.

They hurt me.

Past *and* present tense.

"And of course I had her follow you! You're acting strange. Changing the password on your phone, taking calls at all hours. Meeting with women in the woods. Is it your ex? Are you cheating on me?"

"What?" he snaps. "How could you even think that?"

A hand brushes my shoulder. I jump.

"Don't you think it's time?" Elena's voice floats to my ear, soothing.

Benjamin looks over and does a double take. "What the fuck are you doing here?"

SIXTY-TWO

REBECCA

Now

Elena steps out. In her hand, she holds a syringe—three syringes, actually. Two for Benjamin—he's tall and easily has seventy or eighty pounds on Gwyn and me—and one for Gwyn. She brought them for backup in case the drugs hadn't taken hold to make it easier to get them overboard. To leave them in the middle of the Puget Sound, which if my calculations are correct, is about eight miles wide where we are right now. Sure, a few boats pass through, but with the fog, it's unlikely anyone will see them in time. And it will dampen their calls for help. With the meds, it won't take long.

I draw a shuddering breath, trying to hold my courage intact.

"You're never happy to see me anymore," Elena murmurs. She raises one brow in a classic Elena look. "I told you, Maddy, I never really liked him. And to think, this all could have been avoided."

Shock bolts through me, hot and quick. *Maddy.* I hadn't

planned on her using my old name. I open my mouth to correct her.

"Maddy?" Benjamin's teeth clench in anger, cutting me off. "Maddy is dead. Leave it alone. You and I are no longer family. Why won't you stop calling? And how did you get on my boat?" His eyes flick to Gwyn. "Did you have something to do with this? Are you all in on this together?"

Gwyn stares at me now. She reaches out one hand and grabs my arm. Forces me to turn and face her. I yank away, putting distance between us as much as I can in the small space. But Benjamin's words echo in my mind—*why won't you stop calling?*

"Shit," Gwyn says after a beat. "You're wearing contacts. I can see them." She reaches for me again, and I shake her off.

"Of course, I am. It's that or glasses." I step closer to Elena.

"But you—" Gwyn cocks her head to the side. "You're not her. Not Maddy, but you—" Her gaze flicks to Elena, then back to my face, my body. "But you look like her a little. Like a—cousin, maybe or..."

Benjamin stares, too. "Stop trying to deflect, Gwyn. Did you invite Elena here? I told you I don't want her to be a part of our lives anymore."

Gwyn lets out a slow breath. "What the hell is going on?" She reaches for the seat behind her and lowers her body slowly to sit. "Benjamin, you start."

Benjamin spares her a glance, but his attention is solely on me. Then Elena. Suspicion is in his gaze, but he can't figure it out—his furrowed brow tells me that much.

"Who do you think did it?" Elena asks me. "Or is it fifty-fifty, like we thought? I suppose we have to kill them both, either way. Can't leave a witness." Her voice crawls through me, a kind of creepy I hadn't realized she was capable of. I find myself pulling away from her, too. But maybe it's good. Maybe that's what it takes to go through with killing someone.

Benjamin booms a laugh. "Kill us? Are you kidding me?" The amusement fades from his face when Elena doesn't so much as twitch an eyebrow.

"No, Benjamin, I'm not. You and Gwyn are responsible for Madeline's death."

A moment of silence.

"But—" Gwyn pipes up, reaching for me again.

Benjamin interrupts. "You're as suspicious as anyone, Elena. Why do you think I let you stay close at first? Why on earth would *anyone* stay in touch with someone like you?" Benjamin's words are hard, angry. I'm not sure what he means. In the time he and I were together, they got along fine enough. They even danced at the wedding.

Elena juts her bottom lip out in mock hurt. "You seemed just fine staying in touch with me for the first six months you and Madeline were together. Until right about the time... ah, yes. Until you asked her to marry you. Which was, in fact, part of the plan, so I don't see what the problem was."

"Huh?" I look up, but Elena's still talking to Benjamin. I try to connect the dots, to make sense of their words, but it *doesn't* make sense.

"In fact, if you'd followed the plan, it would have never come to this. You'd be scot-free, with your fucking dream and all the money you'd ever need. You'd have never heard from me again."

The plan? My heart jumbles around in my chest. Gwyn grabs at me again, and I let her, too caught up in my own head to pull away.

"No one would have had to die," Elena continues. "We both would have had what we wanted."

"What is she talking about, Benjamin?" Gwyn's voice drops to a whisper.

Gwyn squeezes my wrist hard. When I look down, I meet her eyes, and I know she knows, or at least suspects, that I used to be Madeline. And all she does is hold my hand, staring at me with wide, unbelieving eyes. My stomach twists, reliving the kind words she's said over the last several days about Madeline, her former best friend—and I form a conclusion.

"Nothing." Benjamin shoves his way past Elena, toward the second steering column inside the cabin, and she takes that moment to plunge the needle into the big muscle in his upper arm. "What the—" he snaps. The effect isn't instantaneous, but his balance starts to go—he reaches for the nearest chair and eases himself into it, his legs no longer holding him.

"Elena?" I say. "What is that?" Another syringe is in her hand, the tip gleaming with a single drop of clear fluid.

She spares a glance my way. "Don't worry. It won't kill him." She turns back to Benjamin. "Actually, tell you what, Benjamin. Since you fucked this up, I'll give you a chance to fix it. You toss yourself overboard, so I don't have to do any heavy lifting, and I'll let one of them live."

Let one *of them live.* She means me or Gwyn.

I can't tell if she's messing with him. Gwyn clutches my hand tighter. Elena turns and points at us. There is nothing kind left in her gaze. Nothing sisterly when her eyes trace over me.

Everything is happening so fast I'm having a hard time keeping up. She was calling Benjamin. She's been lying. But why?

"Who would you like to live? Your first wife? Or your"—she waves a hand—"fiancée?"

I swallow, feeling my palms go damp, examining Elena, waiting for her to share a wink with me—to signal this is just a ploy to get him to talk, that we're still in on this together.

"What the fuck are you—" He presses a hand to his face, wipes his mouth, blinks, tries to focus.

"She's Madeline, you idiot."

"Maddy?" Benjamin's woozy from whatever Elena injected,

but this seems to pull him back to the moment. His eyes go wide, desperate, staring at me like he's never seen me before. He studies my face, my body, his jaw slowly dropping. "You're—" A strangled sound comes from his throat, and he tries again. "You're... you're alive. Is it really you? It can't be you, but is it—"

The hope in his eyes drives a knife right into my heart. The same hope as when he asked me to go to Europe with him. When in this very spot, he tricked me into taking our engagement photo. Suddenly, I don't want him to die. I can't imagine a world where he's not living, even if I'm not Maddy anymore, even if I'll never *be* her again.

He tries to sit up straight, grabbing at the dining table, trying to focus on me, but can't. His voice rises a notch. "Maddy? Is it—is it really you? Gwyn, is it her?"

Elena laughs. "Everyone is obsessed with you, Madeline. Just like it always was. Our father, your friends, your social media followers, the society pages..." Her voice trails off. The two syringes rest in her hand, and now I know who the third one is for.

"You," he says to Elena. "You're the one who tried to kill her."

My gaze flies to Elena. I find her watching me. And now, she does wink—but it's not a nice, sisterly wink. It's a *got you* wink.

SIXTY-THREE

REBECCA

Now

"You're my sister." I say the words, but my body has already gone cold, numb, realizing I was wrong. So wrong. In fact, I've been wrong this whole time. These past three years, exploring first my friends, then zoning in on Gwyn and Benjamin.

"Half-sister." Elena steps closer.

I blink and take a step back. Gwyn grabs at me, tries to yank me behind her, but there's nowhere to go.

"You—" I look left and right, get my bearings. The sky is still dark, gray, and a fine mist comes from the sky, leaving everything damp and slick. We're at the back of the boat, but I see one way away from her—up a tiny set of steep stairs that will take me to the top deck, where the outdoor steering column sits, where an inflatable boat for exploring the shore is tied down.

But to go up there leaves Gwyn and Benjamin—*my best friend, my husband*—alone with Elena.

It still doesn't make sense. I can't quite wrap my head around it—the sister who both loved and irritated me. Who tried to fill the role of mother. Who could tell when something was wrong. And now, I can only think one thing.

Elena tried to kill me.

"You weren't even on the backpacking trip," I say. "You said you had to work."

"Of course, I wasn't." I edge up the stairs as she approaches. "I went home, so when you disappeared I could tell everyone I hadn't even been there. Of course I couldn't have played a part."

My guts twist at her words.

"Then how—"

"It was easy," she said. "Do you think it was a coincidence Kip became your friend? Encouraged you to question your relationship with Benji? Suggested you go backpacking to a cliffside campground for your honeymoon?"

Kip.

Kip, who'd been Elena's resident.

"All Kip cared about was a good review of his residency. Keeping his job so he could help his mom. Getting the fellowship he wanted. He did exactly what I told him to do."

"He's the one who pushed me?" I ask, heart beating faster and faster—betrayed again. The one person who helped me. Who never had his own agenda.

"Oh, no. Not Kip. I knew better than to try to get him to make the killing blow. Besides, I really felt it was better I did that."

I blink, trying to understand.

"He was helping you?" I mumble.

"That's why everyone thought you were having an affair with him." Gwyn says. "Is that why he kept coming around?"

"Just tell them," Benjamin bites out at Elena. "Tell them what we did. Or I will." His hand clutches over his arm, and he tries to stand, but his legs collapse out from under him. I have no idea what she's given him; I search my memory of sedatives used in the office, something I was responsible for cataloging in the months I worked for Elena.

"Tell them what? Everything?" Elena's brows raise. "Well, no one on this boat will live to tell anyone, so I might as well." She lowers the syringe and takes the two steps to Benjamin. Her arm goes around his shoulders, and she yanks him close.

"Sweetheart, if only you'd done as told." Elena looks at me. "Benjamin is the man I dated in college. The one who helped me decide that I was far better without a man in my life. He spent a year convincing me to date him, just like he slowly sucked you in. We came up with a business plan together. Imagined a whole life together. And then? He took the business plan and left me high and dry. He magically got investors he swore he didn't have. Money he pretended didn't exist. He opened *our* winery. I was left with nothing. But you? He wanted to marry you. He *fell in love*"—she uses air quotes—"with you."

"That's not—"

"Quiet, Benjamin. It's what happened."

My throat goes dry. "He's your ex?" The time Benjamin got a call from her at the winery comes back to me. He must have talked to Elena the whole time—the whole time we were together, Benjamin was in contact with his ex. Who was *Elena*. But, how? How was it possible Elena and Benjamin were in on this together?

"She's your ex?" Gwyn repeats after me.

He never stopped communicating with Elena—he's been doing it this whole time. She's the ex Gwyn worried about, too. "Is that why you kept meeting in the woods?" I ask.

"It's not like that," Benjamin says. "That's not—I never cheated. On either of you."

"There's more than one way to betray someone," Elena says. "Why don't you tell Madeline about that?" I look at him, but he presses his lips together, shakes his head, looks away, but then looks back at me, trying to see Madeline in me, I think. My body vibrates with the tension in the air. The desire to climb to the top of the boat, to see if the radio there works, to call for help—the fear that if I do, Elena will toss them into the Puget Sound, that they will drown. That she'll follow me, that I'll be next.

But I also want to know what she's talking about. What happened behind the scenes that I never knew about. The answer to the question I've been asking for more than three years. And behind all that is the knowledge my own half-sister... the one just last night I was so glad to have on my side—I take a deep breath, the memory of a hand on my back shoving me over the cliff—it was Elena's hand. Not Benjamin's hand... though it's becoming more and more clear that doesn't make him innocent. Not Gwyn's hand. Though she was a shitty friend, too.

"Fine. You're a coward, Benjamin. I'll tell her." Elena looks at me. "The reason we went to that bar for your twenty-third birthday was for you to meet Benjamin. *Benji*. You didn't charm him with your looks or your attitude. He wasn't *attracted* to you. He owed me money he claimed he didn't have. He also needed money for the winery. Your mother left you more money than you knew what to do with, so I suggested he take it from you."

The realization slams into me—they were plotting behind my back the whole time I was with him. Every time I told someone how Madeline Hughes had found true love, it was bullshit—he didn't love me. He used me.

My face burns, and I'm not sure if it's from the wind lashing at my skin, or the betrayal. The reliving of those moments I'd considered so special—knowing now they were all an act. Our fairy-tale meet-cute, that first date where we talked and talked. The next time, when he took me out on the boat—this boat—to charm me. The whirlwind trip to Europe. A lie. But how is that possible? How is it possible that every moment we shared was arranged for, and not spontaneous like it felt in the moment?

"You didn't like him, though," I say, grasping at anything to prove her wrong.

"Of course I didn't. You were going to love anyone I disapproved of."

"And then—" I blink, thinking through Elena's evolution of emotions regarding Benjamin. "What changed, then? You acted like you didn't like him, but then you did. And that day at the office you told me I didn't have to marry him. But if I hadn't married him, he wouldn't have gotten my money." It doesn't make sense. Unless she realized he was really in love, and by that time, *wanted* the relationship to end.

"I loved you," Benjamin says. Even with his wilted form, those words come out strong. "*Love* you. Yes, I met you that day on purpose. And yes, the plan was to marry you, to leave you, to take half of what was yours. Elena said you wouldn't want a prenup. She was going to get a cut. But then everything changed for me, and I told her no. Because I really fell in love with you. That's when she started threatening me. Following me. And I guess trying to get you to not marry me."

The words settle.

The past reconfigures itself in my head.

Benjamin. *Benji.* He was Elena's mysterious ex we never met while she chose to not be a part of our family.

"You tried to kill me for the money." I look at Elena.

She smiles sweetly. It looks ugly on her perfect face.

"Partially. With you dead, he'd get the money. Then there was no excuse. And..." Her shoulders rise and fall in a shrug. "I got tired of you getting everything you wanted. You were Daddy's favorite. Your mother left you enough money to live well on, while Daddy wouldn't even give my mother his name. Wouldn't give *me* his name. And then you were going to get the man, too? *My* man?"

"I was never yours," Benjamin bites out. "And I never owed you anything. We broke up. You went to medical school. I opened a business. And then—" He waves a hand. "You wouldn't stop harassing me."

"You used our idea. Our business plan." Elena redirects her attention to me. "And you were just the annoying little sister who had it too easy." She adjusts the plunger to one syringe and slides a gaze in Gwyn's direction.

"It's better this way," Elena murmurs. "You'll still be dead, and I'll still have everything that would have been yours when Daddy died. The business that should have been half mine will go up for sale—not like Aaron is going to want it. Plus the satisfaction that for once, you didn't win."

"Run, Maddy." The words are muted, slurred, as Benjamin mumbles them. But we're on a boat. There is no escape.

"You tried to kill me," I say.

Elena smiles. "You know what they say. If at first you don't succeed, try, try again."

And she lunges.

SIXTY-FOUR

REBECCA

Now

I sidestep her, a move I couldn't have done once upon a time. But I'm fit now—fast. Stronger, too, and I grab the railing, climb the stairs in seconds. She's right behind me, a shadow at my back. My hand slips on the damp rail, but my other hand grabs tighter, and I'm on top of the cabin now. A window lets me see inside, and I catch a glimpse of Benjamin, slumped on the ground. Elena either gave him more drugs, or he fell from his chair. He doesn't move.

I skip up a second set of stairs, heart pounding, head spinning at the revelations. It puts me in the upper steering column, but the fog is dense, claustrophobic, and I can't see anything. My gaze lands on the controls. Once upon a time, I knew how to drive this boat. I grab at the corded black radio, press the button on the side, but come up short—I'm thinking like Madeline. Madeline, who would have called for help.

But there is no help. Even if I could call them—which I can't—they'd never make it in time.

I came here as Rebecca to kill two people.

And instead, Elena is trying to kill all three of us.

Not to mention—I don't exist. Not really, not anymore. And I'm not sure I want to change that. Footsteps behind me, the metallic clang of Elena smacking into the steel rail, also slipping as she rushes after me. I twist—she's there, the half-sister I always felt guilty for not fully embracing. Not that she made it easy.

In that moment I wonder what I could have done differently. If Elena and I had found a way to grow close, perhaps I would be married to Benjamin, living in our house. Maybe I would be pregnant with our child. Would I have never met him, because Elena would have never hatched the plan to begin with?

"Don't do this, Elena." I back up against the steering column. She paces slowly past the seating up top—blue cushions where she sat beside me once upon a time, drinking margaritas and enjoying a sunny day on the Puget Sound.

Everything is colder today. The weather. The water. My sister.

"It won't hurt, Maddy. I know you don't like pain. I'm impressed, actually." She holds the syringe in one hand and gazes at me with cold blue eyes. She beckons at my face. "Impressed you survived. That you somehow convinced someone to do all that. You were prettier before, you know. But this isn't too bad. I could have done it better. I guess it says a lot that you went to someone besides your sister for help. That maybe you didn't consider me family in the first place. Makes this easier on me."

"I didn't go to you because someone wanted me dead. I didn't want you to get hurt by association."

"But you went to Daddy, didn't you? How else could you have gotten help?"

The truth sits between us a long moment. "Did you kill him?" I ask.

Elena lets out a halting laugh. "No, I didn't. But thanks for thinking so much of me."

"With all of us dead, you're guaranteed the money," I say.

"It wasn't just about the money. It was about Benjamin. About you. Your bullshit. You always came out on top. Daddy married *your* mother. She left you a ton of money. And all you ever did was look pretty. You never did a real day of work in your life. Just took pretty pictures of your smiling face for your adoring fans." She flutters her eyelashes, rolls her eyes. She adjusts her grip on the syringe, and I see the moment she decides to lunge. I dart to the side, stepping up and over the rail of the captain's deck. I maneuver over, and her hand grabs mine. I dangle, and she aims for my arm, like she's got a knife instead of a five-milliliter syringe full of god knows what. I let go with my opposite hand, and she can't hold all of my body weight. She lets go, and I drop to the deck below, nearly sliding off the edge and into the Puget Sound.

My feet find purchase along the edge of the boat, and I tiptoe around to the back. She'll be here in seconds. Gwyn watches us with eyes as round as saucers.

"Maddy—"

"Get in here," I snap, stepping over Benjamin's unconscious form to the interior. I slam the door shut, lock it. I do the same with the windows, cracked open, then secure the side door, closer to the bow, locking us in—locking Elena out. Gwyn presses palms against the nearest window, searching for Elena, I assume.

"I can't believe this is happening," she manages. "I can't believe you're—you're you."

Benjamin stirs. "Maddy?"

"Quiet, both of you." We're about to be offed by Elena of all people, and they're still going on about how I'm me.

A thump from overhead. Gwyn and I both spin in jerky circles, searching for wherever Elena's gone. We're trapped in here, like a glass cage, and the moment we try to escape, she'll have us. The syringes. God, what if she has a gun or a knife? My gaze drops to the cabinets and storage of the boat, trying to think if there's anything we can use as a weapon.

A slam against the back door draws my attention. Elena, her fists against the glass. Stuck outside, locked out of the cabin. Her gaze is full of venom—I can see now what I somehow never noticed before. She hates me. Absolutely abhors my existence.

Every time I can remember she treated me with kindness, she was only moving her own plot forward—to drive me to marry Benjamin. So he could divorce me. I wasn't even sure that's how divorces work in Washington—Daddy had never given over any more than he'd wanted to any of his wives, though maybe that was due to prenups.

"God, I've always hated her," Gwyn mutters.

I look back toward the inside controls at the front of the boat. I can figure it out. I look at them—Benjamin, Gwyn. The husband, the best friend. Guilty of plenty.

But not of trying to kill me.

SIXTY-FIVE

REBECCA

Now

Elena doesn't stay at the back for long. She scales the side of the boat, moving along the windows until we're a few feet apart, only the glass separating us. I wish more than anything I'd gotten that syringe away from her. That I'd somehow gotten *her* to consume part of the bottle of wine. Anything to make this easier.

"What do we do? Maybe I can break a wine bottle and we can use the glass as—" Gwyn does a stabby motion with her hand. "Like as a weapon."

"Let me in, Maddy," Elena calls. "You can't stay in there forever." When I flip her off, she cackles. "Gwyn? Oh Gwyn? I know you don't really like her. Let me in. I'll let you live."

I heave a breath and try to think. Gwyn starts to speak again, but I wave her off. Focus on Benjamin on the ground, on the crazed woman outside the cabin who's staring at us with gleaming eyes. The boat rocks gently in the dark waters of the Puget Sound. The fog has settled thick around us.

I go to the steering column. I wouldn't know which way to

go if it weren't for the navigation system, but as it is, I punch in buttons and spend a few minutes figuring it out. We're in one of the deepest sections of the Puget Sound. One of the widest areas, too, almost nine miles from one piece of land to another, and we're a full three miles from the closest shore.

Far enough away there's no chance she'll survive the swim.

"Can you drive this?" Gwyn whispers. I startle, and she's right at my shoulder. "Sorry."

"Do you know how to?" I ask.

"No. I haven't been on it since—" She motions at me. "Three plus years. Since I was out with—you."

I nod. Try not to catch the emotion in her gaze. I have to pay attention to what I'm doing, or I'm likely to kill us all hitting the rocky outcrop of an island, or hell, another boat.

Not to mention, what I'm about to do. I take another look back, at Elena, who's still watching us from just outside the cabin. One hand presses to the latch, trying to open it, but the lock holds. Elena starts to edge around the side of the boat, clinging to the rail precariously as she moves toward us. I reach out, make sure the nearest window is still secured. I watch her.

My breath catches in my throat, but I know I won't hesitate. This is the only way to survive. I wait until after she gets close to the side door, putting us face to face. Behind me, Benjamin is still in and out of consciousness—offering input like "Fuck" and "Where are we?" and "Is it really you?" from time to time. Gwyn goes to kneel beside him, keeping a nervous eye on Elena.

"Why don't you call for help?" she asks.

I ignore her.

Ignore Benjamin's murmuring, too. There will be a time to deal with the man I loved, and now is not it, as much as I want to yell at him—rage at him. Call him an asshole for what he's done. For destroying what we could have had.

"What do you want?" I call the words through the closed

window to Elena. The wind has picked up, and the water is taking on a certain choppiness that leaves the boat in that constant motion that leads to seasickness.

"I want to talk. You clearly don't want to die. And I can understand that. I don't actually need you dead, anyway. You don't want to be Madeline anymore, do you?" Her gaze shifts beyond me, to where Benjamin and Gwyn are in the cabin. "Help me toss them overboard. You go on being Rebecca. Leave town. Find another assignment somewhere else. I'll even give you some money to get you started."

It's not a bad deal.

But she's forgetting one thing.

I came here to avenge Madeline. To kill her killer.

This boat is not fast. It's designed for pleasure, for rambling through the Sound at an easy pace, spending the night anchored offshore. People live in boats like this one. It's not speedy, but it's not slow, either.

"Meet me at the back." I point back toward the door she pounded on seconds ago. She'll have to shimmy along the edge of the boat again to do it. And the moment she begins heading back, I press the button labeled *Start*. Touch my fingers over the joystick that controls forward thrust. All around me, the vibration of the engine starts up, grumbling, preparing itself.

"What are you doing?" Gwyn asks, still on her knees beside Benjamin.

I glance back at Elena, now behind me—she stops. Looks at me through the window, realization dawning over her face, followed by panic.

"Bye, Elena," I mouth. And I punch the boat forward, twisting the wheel hard. I don't stop to check, because I can hear the splash of her body hitting the water. It's sickening in a way, but no more so than shoving your own sister over a cliff to her death. I want to navigate back to the marina. I want to dock the boat and leave the past behind me, Gwyn and Benjamin included.

But I'm living proof that sometimes things don't go as planned. Sometimes people don't die.

So I let the boat slow, turn it ever so slightly, until I can see her form bobbing in the distance, her arms chopping in the water, panicked. The water is icy cold—too cold for her to survive long. She'd told me herself, a person might last a couple hours at the longest. I check the time—11:47 a.m.

Gwyn gazes at me with shock all over her face, but she doesn't say a word—doesn't so much as suggest we pull Elena out of the water. If anything, she looks afraid, which works just fine for me. I ignore her, ignore Benjamin, stepping around them to the fridge and retrieving the last wine bottle. First, I check to make sure it's unopened, because apparently no one can be trusted—the cork and foil wrap are still intact—and then I open it. Pour. And step back outside, into the cold, to watch Elena.

"Maddy!" Her voice echoes through the mist, but Madeline is dead.

I take a seat. Cross my legs. And wait for her to die.

SIXTY-SIX
REBECCA

Now

Benjamin wakes with a start—I've drained my glass twice, but I'm not sure if the fuzzy warmth filling me is the alcohol or the knowledge I've finally put the past to rest. One more glass, and I might not mind so much it was my own sister who tried to kill me.

Gwyn tries to mother him, grasping at his arm, but he shakes her off. "Where is she? Where is Elena?" He half staggers out the door.

I don't turn. I don't look him in the eye. He knows who I am. Who I once was. And facing him is too much like facing the man I used to love. If I look at him, I'll think about how I was wrong this whole time. How he never stopped caring about me, about Madeline, how he tried to find out what happened.

How really, nothing changed between us.

Except, everything changed. I'm not her anymore. I will never be her again.

I exhale what feels like a mountain of grief, setting it out across the water in the Puget Sound for it to sink to the bottom and disappear. No matter what feelings I once had, I can't have them anymore.

"There." I point to where minutes ago she dipped beneath the water and didn't rise. At first, she fought—tried to swim. First toward the boat, then away. But the cold got to her and soon she was just trying to stay afloat. Calling to me every now and then. Gwyn even came out, using a soft voice, saying, "Maddy, we need to get her out. She'll die. You don't want to kill your sister."

I hadn't answered the latter. To the former I'd merely said, "My name is not Maddy."

I stare out at the water. Elena will stay underwater for at least three days before decomposition builds up enough gas to make the body surface. But no one would have known why she was out here—no friends, no family. I think of Kip, of his betrayal. Relive every moment he wanted to hang out, or the fact he signed my marriage license, or—

"She's gone?" Benjamin asks, interrupting my spiral.

"She's dead," I say. "I watched her go hypothermic and go under. I'm waiting a few more minutes, and then we can leave."

"We could... pull her out, still," he murmurs. "I read an article. People who drown in cold water have a better chance of survival. The cold water keeps oxygen—"

"No."

"Madeline, we're not killers." He sits heavily beside me—too close—and I edge away.

"Don't call me that." I pour more wine, then hand him the bottle. He stares at it a long moment, then takes a sip. "We're not saving her," I continue. "You get in the water, I leave you, too."

Benjamin absorbs what I say, seemingly at a loss for words. His mouth opens, closes, and he finally settles on, "I'm sorry. I was an idiot. I didn't know what to do, though, and I didn't want to lose you. She wouldn't stop harassing me for money.

Following me everywhere. She was pissed when I broke things off, but what I told you about the constant paranoia and jealousy—that was all true. I should have known better. That... that making you fall in love with me wouldn't work. That she would lose it." He drinks more wine. Spares a glance back at Gwyn, who's in the boat, out of earshot.

"I never lied to you, though. When I told you I loved you that first time, I meant it. It was almost like without meaning to, Elena set us up... *for real.* And after the first few months, after Europe, actually, I realized I couldn't go through with it. I realized I really did want to marry you, and that I wouldn't want to ask for a divorce. So I told her. She started showing up at odd places. Following me. Calling me." He sighs. "I should have just told you. But how could I? You would have hated me. And then you died. And..." A beat of silence.

"I never seriously considered she had a part in that. I couldn't see how Elena could have pulled it off. Sure, she was jealous of you, but she was your sister—I figured she still loved you. Besides, they said you fell. Your stuff was missing. We assumed you had it with you. You were always carrying the camera around. Always had the journal nearby."

He casts a look back at Gwyn and asks softly, "You think Gwyn was helping Elena?"

"No," I say. I think about Gwyn asking me for help, asking me to spy on Benjamin. "I think Gwyn suspected you of something—cheating on her. Maybe of killing me. And I think Elena wanted it to look like she was in on it."

Benjamin rubs his jaw. "I thought she was. At least, I started to wonder. Elena came over a couple times. She could have planted the camera then."

I consider Gwyn's lies—stringing me along so I'd consider helping her spy on Benjamin. No doubt she suspected him of something, and I tell him as much.

Benjamin nods. "I think we both wanted to find out what

happened to you. The police said a body would wash up after six months or a year. And then it never happened." I can feel his eyes on me, but I keep my gaze trained to the cold, inky water where Elena submerged. "I think we both suspected each other. Were trying to catch each other as your killer."

That's why Gwyn wanted me to follow Benjamin. That's why Benjamin was watching Gwyn. I almost laugh at how ludicrous it is—Gwyn and Benjamin were *engaged*, and both thought the other played a part in Madeline's death.

"That's why you were together?" I ask. "Because you both wanted to figure out what happened to me?" I snort. "Right."

A long, slow sigh. "No. That's not why we were together. At least, not at first. I mean—I don't know, Mad—fuck. What do I call you?" I don't answer, and after a moment he says, "I wanted to like her. I wanted to love her. I *did* love her, but not like I loved you. In a way, she was the best way to stay close to you." His voice breaks. "I loved you, Maddy. Fuck it. Get mad if you want. Our vows said until death do us part. You're not dead. That means you're still my wife."

His hand finds mine. I let him hold it because I know it's the last time he ever will. And some part of me wants, wishes, I *could* go back—I could be with him again. He's the only man I've ever loved. But he betrayed me—every moment we spent together was a *lie*—and I can't get past that.

"You both looked guilty as hell," I say. "I thought one of you did it. Maybe both of you. Getting engaged. Being together in our home." My words almost break at that. *Our home.* I can't think of it that way, though. "It seemed like you needed money for your business. And I found the emails." I turn now and look at him. "You let her flirt with you for months when we were together. When we were engaged. Were you having an affair, too?"

Benjamin opens his mouth, snaps it shut. Lowers his head all hangdog.

"I don't know what to say, Maddy. No, I never cheated on you. It was just... banter." He scowls. "Like you were with Kip."

I stare at him. "I was friends with Kip. I never flirted with him."

"Right."

I snort, shake my head. "What's your excuse for why you were meeting with Elena in the woods all this time?"

"She was demanding money again. She didn't need it. Just felt entitled to it, I guess. Hinting she could make it look like I'd killed you. She knew too much. I started to think she and Gwyn were in on it together. That's why Gwyn wanted the interior design job, why she pursued me the way she did. All the flirtatious emails. The fact Gwyn was jealous of you. It made sense they would team up since they both seemed to want something from me."

I exhale a long, slow breath, thinking back to the early days, when Maddy and Benjamin first met. "I just can't get over that all those moments—they were all bullshit." I let the anger show through now. "My red heels. Kicking you. I thought it was wild we went to Europe so soon. I thought it was..." I search for the right word. "Fate. I spent my whole life thinking I shouldn't get involved, but then I met you. Guess I was right. Love is a lie." I pause. "Is that how you got my number when I gave you the wrong one? From Elena?"

His silence tells me the answer is yes.

"It was all a setup." I yank my hand from his.

"It started that way, yeah." His voice is low, shame filled. "But like I said, I told Elena I was done. She just... she wouldn't let it go. How did you—" With his other hand, he reaches over, touches my chin. "You don't look like you."

"I was pushed over a cliff," I say. "There was a lot of damage. I asked them to make me look different. And I changed myself, too. I didn't want to be the skinny little twentysomething anymore. I wanted to feel strong. I wanted to be in shape.

I learned to move differently." I blink. "I got contacts. Dyed my hair, cut it. Got implants here and here." I touch my cheekbones, my jawline.

"I can see it now. But... just barely," he says. "And that makes me sad."

I look out over the water again. Elena is gone for good.

I stand and turn away. I turn to go to the steering column, but not before saying, "Well, I'm not Madeline anymore, and you're not my husband. So I don't care what you think."

SIXTY-SEVEN

REBECCA

Now

The boat slides easily into the slip. Benjamin calls something to me as I leave the cabin, but I don't stop. I take one last look at Gwyn, who's watching me warily.

In a different world, I might thank her—might stay in touch with her. After all, though she was not the best friend in many ways, and though she flirted with my husband, she never betrayed me, not really. She's the one person who never stopped trying to figure out what happened to me, even if that meant getting close to my potential killer. I won't forget that. But she doesn't have a place in my life anymore.

My phone rings before I can leave, and I look down to see the hospital's phone number. Probably, Riley. Maybe, the nurse manager. Ready to call me out on not being the real Rebecca. Maybe, to ask me to come in, where police will be lying in wait to ask me questions about what happened to her—how I came to take over her identity. I hit end and toss the phone in the nearest trash bin. I won't be needing Rebecca anymore.

I take a last look at the marina, at the Puget Sound. I move from the boat to the dock and jog up the pathway to the parking lot where my car waits. The streets are clear on a Saturday—the only traffic is on the highway, or near Pike Place, and I steer clear of both. Instead I direct myself toward a house I haven't entered in more than three years, just a block down from where Gwyn and Benjamin now live. Daddy's house. And it became Elena's when he died.

I pull on a hat, put my hair down, and I could almost be the likeness of my half-sister. The keypad code hasn't changed, and I dial it in as though I belong. Inside, I pack her bags. I find the emergency cash in the same place she kept it in her apartment—tucked inside a sock in her drawer. I roam the hallways, putting to rest the ghosts of Madeline. Saying goodbye to my father. Taking a photo of my mother from my old bedroom, a dust-filled space I suspect no one has entered since I last left. When I leave here, I won't return. Madeline won't return. Elena certainly won't, either.

I take other things, too—Elena's credit cards, her birth certificate and Social Security card, locked in Daddy's safe. I take a copy of her medical license. I pack these things into my car and stay until dark, then I pull on running shoes and go for one last run. This time, I don't go by Benjamin and Gwyn's. They are in the past, and their business no longer concerns me.

It's only the alley behind Chris's house I'm looking for. And when I get there, I don't watch from afar—I open that side gate, like I've dreamed about doing more than once. It creaks, alerting both Chris and his dog to my entry, and they turn to look at me. Izzy rushes me, all energetic yips and licking, and within seconds, a tennis ball is in my hand.

Chris stands on the other side of the yard, watching me, almost like he expected me. His lips curve up in a faint smile. I considered avoiding him. Not coming back here. But he helped make me into Rebecca, and never breathed a word of it to Elena, who was shocked when she realized I was alive. And then the other night he chased me down the alley—I'll bet he knew who he was chasing. I just need to know why he did what he did—and then after that, helped me.

"Madeline," he says.

"Kip," I reply, and even if I'm grateful to him, even if I owe him, I can't keep the ice out of my voice.

"I never meant to betray you." His words come out fast, sharp. "I didn't know what she was going to do. And my career as a doctor was on the line, I just—I thought she was jealous. That's why I tried to stop you that night. To tell you everything."

I wait a beat, staring at him, confronting this last person in my life who led to Madeline's death.

"I didn't put it together until I saw you with her a couple nights ago," he continues. He searches my gaze, looks me up and down, putting together the pieces of how I look now. He last saw me after the accident—before my face was operated on. Before the implants. Before I became Rebecca. Although, that's not totally true, either. He's seen me since, watching him.

"You saw us?" I ask.

"I was following you," he says. "Please believe me. If I'd known before, I would have warned you. Once I figured it out, I tried to warn you."

I find a place to sit on the porch. When his dog comes up to me again, I pet her absently, turning his words over in my head.

Kip finds a spot beside me. "She made me suggest Benjamin might be cheating on you. Made me suggest the Wonderland Trail for your honeymoon. But I had no idea... I mean, I kind of thought Benji wasn't good enough for you, so it didn't bother me to suggest he was cheating on you. Hell, I thought he might be." Kip pauses, eyes lowered. "And I thought Elena just wanted you to have a miserable honeymoon in the forest. You're not much of an outdoors person. But I thought you'd like it once you got out there."

He blows out a breath. "She threatened to get me kicked out of the program. Med school, two years of residency, they would have been for nothing. My student visa would have been revoked. I would have had to go back to my mother having wasted six years of my life and penniless. Hell, in debt. I wouldn't have been able to take care of myself, much less help her." He takes a long draw off his beer.

"Elena also said if I helped her, she could guarantee me the fellowship I wanted after graduation." He swallows, as if embarrassed on this last point. "Anyway, I'm sorry, I really am. I didn't see any harm in what she asked. And she didn't go on the trip, so I never imagined she could have played a role in your death. But... I mean..."

I stare at the man I've watched for the last couple months. He started as an unexpected friend and ally. He ended up helping me become Rebecca. Saving me, in a way. Part of me wants to tell him to go to hell, too—he lied to me. But after I crawled up the cliffside and got myself out of the wilderness, then found him in his shitty apartment in the days after my disappearance, he didn't ask questions. He believed me when I told him someone tried to kill me—believed I was in danger and had no one else to turn to. He just got me help, connecting me to surgeons in Mexico who could help me without all the red tape of the American medical system. And he never shared that with Elena. Never told her I was alive, or back. And now, I can't help but think he's known I've been back in Seattle for a while now. And apparently, he would have told me if only I'd stopped and listened.

He blinks at me, waiting for me to respond. "They did a good job with your face. You look—not like you."

"I know." I breathe out through the emotion—a swirl of relief he never meant for it to happen the way it did, and that sitting here beside him feels as easy as it always has—and accept the beer he offers.

"I believe you," I say. "And thank you. For everything. How did you know something was happening?"

"I've seen you watching me, but I didn't realize who you were at first. Then I saw you in the hospital, working as a nurse. I asked who you were, and they said a travel nurse, and—somewhere in there I started to suspect. Then I saw you with Elena. That confirmed who you were." He breathes out in a sigh. "I tried to warn you the other day. Tried to tell you what she'd wanted me to do. I didn't know..." He gives me wide eyes. "Was it her? Is she the one who tried to kill you?"

I nod.

"What happened?" he asks.

"She's gone." I sip the beer, and don't give him details, because no one needs to know any more than they already do. Neither of us speaks for several minutes. The energy between us settles, becomes companionable again. We watch the dog run in circles. I try to imagine a future where this could be a part of my life. But it's not my life. Kip has never been more than a friend, nor will he ever be. But at least, after all of this, I have a friend. Someone who helped me. Someone who tried to warn me.

I try to decide how I feel about him doing Elena's bidding—but suggesting a honeymoon in the forest is a lot different than creating a whole relationship like Benji had—setting me up to fall in love, with the plan to leave me and take half of what was mine. Benjamin had acted out of selfishness—the desire for money. Kip had acted out of self-preservation, and to protect his career, his mother.

I wasn't happy about either of them, but his, at least, I could understand.

"How can I make it up to you?" he asks.

I exhale, lean closer to the fire to warm myself, think about it.

"I think I need to start over again," I finally say.

"Okay. How can I help? I'll do anything."

"Last time I became Rebecca. A dead girl. A nurse."

"You were good at it," he says with a smile. "I would've never guessed you hadn't had formal training."

"I think..." I dig in my pocket. Hold out the driver's license I took from my father's house. "I think I could be her. Take off. Start over."

Kip goes still. "Another dead girl?" he asks.

I nod.

He clears his throat, takes a long sip, grabs the ball from his dog, and throws it. We watch as it bounces off the fence line and his dog catches it midair.

"Think I could pass?" I ask.

A half laugh. "Definitely." He gives me a once-over then looks at the ID again. "The likeness is there. Just tell me I won't have to start calling you Elena."

A LETTER FROM JESSICA

Dear Reader,

Thank you for spending these hours with my book, my characters, my story. I hope you enjoyed them, and if you did, I'd love it if you took a moment to leave me a review on Amazon or Goodreads. You can find out more about my latest releases by signing up here. Your email address will never be shared, and you can unsubscribe at any time:

www.bookouture.com/jessica-payne

I'd love to connect with you—my personal newsletter is another great way to stay up to date with my upcoming books, behind-the-scenes author stuff, book giveaways, writer life, and more. I'd love for you to join me:

https://jessicapayne.net/newsletter

Readers are the heart of the bookish world—the reason it exists. As a reader myself, I understand what it's like to get lost in a book. I'm grateful I get to be a small part of this bookish world we all share, weaving stories and characters and twists and turns. It truly is my favorite part of my day, sitting at my computer and writing about these fictitious lives that feel so very real.

This is a book inspired by a very Covid lockdown-oriented

part of my life. I had an eighteen-month-old and a husband working eighty hours a week, which meant I rarely got time to myself to run when I wasn't pushing a running stroller. But Sunday mornings were mine, and I'd escape the house at 6 a.m. to run the streets of San Antonio, our temporary home, by myself. It was still dark out, and I ran among the shadows, the *thud-thud-thud* of my feet the only sound in the otherwise silent morning. Golden light shined out of open windows from nearby houses. The human eye is naturally attracted to this light, and while I'd quickly look away, conscious I was literally looking into someone's private home—I couldn't help but wonder about a character who might purposefully hide in the dark, might purposefully stare inside. She would have secrets, of course, and some type of agenda. A character was born, an idea spinning into threads of story. The book itself took much longer to write, but this is where it began, and I still remember those dark mornings on my own. They were simultaneously eerie and wonderful, and this book was born there.

I can't wait until we meet again in my next book!

Jessica Payne

facebook.com/authorjessicapayne

x.com/authorjesspayne

instagram.com/jessicapayne.writer

goodreads.com/authorjesspayne

tiktok.com/@authorjesspayne

ACKNOWLEDGMENTS

Thank you to my amazing agent, Kimberly Brower, who helped every step of the way. This book wouldn't be what it is without your insight and advice.

Thank you to Joy Kozu for your reading and recommendations.

Thank you to Kelsie Marsden, my editor, with whom this is my fourth book. We've done a lot together, and I appreciate you.

Thank you to my husband, Virgil, who is incredibly supportive.

And Emma, who regularly makes me feel like a very cool author mom.

Thank you to Sara Read, my author wife/critique partner/friend. One of my favorite memories is discussing this book over coffee as the sun rose, and the rain created the background music to our morning.

Thank you to Jaime Lynn Hendricks, my friend and critique partner who is *always* honest—always.

Thank you to Ande Pliego, Mary Keliikoa, Mary Boone, Shay Galloway, Tobie Carter, Tracy Grant, and Tara Goedjen, all of whom are amazing author friends.

Thank you to Aleida—trusting my daughter is in good hands and learning and loving to learn while I work on my books makes all the difference. You've been such a blessing to our family.

Thank you to Browsers Bookshop, the booksellers, and Andrea, for the amazing ongoing support.

Thank you to Pierce County Library and the wonderful librarians who work there.

Thank you to Lilst Kitty, the strangest, best cat ever.

Thank you to my Porch Crew, who, as always, provide so much support and love and cheerleading. I still can't quite believe how much I lucked out to move in next door to you all.

To #MomsWritersClub, this amazing group of women who have created my writing circle. We're going through changes these days, but I still appreciate each and every one of you.

PUBLISHING TEAM

Turning a manuscript into a book requires the efforts of many people. The publishing team at Bookouture would like to acknowledge everyone who contributed to this publication.

Audio
Alba Proko
Sinead O'Connor
Melissa Tran

Commercial
Lauren Morrissette
Jil Thielen
Imogen Allport

Data and analysis
Mark Alder
Mohamed Bussuri

Cover design
Eileen Carey

Editorial
Kelsie Marsden
Jen Shannon

Copyeditor
Ian Hodder

Proofreader
John Romans

Marketing
Alex Crow
Melanie Price
Occy Carr
Cíara Rosney

Operations and distribution
Marina Valles
Stephanie Straub

Production
Hannah Snetsinger
Mandy Kullar

Publicity
Kim Nash
Noelle Holten
Myrto Kalavrezou
Jess Readett
Sarah Hardy

Rights and contracts
Peta Nightingale
Richard King
Saidah Graham

Printed in Poland
by Amazon Fulfillment
Poland Sp. z o.o., Wrocław

37403000R00194